ANNASLAND

THE ANTLANDS SERIES / BOOK 2

ANNASLAND

GENEVIEVE MORRISSEY

ANTLANDS.COM

To Deer. He knows who he is.

CHAPTER ONE

Sometimes I still dreamed I was back in the Valley, kneeling in mud and blood with my friends lying dead all around me. Twenty years ago I killed a lot of Ants—and my better self—in battle there, and I left the battlefield by way of a dark road. I followed that road for many years. It didn't take me home.

On the morning I kissed my weeping mother and rode out of Evergreen for the last time, I stopped as soon as I was out of sight of the forest pickets and cut off my braids with my knife. I was a Man now, on my way to be married to a Daughter of Men, and I wanted to look the part. I wanted to have two names like a Man, too. I wanted to call myself River Wolfson, in honor of my father, Wolf. But my mother told me I was disgracing my father by leaving the forest, so I settled for River Evergreen instead. I never liked the name, and it never felt like mine, but the first two days after I took it were the happiest of my life. I spent them with my new wife, Sarah, and we were young, we were free and whole, and most of all, we were crazy in love with each other.

On my third day as a married man, I went with Sarah's brother Dan, my best friend and business-partner, to where the Allied Armies were assembling in the Valley to make war against the Ants.

The Foresters might have sent me into exile, but they weren't above taking advantage of the fact that I knew both their language and most of the tongues of Men. Though I wore a sword and knew how to use it, they assigned me to a place in front of a telegraph key at a table positioned so it had a view of the whole battlefield. The generals of Men and Foresters stood to observe the action on a platform above me, and it was my job to relay their shouted orders by telegraph to the captains in the field.

The Ant soldiers marched in from the west, and there was no doubt they'd come to fight. Their weapons were already in their hands. We watched as they warily scouted the ground, their minds working, Ant-fashion, in unison. It was clear they were afraid of the broad river that blocked their escape to the south. They crowded to the farthest edge of the field to get away from it. But they were unsuspicious of the line of uprooted bushes along the top of the rise to the north. The bushes concealed twenty large cannon—crude by today's standards, but plenty deadly—and troops the Men held in reserve, but all the Ants saw was that the army that faced them was reassuringly smaller than their own. Satisfied, they ranged themselves in their usual battle-lines.

Before they could move to engage us, General Cade of the Foresters gave the order for the great guns to be fired.

At the first barrage, the Ants froze, and when we saw them just standing there, witless with surprise, we Allies let out a roar of our own that was almost as loud as the guns. We waited for the cannon to finish its bloody work and watched, amid choking smoke and the screams of the wounded, while the Ants considered their situation.

Their choice must have seemed clear: They faced artillery to the north, a river to the south, and an army in front of them. Before the gunners on the hill had rammed home the shot for a second volley, the Ants turned around in a body and started back the way they'd come.

But by then we'd erected an obstacle in that direction, too. In the Ants' path, a team of Men that included Dan had raised a fence of heavy wire. The Ants had no way of knowing the fence was connected to a human-powered electrical generator, but they were distrustful of it. When they saw it, they stopped their headlong rush and waited while one or two of them reached tentatively to touch it. Exactly as Dan and I had hoped (we hadn't had time—or the means—to really test it), the fence-wire emitted showers of sparks and a sharp crackle, killing one Ant, I think, and terrifying them all. Just then, a second volley of balls and exploding shells landed in their midst, and the Ants, who were usually silent creatures, cried out with one voice in despair.

Mad with fear and thwarted by the fence, they rushed toward the river, then stopped—Ants can't swim—turned again, and made a feint at the Allied ranks instead. In response, the human soldiers stood as ordered, unmoving, and the Ants, seeking an easier way, wheeled north again, toward the rise. The cannon answered their charge with more fire and death. The Ants spun west—but on that side, of course, was the fence.

With mounting panic, the Ant-soldiers whirled like leaves in the eddy of a brook, slashing ineffectually with their weapons. Seeing them, I almost laughed out loud. Everything was going exactly to plan.

Then, just as the generals on their platform called down to me to order the cannonade to cease and the Allied soldiers to advance, the collective Ant-brain apparently issued an order of its own. Of the obstacles they faced, armed men was the one with which the Ants were most familiar. Turning one last time, they hurled themselves with unimaginable ferocity on our armies, and from that moment, all their efforts to attain victory or escape were focused in that direction.

I looked on helplessly as General Cade, standing forward of his line, was among the first to be struck down. Even before he fell, one of my best forest-friends, Swan of Evergreen, was fighting his way up from the rear, frantic to reach his general's side. Swan went down too. I jumped to my feet, my hand on my sword.

Someone on the platform above barked at me to sit down; that I had a job to do; and I obeyed. Whether the command came in Forester or another language, I could never remember afterward, but I'd never willingly taken an order from anybody since.

The only help I could give was to signal repeatedly to the field-captains to stop the Men who carried hand-cannons from using them. Small arms were a recent re-invention of an ancient weapon, and too primitive to be effective, but the noise and spurts of flame they produced seemed to be frightening the Ant-soldiers into concentrating their greatest fury on the Forest Army, where they faced only the familiar sword, bow, and lance.

I signaled—but the Battle in the Valley had degenerated by now into a melee of individual combats, and the gunfire continued. I watched the carnage with mounting anguish. Unless the Ants could somehow be persuaded to turn in another direction, the Forest Army would be annihilated.

The plan of battle called for the Ants to be confined in the Valley until they had been exterminated down to the last soldier, but it was evident to me by now that no more Ants could be killed with bolts of electricity or persuaded to drown themselves in the river. Since the two armies were now fully engaged, further cannon-fire or more volleys of hand-thrown exploding missiles (my own invention) would be as likely to kill friends as enemies. The Ants would have to be dealt with one-by-one by individual soldiers—and the soldiers of the Forest, exhausted and demoralized by the slaughter among them, were at the forefront of the battle. I watched in torment as one friend after another fell.

Finally I turned to the generals and begged them to allow me to telegraph to have the fence at the Ants' rear lowered. It might relieve the pressure on the Forester's line, I said.

The generals could see the appalling slaughter for themselves, but lowering the fence would give the Ants a means of escape. After a discussion that seemed endless, they reluctantly gave permission. I sent the signal, then watched with a spyglass as Men rushed to carry out the order.

The fence was down, but the Ants didn't immediately notice that the way to their rear was now clear. Their entire attention remained focused on forcing a breakthrough in the opposite direction. Frustrated, I signaled again and again to the Forest Army, the only ones whose discipline still held, to do something—anything—to turn the Ants around, but the forest soldiers were too hard-pressed to do more than stand as they were and keep fighting.

A commotion behind the Ant Army caught my eye. Brandishing the sword

Foresters had once given to his stepfather, Dan was leading a handful of Men in a charge at the Ants' rear.

The Men were few, but they were valiant. When they couldn't get the Ants' attention by shouting, they attacked the rearmost soldiers of their line. With my heart in my mouth, I watched as, more irritated than injured, twenty or so Ants turned to face my friend. Dan fought courageously—all the Men did—until finally the Ants looked past them and recognized there was a clear path out of the killing-grounds.

Since Ants are telepathic, the realization they could escape traveled almost instantly from the few Ants' brains to the many.

It would be inaccurate for me to say the Ant Army then *began to retreat*. In an instant, they *were retreating*, leaving the field of battle as fast as they could. Seeing this, the generals above me began arming themselves to rally their troops for pursuit. They released me from my duties, and, able to draw my own sword at last, I ran behind the fleeing enemy. I struck them with impunity. Their whole attention was on getting away. They didn't bother to fight back. By the time I reached Dan, my hands, my clothes—my soul—were sodden with the blood of those I had slaughtered.

Dan was alive, but just barely, with many wounds and shattered legs. As I knelt beside him and did what I could to help, I begged him aloud to please, please just live. One or two of the other Men showed signs of life, and I bandaged their wounds, too. I couldn't look at the torn remains of the rest.

The Allied Armies, reinvigorated by the Ants' retreat, chased after them, determined to cut down as many as they could before the enemy scattered too far or found cover. In their wake, the Men's medics and the forest infirmarians swarmed onto the field to carry the injured away to field hospitals. I saw Roar of Evergreen bend over General Cade, then turn sadly away, but Swan, at least, wasn't dead after all. As Roar lifted him onto a litter, Swan was holding to his chest the gory stump of what had been his right arm, from which white bone protruded.

I was unhurt but afire with rage, and as the Ants rushed toward the hills, I swore in the names of the dead that I wouldn't go home again until the last remaining Ant on the continent was dead, too. To kill them might take months, or even years, but it seemed like a debt I had to pay. I could only hope—and I did hope—my darling Sarah would wait that long for me.

*

For the next twenty years, the memory of the Battle in the Valley was like all the other scars I brought home from the war—an ugly thing nobody talked about.

Meanwhile, D&R Enterprises, the company I owned with my friend Dan, flourished. After I came home from the army, we moved quickly from telegraphy into radio, and since a legless man in a wheelchair couldn't get around too easily, I did the necessary traveling throughout the continent to put up broadcast towers. Dan stayed at our workshop in Fortress City, supplying everyone who would pay with radio receivers and reliable power, and combing Ancient Texts to find more useful things we could reinvent.

We usually had more business than we could handle, so when we were approached about a partnership by the biggest shipping company on the continent, Dan and I told them we weren't interested. Neither of us knew anything about ships or shipbuilding, and we weren't inclined to learn. But the shippers persisted, and eventually I saw interesting possibilities in the project. I'd always had an urge to go exploring. Throw in a chance for me to explore, I told the shippers, and we have a deal.

Naturally the shippers didn't want to explore. They just wanted us to help them build a coaster that could make the trading circuit of the continent in less time with more cargo. The compromise we finally worked out was that Dan and I would oversee the construction of a vessel built to our specifications but paid for by the shippers, and in return for a chance for me to take her on a couple of exploratory cruises before we surrendered her, Dan and I would design, manufacture, and fit her with a workable engine and a new means of navigation. *Muriel* was the first steel-hulled ship produced since ancient times, and I won't deny I was as proud of her as though I'd built her with my own hands.

I didn't, naturally. I didn't know anything about naval architecture. Experienced shipwrights drew her plan, and her hull was constructed by steelworkers, some of whom wondered aloud in my hearing whether something as heavy as the *Muriel* would actually float. When the steelworkers were finished, dockyard joiners furnished her interior, grumbling the whole time that the ship's steel knees and engine compartment got in their way. In point of fact the *Muriel* was nothing more than an outsized wooden boat encased in a metal shell. Only her engine was novel, and the engine was Dan's design, not mine.

But I oversaw the whole project, and I provided the impetus, through a million complications and delays, to see it to completion. Looking around her, I was completely satisfied with my work.

Muriel had passed her sea-trials, and I was going to take her out on a real voyage as soon as she'd been provisioned. Only first, the shippers insisted, she had to be fitted with a few cannon for protection.

I was not a great lover of guns—which probably sounded ironic coming from somebody who'd used them as much as I had. I could respect a bow, or a knife, which required skill and a certain degree of courage (or at least nerve) to use, but any fool could shoot a gun, and nobody liked to shoot guns more than fools did. There was no resisting the shippers in the matter though—I knew, because I'd tried—and I was watching from the shore as a cannon was lowered through the *Muriel's* main hatch when a voice beside me exclaimed, "Oh, I see! Those slides are mounted to the deck, I suppose, to absorb and direct the cannon's recoil."

I didn't bother to turn. Since the day we'd laid her keel, everything we did on the *Muriel* attracted a gaping crowd. "Right, right," I agreed distractedly. "It's safer than the old blocks and about twice as fast to load."

Then I stopped as it dawned on me the voice and accent were familiar. I looked and heard myself say, "Teacher... Teacher."

Except that his hair was now white, Deer hadn't changed much. He smiled broadly and put out both hands to me.

I didn't take them. "What're you doing here?" I blurted instead.

"I came to see you," Deer said, his smile fading as he lowered his hands. "And her." He gestured toward the *Muriel*. "She's beautiful. You must be very proud."

My mouth was hanging open. I shut it. "Yes."

Deer hesitated. "Perhaps this isn't a good time," he suggested. "Later, maybe? Let me be perfectly straightforward, River; I want a favor of you. You may refuse me, but I hope you can find time to hear me out. You're very busy, of course."

I'd begun to collect my wits by now. "No. I mean—yes, I'm busy, but we can talk. I don't need to watch this. I don't even want to, now that I think of it." We stood for a moment in awkward silence before I thought to add, "Come aboard, why don't you? I'll show you around the ship."

Deer's smile broadened again.

At his feet lay a doeskin travel-bag no different from the one I carried out of the forest when I left it twenty years ago. "Let me get that, sir," I said. "Come this way."

The "sir" was inadvert, and I winced to hear myself say it. The last thing I wanted was for Deer to think nothing had changed from back in the old days. I was a Man now, and a pretty successful one, too. "How is it you're here?" I asked him, trying to sound polite, but distant. "Have you Foresters changed the rule about the master never leaving his forest?"

If Deer noticed the deliberate chill in my voice, he didn't let on.

"I'm no longer forest master. I retired last year. I only recently heard about your ship. Is shipbuilding a new enterprise for your company?"

Everybody asked that. "No. The ship belongs to somebody else. D&R's business is mostly radio."

"Ah, radio!" Deer said, brightening. "I enjoy your radio. I like the musical programs."

Nobody in Evergreen would have listened to a radio in my day, that's for sure.

I didn't say anything more until we were aboard the *Muriel*. When I announced, "Here she is!" I couldn't keep the pride from my voice.

"Fascinating!" Deer looked around. "This oak is from Northland, I believe."

On a crowded ship with about three hundred new things to look at, trust a Forester to notice the wood first.

"Right," I said. "Old growth." As if Deer wouldn't have figured that out already. "So—what's this favor you want?"

"Can we wait a moment before we get to that? I'd like to know first how you are. Are you well? You look well."

I laughed, embarrassed. "Sorry. Businessmen have trouble with the social niceties. Let me think…" I tried to remember how things were done in Evergreen. "I should offer you something to eat and drink, I guess. What would you like?"

Deer said he only wanted water, which I supplied, and as he drank, I answered his question.

"Yeah, I'm well. Busy, as I said. How about you? What're you doing now you're not forest master anymore? Have you gone back to teaching?"

It was Deer's turn to look proud. "I have. We have quite a large school in Evergreen. How are your children, River?"

I love my children very much, but for various reasons, I didn't want to talk to Deer about them. I squinted toward the horizon. "They're good," I said vaguely. "My daughter, Laura, just got married, and my son, little Bobby, works for D&R now, in Fortress City. More water?"

I could feel Deer studying me, but I wouldn't look.

"How's everybody in Evergreen?" I added quickly, "I heard you got married."

This was old news, but successful as a distraction. "Yes, Bellflower and I married during the war—about ten years after we should have, according to Leaf." Deer smiled. "My wife sends her love."

"Thanks," I said sincerely. I'd always liked Bellflower. "Give her mine, too. Care to see the rest of the ship?"

"I'd like nothing better!" Deer exclaimed.

I led the way, explaining the functions of the various parts of the *Muriel* as we passed them, and when the conversation looked like it was veering toward subjects I didn't care to discuss, I sidetracked Deer by asking about old friends in Evergreen.

The few who'd survived the war seemed to be doing all right.

"For Swan's sake, we built stairs in place of the ladders in the library," Deer told me. "They seem to have caught on. We have many stairs in the forest now. And electric lights, of course."

"I heard that. What's your power source?"

"Water turbines. They've rather spoiled the look of the waterfall, I'm afraid, though the light is welcome—especially in the schoolhouse."

"You have a schoolhouse now?"

"Oh, yes. We outgrew the library some years ago."

Deer explained, and it turned out the Evergreen school really was big, just as he'd said. In an agreement with neighboring villages of Men, the Foresters were educating Men's children as well as their own. Apparently, the Men's children were permitted to come right into Evergreen. I was dumbfounded by this news.

"We made an agreement with the Men," Deer told me. "We offered our school to their children in return for their own assurances that they would otherwise respect our borders. Our game and timber are a constant temptation to them. So far, at least, they've kept the bargain."

I shook my head like I doubted this, but what I was really thinking was that Deer had been incredibly clever. He'd arranged things so Men's own children—with their Forester school, and their little Forester friends, and their Forester teachers who no doubt indoctrinated them thoroughly with Forest Principles—would be his adorable little allies in keeping their fathers' greedy hands off Evergreen. Deer had taken what had happened to Broadleaf Forest as a lesson.

I stifled a laugh. "Feel like going down to see the engine? All Dan's design, by the way."

"I'd like it very much!" Deer said happily.

Once we were in the engine room, he was puzzled by the *Muriel's* lack of an obvious means to charge her batteries.

"This is the battery array, is it not?" He peered closer. "And those, I think, are the turbines. But what turns the turbines? Is it the sails?"

"No. The *Muriel's* masts are for emergency use only. At her bulk, I'm told she'd need at least one more mast and a lot more canvas to be a good sailer. Guess again."

"Is it the motion of the ship against the water?"

I admitted regretfully it wasn't. "That would be great, and we tried that first, but we couldn't make it work. No, the turbines are turned by steam."

Deer's face fell a little. He was too polite to say so, but I knew he thought steam power was a terrible idea.

We modern Men knew from the writings of our ancestors there was a great "steam age" in ancient times. But that steam age could never be repeated—or at least, not on our continent. Our continent couldn't support trees enough for wood to heat thousands and thousands of boilers. Whether it might be rich in coal or in whatever "oil" it was the Ancients also used for fuel, we didn't know, but we did know the extraction and processing of either of those would likely require technology beyond our capabilities.

But as Dan Farmer figured out while he was still not much more than a boy, batteries weren't difficult to make, though they were difficult to make well, or small, and turbines to charge them could be turned by any swift-flowing watercourse or stiff breeze. Thanks mainly to D&R, wind- and watermills had become features of every continental landscape.

"No need for us to cut down a single tree, Teacher," I assured Deer. "The ship's liquid-fueled." I slapped my hand against a tall, upright iron apparatus he hadn't asked about yet. "This is where the heat comes from to make steam."

Deer had never heard of liquid fuel before, except maybe the little lamps Foresters used in my childhood with a wick to melt greasy lumps of goose-fat to liquid oil.

"This is Dan's best invention ever. Or best re-invention, anyway. We mostly just re-implement ancient technologies. The *Muriel's* fuel is fermented from plants, and then distilled like spirits." I grinned. "You remember how good Men are at distilling spirits, right?"

Deer agreed wryly that distillation was a branch of chemistry at which Men excelled.

"We burn spirits for fuel. It's handy that we don't have to make these particular spirits taste at all good. Anything flammable will do."

I opened the front panel and invited Deer to inspect the whole system at close range.

Deer studied the burner closely. "What plants do you use?"

"That's the best part," I said. "We use waste. We distill stuff nobody needs into spirits nobody wants to drink. Then we store the spirits in those tanks back there, and to make the turbines go, we feed the spirits into the burner. The burner boils water to make steam, and the steam turns the turbines. The turbines charge the batteries, the batteries power the *Muriel's* propeller, and the propeller pushes us through the water. Brilliant, right?"

Deer agreed that it was brilliant and added a few flattering adjectives of his own. "Will you be able to make long voyages?"

"Pretty long, because we can refuel along the way. We carry all the equipment we need to distill spirits right here on the ship."

After looking some more at the engine, we continued our tour. By now I'd forgotten my earlier misgivings, and we talked with a freedom that was almost like old times.

Deer wanted to know if I was going to be captain of the *Muriel*.

I laughed at the suggestion. "Me? No. I don't know anything about captaining a ship."

"But you will be sailing on her?"

"Oh, definitely. But just as Supercargo." By now we were standing at my cabin door. I waved him in. "I think you'll be impressed. The actual space is small, but it's got everything I need."

Smiling, Deer entered.

I saw him look twice at my bed, and all the self-consciousness I'd felt earlier came back. It was unmistakably a forest bed, with hand-loomed linen sheets and a cover of squirrel-fur.

"Fisher's," I explained uncomfortably. "He left his room at the library to me when he died. He gave the rest of the library to the city, but he left that one room to me." Before Deer could answer this, I added, "The fact that I have it here doesn't mean I want to be back in Evergreen or anything. My mother wove the sheets, that's all."

"She was a fine weaver," Deer said gravely.

He sat where I pointed, and I took the chair opposite and put his bag on the floor between us. Neither of us spoke for a moment.

"How is Sarah?" Deer asked suddenly.

Sarah was at the top of the list of things I didn't want to talk about.

There was a greasy machine part lying on my desk. I picked it up and held it out for Deer's inspection. "It's a bearing," I explained. "See? But it's broken."

Deer just looked at me, and I laid the part aside again.

After a minute, I said, "Sarah's fine, I guess. I haven't seen her for a while."

"You parted?" Deer asked quietly.

"Yeah, we parted. About a year ago."

"I'm sorry."

"Not Sarah's fault," I said quickly. "Mine. First the war kept me away, and then afterward I was gone a lot on business. She got tired of it."

"I see."

"She got tired of being alone, and—we grew apart. That's all. It happens."

"I knew after the Battle in the Valley you continued to pursue the Ants." Deer folded his hands together. "Roar told me he thought you went because you felt partly responsible for the fact that our casualties were so great. Is that true?"

A change of subject was in order. "How is Roar? We haven't talked about him yet."

"Roar's fine. Was he correct? Is that why you went away instead of home to Sarah?"

I took a deep breath. "Look: I *was* responsible for a lot of those casualties because I waited too long to ask for the damn fence to be let down. But it was a long time ago, the Ants are all gone now, and my marriage to Sarah is finished. Let's not waste time discussing the past, all right?"

Deer wouldn't let it go. "After the Valley, were you in many more battles? Were your casualties heavy?"

The question annoyed me.

"You're thinking of another kind of war," I said coldly. "The kind you fought. We took some casualties, sure—but mostly, we killed them, not the other way around."

"Ants?"

"Yeah, Ants. Who do you think? Cold, starving Ants, a lot of them."

"Tell me."

"Tell you what?" I leaned back in my chair, avoiding Deer's eyes. "What don't you already know? You went to war."

"As you said, I went to a different war. Tell me about your war."

Deer had always been obstinate. I remembered that now. And nosy.

"War?" I repeated, sneering. "After the Valley, the only war on the continent was between nations of Men." Somewhere in the last few minutes—I had no idea when—we'd both switched to speaking Forester. I was surprised at how easily it came back to me. I hadn't spoken it for years. "Where I was, there wasn't war, there was slaughter. We found Ants in little groups of twenty or thirty and some of them weren't even armed. By the second year, a lot of them weren't armed, in fact, and some of them didn't even have clothes. They were cold and starving and scared to death, and we didn't kill them in battle, we executed them."

I realized suddenly I was shouting and struggled to lower my voice. "One group I remember had a young one with them, a female. I don't know what she was even doing there. She was no soldier. I guess the others just hadn't wanted to leave her to starve in the Antlands. Not only did that group not fight us, they didn't even try to run away. They just looked at us. They looked at us, and then they shut their eyes, put their arms around each other, and then one of them put her hands over the young one's face. I'll never forget that. They wanted to spare her from seeing death coming. She knew what we were going to do, though. They all knew."

"You killed them?"

"I helped. I didn't want to, but shit, yes, I killed them. That was my job."

Once I started talking, I couldn't stop. I told him more things; unspeakable things. Terrible things the Ants did, terrible things my men and I did to the Ants. It was ugly stuff, and I'd never told a soul about most of it before. I thought I'd forgotten it, in fact, but as I spoke every incident came back to my mind as clearly as though I were right there, watching it happen. I talked until I was sick of the sound of my own voice, and if Deer answered any of it, I didn't hear him.

Finally, I said, "When the Ants were all dead, I went back to Fortress City. I'd hardly been home for two years. I was ashamed to face civilized people. I wasn't human inside anymore. I was an animal. My men and I—!"

I had to stop to get my breath. "The truth is, my men and I were no better than the Ants."

"You were soldiers," Deer said quietly.

I waved the remark away. "We were *killers*. And when I got back, my little girl, Laura, didn't know who I was. She kept asking Sarah, 'Mama, who's that Man?'"

Deer started to say something, but I wouldn't listen. Suddenly, I wanted to tell him the worst and have it over with. "I won't lie to you," I said. "That really hurt. I tried to laugh it off, but it hurt. But then instead of staying home and making it up to her and Sarah, I ran away. I started traveling. It was business, sure—but somebody else could have done it. I wanted to go. I couldn't be home for more than a month or two before I wanted to leave again. Despite Sarah. Despite Laura. She was so beautiful and sweet, like her mother... But I was gone when she was little, so we could never be as close as we should have been. But I could have been close to my son, at least. I could have stayed and been close to little Bobby. Instead I kept going away. It's a wonder when my children saw me they even knew who I was. They didn't know who I was, in fact. They still don't know. And that's best. That's the way I want it."

Deer didn't say anything, but I knew what he was thinking. Any child born in a forest is loved and nurtured by all, and no one who has children ever travels to get away from them. I'd had two young ones, and I hadn't valued them. Deer was thinking Evergreen was lucky to be rid of me. I waited for him to tell me so. I would have welcomed it if he had.

But instead, when he finally spoke, it was just to ask me calmly, "Your children are both living?"

As if I hadn't been clear on the point. I kicked his bag aside—viciously.

"Yes," I snapped. "I told you before—they're fine. That's all Sarah's doing, by the way; not mine—in case you weren't listening."

"I was listening. Then whether the situation is a bad as you believe it is or not, since your children are alive there is still a chance for you to become closer, isn't there? Assuming you want to be closer."

"Of course I want to be closer! I'm just a bad father, not a monster. They don't want to be closer to me."

"Have you asked them?"

My patience was gone. "Look, this conversation is over, all right? What my children want—or I want—isn't your business. Let's move on to the 'favor' that brought you here in the first place and get this over with." Not that I was in any mood for granting Deer "favors."

"I didn't realize it before this moment," said Deer, "but the two matters may actually be linked. Your relationship with your children and their mother isn't complete and immutable. As long as you live, it will be an ongoing project. Meanwhile, there is some unfinished business in their lives that I suspect must trouble Sarah, at least. If you were to help her with that, it might be a means of bridging the gap between you."

I was suspicious, but he had my attention.

"What 'bridge?'" I asked warily. "What 'business'? Did anybody ever call you a schemer before, Deer?"

"Yes. Your mother. In this case, I'm talking about the fates of John and Muriel Seaborn."

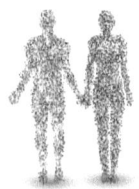

CHAPTER TWO

I leaned back in my chair, and all the breath left my body in one long sigh.

"Oh, gods… John." I rubbed my face. "And Muriel."

Muriel was my mother-in-law. Without needing one minute's discussion to make up our minds about it, Dan and Sarah and I had named our ship for her.

She was a sweet lady. A little insecure, like my own mother, and inclined to be nervously fluttery, but unlike my own mother, always watching out for everybody else's happiness and comfort. If anybody was going to remember what you liked to eat, or which chair was your favorite, or that you'd mentioned you wanted some new thing, it was going to be Muriel. She'd see to it you got whatever it was you wanted, too, even if it meant she had to give up something of her own.

John Seaborn had come to live in the Farmer house as Dan's tutor after Dan's father was killed in the Penultimate Ant War, and though he was a cranky old fellow generally and never minded giving anybody else the rough side of his tongue, he was always tender with Muriel, whom he adored. He was a demanding but loving stepfather to her children, too. He valued them because they were hers.

On the day the Ants broke out of the Antlands and began advancing on the Valley, where we Men and Foresters hoped to annihilate them, John and Muriel made a run for the coast.

The reason they went was never quite clear to the rest of us. In one way it made sense: The coast was farther from the battlefield than the Farmer home was. But in another way, the decision was incomprehensible. John and Muriel weren't particularly afraid of the Ants, for one thing; and for another, they left Sarah, her sister Elizabeth, and Elizabeth's three children behind in Fortress City.

After the Battle in the Valley, we all assumed John and Muriel would come back home. I gave letters for them to people who were headed coast-ward, breaking the bad news about Dan's legs and the good news that they were going to be grandparents again (twice over, because both Sarah and Elizabeth were pregnant), and we looked for them every day.

Over a period of about a year, we received twenty or so letters back. They'd gotten our messages—Muriel was half out of her mind with worry about Dan—but they wrote that they couldn't come home yet. Soon, soon, they said. Keep the home fires burning; we'll all be together again very soon. They sent their love, and in Muriel's case, lots of loving advice: Keep warm; eat well; wear clean socks.

And then—nothing. For twenty years.

The wound was still raw for me; I could only imagine what it was for Sarah and Dan and Elizabeth.

"I don't know what you could possibly tell me to say to Sarah that would help," I said slowly. "Honestly, I think it might be better not to bring the subject up at all. You have no idea how hard it's been."

"No one can truly know another's pain," Deer agreed. "But what if you could tell Sarah where her mother and stepfather went and why they didn't return? Wouldn't she want to know that? It's possible Muriel might still be alive. She was younger than I."

"If Muriel were alive, she'd be with us," I said firmly. "Nothing could have kept her away."

"But something *did* keep her. Something unanticipated. That's the favor I came to ask of you, River. To find out what happened to John and Muriel."

My eyes narrowed. "What happened to them? You know more than you're saying, don't you?"

Deer took a breath to answer, then stopped himself. "No one else on this ship understands our language?" he asked instead.

"Of course not." I sat up impatiently. "Who'd bother to learn it? What do you know?"

"I *don't* know where John and Muriel went," Deer said hastily. "At least, not precisely. You will have guessed for yourself they were not really bound for Coast-town when they left Fortress."

Actually, I hadn't.

But I didn't like to admit it, so I said, "Well, sure. So where were they going, then? And what happened to them when they got there? If they did get there, I mean. Wherever it was."

"Let me start from the beginning. You knew John Seaborn was not Anna's father?"

Anna.

Anna of Evergreen was my first love. She married Heron, my best forest friend. Put that way, the story sounded like someone's life-blighting tragedy— but it wasn't. Anna may have been my first love, but I was long over her and head over ears for Sarah by the time Anna and Heron married. I danced at their wedding quite happily, in fact, the night before I left the forest for the last time.

Though she'd been raised in Evergreen, Anna was a Daughter of Men. Specifically, she was the daughter of John Seaborn. Or so I'd thought.

"He *called* her his daughter."

"She was the daughter of Margaret, his first wife," Deer said. "Her real father was an Ant."

My knees went cold.

"Oh, gods," I breathed. "An—!"

Everything became perfectly clear. "Of course she was. How didn't I see that? It was right in front of my face."

It was Anna—not scholars like Deer or John Seaborn or (at one time) me—who discovered that Ants were telepathic. Anna knew it because she was a telepath herself. She led us to other human telepaths, and the Allied Armies had the upper hand at the Battle in the Valley because Anna and the other telepaths together had plumbed our enemies' minds, taught us their secrets, and showed us how to fight them and win.

"Those other telepaths—them, too?"

"Yes. They were all half-Ants."

"How did—"

"You can guess how," Deer interrupted, with a grimace. "Apparently, Ants sometimes returned for young ones begotten in that way. The Ants who destroyed Anna's village were there to retrieve her. In Anna's case, her injuries obliged them to leave her for us to find, but we think this admixture of human blood in the Ant line accounts for the subtle differences between individuals among them."

Ants were originally all descended from one small group of clones—"clone" being a word, a concept, we learned from the Ancient Texts. Our long-distant ancestors had cloned Ants to be workers, lost control over them, and ended up being nearly exterminated by their own creation.

I had to stop and think about all this for a moment. It was news, and yet in a way I felt like I'd known it all along.

"Where do John and Muriel come into this?" I asked finally.

"By the time of the battle, we had nearly sixty captive Ants, as you'll remember. They and the seven half-Ants we also had working for us were under Anna's command. We used all of them to draw the Ant Army into the valley. Anna and the others took a path just out of the Ant soldiers' reach, and mentally directed them to follow."

"I heard that." I shook my head. "I still can't believe it worked."

"Anna and the others told the Ants they were leading them to a place where they could live out their days in peace and plenty. The message was true—and indeed it *had* to be true to convince the Ant soldiers. Telepaths, of course, cannot deceive each other. There was such a land as Anna described, and the

Ants were going to it. But only her Ants. And John and Muriel were going with them."

I started, and then my face began to burn. "No."

"It was by their own choice," Deer said, watching me closely. "They wanted to help."

"No."

"River, they never intended to *stay* with the Ants."

Even in my rage, I recognized Deer was speaking gently. He must have understood how painful it was for me to hear that while I was killing Ants—and part of myself—John and Muriel were choosing Ants above their own children and saving them.

"It was only going to be for a short while. They had become fond of Anna's captive Ants, and anyway, John felt he owed it to Anna for having thrown off her mother. He abandoned Margaret for giving birth to another Man's child, as he believed Anna to be, and that was how she happened to be living in a frontier village when the Ants raided it."

While I was still mentally resisting this information, Deer added, "Posthumous went to stay. He told me frankly he expected to die on that island. But John and Muriel—and Anna and Heron, too—were going to get the Ants established, and then they were going to come back."

"Wait—!" I gasped. "Posthumous went? To an island? Where?"

Posthumous had been the forest master of Evergreen before Deer. The day after Anna and Heron married, he retired and left Evergreen to join his daughter in Beechlands Forest.

He left Evergreen, but never reached Beechlands. I remembered that now. Another loss among so many in the Final Ant War.

"What island?" I repeated grimly.

"I don't know."

"Don't give me that, Forester," I said tightly. "What island? Where?"

"I don't know," repeated Deer. "It was an island John knew of, a few days' sail, he said, from the island of his birth. He said it would meet all their needs, but he would tell no one exactly where it was, save the young Man who was captain of the ship that was to carry them all there. That Man, you see, was brother to one of the half-Ants and could be trusted to keep the secret."

"But Sarah couldn't. Or Dan. Or me."

"Nor I," Deer pointed out. This argument, at least, seemed valid. "John reasoned it would be easier for us if we didn't know. No one could press us for information we didn't have. Only a few people were permitted even to know Anna and her party were not lost in the war, as most assumed. Even Bellflower didn't know it until a few days ago. John made me swear not to tell."

It was just like John to decide what was best for other people, of course.

"When they didn't return, I made inquiries."

People I loved had been wiped from the face of the earth, and Deer had made "inquiries." At that moment, I almost hated him.

"What good did you expect that to do?" I sneered—not bothering to keep my tone respectful. "What kind of 'inquiries' could you even make without telling anybody what you were inquiring about?"

"I knew the name of the ship. With that much I was able to discover quite quickly that it had not been seen in any port since a year or so after the Battle in the Valley. I knew by the letters I received from Posthumous that the party arrived safely on John's island, and that the ship made at least two successful trips back before—"

Deer looked away suddenly. His lower lip shook.

"Before the ship was lost," I finished for him.

Deer nodded miserably. "We must suppose it was. River, I am tortured by the thought they might think we abandoned them!"

I softened. Posthumous had been like a father to Deer after his own father was killed by Ants, and Heron was Deer's only nephew. Deer and John somehow managed to be friends, and everyone loved Muriel, of course.

And Anna had probably been more to Deer than all the others put together. Though she always called him "uncle," I think to Deer, Anna was the daughter he'd never had.

"I'm sorry." I meant it. "The captain of the ship… he hadn't told anyone else where the island was?"

"His crew, I suppose, must have known. But they were lost with him."

I thought about this.

After a long moment, I said, "Seems like you could find the place, though."

"I thought so, too. I hired ships to look for it, in fact."

"You hired ships?"

"Well, I'm not a sailor myself." Deer shrugged apologetically. "I felt the relinquishment of Broadleaf provided good cover for the undertaking."

I saw his point.

A few years after my mother died, the citizens of Broadleaf Forest, pressed on every side by nations of Men, voted to sell their land and disperse themselves among the other forests. The decision marked the end of an age. Broadleaf was the original Forester homeland and had existed for almost a thousand years. At the time all I could think was that my mother would have died a second death if she'd known how many of her friends elected to go to Evergreen, where Deer—whom she hated—was still Master.

Deer explained, "I suggested to my councils it might be prudent, if worse came to worst for Evergreen, to have a place prepared for us to go. When they agreed, I sent pickets to hire ships to explore for one. I knew the island we were looking for was near John's former home, so I directed the search be made in that area—though without saying why."

"But you didn't find it?"

"No. There are many islands, and the Men who sailed the ships were willing to risk themselves only so far and no more. But your ship is powered, and capable, you said, of long voyages. You may succeed where I failed."

I mentally poked at the fire of my earlier rage at Deer and John—no use even trying to be angry with Muriel—and was surprised to find it was dead out. What was done was done, and a few Ants one way or the other didn't really matter. We already knew there were plenty of Ants left elsewhere in the world by the fact that no humans from other continents ever came to ours.

Deer was right. I might succeed where he'd failed. Using the *Muriel*, I might *find* Muriel—and John and Anna and Heron, too. At any rate, trying to find them seemed like a better use for my time than anything else I was currently doing.

"What were you planning to tell the captains of your rental ships if they had found that island?" I asked, beginning to smile. "Were you going to flat-out lie about the Ants, or just hide them under rocks? You'd better tell me, because if this works, I'll have a captain and crew I need to deal with, too."

Deer's face lit up. "You'll go?"

"Sure, I'll go. Why not?"

Deer was spry for his age. Before I had time to blink, he'd jumped up, grabbed both my hands, and embraced me where I sat, cheek to cheek in the manner of the Foresters, who are still my people, forever my people, even though I chose to throw in my lot with the Men. How could I ever have forgotten—or doubted—my people?

Almost despite myself, I clung on. If Posthumous had been a second father to Deer, Deer had been one to me, and I was suddenly ashamed of the long silence between us. Deer had written to me a few times after I left Evergreen, and I'd never answered.

"I'll find Anna and Heron for you, Teacher. I'll find them and the others, and I'll bring them home. I owe it to you for hearing the worst about me without flinching."

I laughed outright then and stood up, drawing Deer up with me. "And now I know the worst about you, too, Teacher. You, the famous Deer of Evergreen, are an unrepentant liar." When Deer protested that he wasn't unrepentant, I corrected myself. "You're right. According to Forest Principles, you're actually a violator of oaths, which is worse. As I recall, you and all the other important Men and Foresters took a sacred oath to wipe out all Ants, and now it turns out you knew damn well the whole time you weren't going to keep it."

"I question the sanctity of oaths in any case," Deer said, looking wounded, "and I took that particular one under conditions of some duress."

"I know why you took it. You took it because Men and Foresters don't trust each other without a lot of swearing and promises and oaths. Well, whatever. All I can say is it's made me a new man to know you lie just like the rest of us when it suits you."

I put my arm around Deer's shoulders as familiarly as if we'd been equals.

"Come on, I'm starving. Let's go get something to eat."

Deer pulled back, eyeing me warily. "You were serious when you said you'd attempt to find John Seaborn's island, weren't you? You didn't mean that facetiously?"

"I was serious. I was dead serious. But I'm also hungry, so come on."

"I can't begin to express my gratitude, River."

"Fine, fine." I nudged him along. "Let's eat."

That's what I said.

But deep down, I knew I should be the one thanking Deer. I'd failed Sarah; I'd failed Laura and little Bobby; I'd failed a lot of people. But in my business undertakings, I'd always had success. If I could succeed in this bit of business— if I could find John's island and maybe bring Muriel home—it might go a long way toward making up for my deficiencies as a husband and father.

And if I found Ants on that island and let them live, it might in some way make up for the skinny little knock-kneed female I'd slaughtered, too.

CHAPTER THREE

Deer stayed with me for three weeks, until the *Muriel* was nearly ready to sail. We spent our days together at the docks and our nights sitting up late in my cabin poring over every map and chart of the North Ocean we could manage to get our hands on. There weren't many, and they were all worryingly incomplete, but they were all we had, so I did my best to comb every bit of information I could get out of them.

"I'm having to talk pretty fast to justify our projected route to the shippers," I confided to Deer. "Before you came, we had it all settled the *Muriel* would go south."

"What's of interest to the south?"

"Nothing. But the weather in the South Ocean's better, and there aren't as many islands or pirates there. Sailors don't like storms, of course; they hate pirates; and they don't like islands because islands might have Ants on them. We're having trouble putting together a crew."

"Would more money help?" Deer reached into his jacket.

"You Foresters are so materialistic," I grinned. "You think money will solve any problem. No, that's all right. We're fine for money, I think."

Two days later I found myself paying a bonus in antique gold coins from a Forest money pouch to secure the services of a stinking, profane old seaman to be the *Muriel's* new captain.

"He was the only serious applicant we had," I complained to Deer, returning his pouch to him significantly lighter. "The rest were all drunks or just boys."

Deer said he thought the fellow would be all right, once he'd had a bath.

"Not much chance of that," I muttered. "Sailors spend their lives trying to stay *out* of the water."

I was right. Despite the hints—and eventually, outright pleas—of the crew, anybody who wanted to find Captain Alcock could track him by sniffing the air.

The only good part of the whole business was that we also acquired a first mate in the transaction. When Captain Alcock came aboard, he brought his former second mate with him, who signed on with no more bounty than the promise of promotion.

The two made an odd pair. In fact, it would be hard to imagine two Men more completely opposite in every way than the captain and his mate. Captain Alcock was big and muscular and dirty; Mr. Jameson was slim and fastidious— or what passes for "fastidious" among sailors, anyway. The captain was loud, obscene, and forceful; the first mate soft-spoken and mild. I thought he was too mild for the job, in fact. Sailors in general tended to be independent-minded, and the *Muriel's* crew was not exactly the pick of the stock.

But Deer made the point that Captain Alcock had a few other deficiencies besides his standards of hygiene, and that, since Mr. Jameson seemed to have exactly the opposite deficiencies, the two Men might balance each other out.

Deer was right. The *Muriel's* crew shaped up nicely despite the comic disparity between the captain's relentless verbal (occasionally physical) pummeling and his mate's mild persuasions.

*

I was sorry when Deer said it was time for him to go.

We were standing dockside when he brought the subject up, admiring the *Muriel* from there and watching as her sailors practiced putting her sails up and down. Sails were something they were used to, and they performed well, though one would never have guessed it from the steady flow of curses emanating from Captain Alcock. To oversee the engine, on the other hand, we had only Mike, a D&R employee who related well to machines but who would happily go for weeks without talking to another living being. I suggested to Mike once that as soon as we were underway, he should pick a couple of likely sailors to train as assistants, and he looked at me like I'd recommended we store the powder for the guns next to the ship's burner. He didn't refuse me. To refuse would have required him to actually speak.

"You sure you won't come on the voyage?" I asked Deer—not for the first time. "There's room for Bellflower, too."

Deer smiled wistfully. "Thank you, but no. This has all come too late for me, I'm afraid. I have a place for my tree all picked out in the Memorial Grove. I expect my ashes will be put there soon."

I wanted to deny this. I wanted to insist he would live another hundred years, at least.

But I couldn't. "You know I own the one at Broadleaf?"

"The Memorial Grove?"

"Yes. Silverbirch and I made a deal. I bought that part of the forest. We put it around that I paid a fortune for it, but it was a token, really. The real price was that I promised it would never be built on or logged."

Silverbirch was the last Master of Broadleaf. His tree was close by my mother's.

"My mother and brothers are there," Deer remarked, staring seaward.

"My brother Robin, too." I followed his gaze out to memory. "There's a tree for my father, but he's not really under it."

"No. He was buried in the field," Deer replied quietly.

That was all he said, but suddenly I knew what my mother had always had against him. She hated Deer for having my father buried in the field.

She never told me she'd wanted my father's body brought home. She probably never told anyone. It's a Forest Principle that when life is extinct, a body is just an empty husk, and my mother would never have admitted, even to herself, that her natural instincts didn't perfectly align with Forest Principles. But for some reason she'd wanted my father's empty husk near her, and by order of his commander, General Deer, she'd been denied that.

I wondered briefly if Deer knew, and then decided he did. He knew everything about people, it seemed, including things they didn't know about themselves.

On the *Muriel*, the sailors were dispersing to other tasks.

"Do you think..." ventured Deer hesitantly, "do you think your mother found peace before she died, River? She lost so much, but you gave her two beautiful grandchildren. Did she take consolation from that, at least?"

I owed him the truth. "She never forgave you, if that's what you mean," I said bluntly. "She blamed you for the loss of my father, my brother Robin, and me too."

And for everything else in the world that didn't suit her, I think. I didn't say this aloud.

"Oh, yes; I understand that. She made that very clear. But did she find peace? Silverbirch thought she did, but you knew her best, of course."

I considered the question. "Peace? I don't know. Near the end, she forgot what she'd lost. Maybe forgetting was a kind of peace for her. Sometimes when I visited, she called me Robin, and sometimes when I brought Bobby with me, she thought he was Robin, and I was my father."

"I wrote to her..." Deer murmured. His voice trailed off as Captain Alcock's roar carried across the water to us.

"Move that keg, you crook-backed cripple, before I use it to bung up your—"

Though this exhortation had no discernable effect on the sweating sailor it was directed toward, the remark at least had the effect of dispelling our somber mood. I stifled a laugh, and even Deer smiled.

I studied him surreptitiously. We might be gone a year or more. Assuming I did find Anna, I wondered whether he would live to see her again. And what about Anna's foster-mother, May? She was ten years younger than Deer, but he'd told me her health was failing. Some days she needed Snow's help just to move between her bed and a chair.

Coming to a sudden decision, I said, "You know my warehouse in town?

Let's go there right now. I've got something I want to show you."

"All right," Deer agreed pleasantly. "What is it?"

"Too many ears out here," I said, looking around. "Let's get to the warehouse, first. And prepare to be amazed."

Examining the boxy device, Deer asked dubiously, "It's a radio, isn't it?"

I laughed. "Don't sound so disappointed. Yes, it's a radio—but a new kind. New to our world, anyway."

"Something of the Ancients'?" Deer peered closely at the dial.

"Of course. Look—I'm not going to explain the whole thing to you, all right? I mean, I will if you really want me to, but it's not necessary for you to know how it works to appreciate it."

"That's fine," said Deer absently. "What are these numbers?"

"Those are the radio-wave frequencies the set broadcasts and receives. The important thing to notice is those are *short* wavelengths."

I could see he didn't understand, and I didn't want to spend hours teaching him. "Let me just skip ahead to the good part. Have you ever asked yourself why, after all these years of ships hugging the coasts, we've suddenly built a great big expensive ship we're willing to risk in open, uncharted waters?"

"Not really, no," Deer admitted sheepishly. "I was just so glad to hear about the *Muriel* I didn't think to question anything. What has changed? Why now, and not ten years ago?"

"This radio is why," I said, patting it. "All the radios D&R—or anybody—has made until now have used longwave frequencies. This is a shortwave system."

"Wave—?" Deer asked uncertainly.

I knew a lot of the words I was using were strange to Deer. They were strange to me, too; clumsy translations of ancient words whose derivations were not always entirely clear. But I figured if I kept talking, he'd get the drift.

"Long waves travel outward from a radio transmitter in straight lines." I gestured with my hands to illustrate what I was saying. "And if they're not picked up by a line-of-sight radio receiver, they dissipate. Shortwaves, on the other hand, go up, bounce off the upper atmosphere somehow, and come back down. They can go all the way around the earth bouncing like that. Or at least, that's what the ancient texts say. We aren't exactly in a position to confirm it, but the radio works, and that's enough for us."

Deer looked blank. "These 'short' waves relate to the ship—how?"

"Well, as I said we can't check whether shortwaves will really travel all the way around the earth, but on the other hand, we don't care whether they do or not. It's enough for us that they can travel between the continent and a ship at sea, even when that ship has passed beyond the horizon. That's how we're going to navigate the *Muriel*, Teacher. She's going to be able to track her position relative to a fixed position on the continent."

Proud and happy, I leaned against the wall and crossed my arms—a sloppy, un-self-respecting posture that wouldn't have been tolerated in Evergreen. "See, the idea is to send the *Muriel* out and bring her safely home to demonstrate the feasibility of large trading ships that can safely sail out of sight of land. Once people get comfortable with the idea, the shippers will build more big ships, trade will increase, and prices for goods imported from other parts of the continent will go down."

Deer looked at me sideways.

"That sounds very nice for the shippers," he said stiffly.

I laughed. "Yeah, that's not *my* plan. It's just part of the deal I made with the shippers. If Dan and I keep shortwave radio a secret for five years while the shipping company that backed the *Muriel* gets a head-start on building big ships, I get to take the *Muriel* out exploring for a couple years before they take possession of her. Here's where you come into it, Teacher. See this set? I'm giving it to you."

"The radio?"

"Yes. I'm going to show you how to use it, and then I'm going to pack it up and send it back to Evergreen with you. A secret's always safe in a forest, right? Once you're back in Evergreen, you're going to turn on the radio at a certain time every day, to a certain frequency I'm going to tell you about, and every day, we'll talk. You'll know when I find Anna, because when I do, Anna's going to talk to you on the radio."

"Anna?"

"Anna herself. You won't have to wait until she gets home to talk to Anna—or Heron, or whoever else is on that island. Within a day or two of us finding them, everybody in Evergreen will be able to talk to everybody on John's island just like you were all in the same room together."

"Anna." Deer's face went as white as his hair. "Heron."

"Sit," I ordered, pulling a chair over. "Let's have a lesson now. We'll talk more about Anna and Heron later."

A few days later I sent Deer off with the radio and a D&R employee to carry it to Evergreen for him. I met him at the warehouse alone first, because there was something I had to tell him before we said goodbye.

"You're not going to like this," I confessed, "but I wrote to Sarah about John and Muriel and the island. I asked her to tell Dan and Elizabeth, too."

Deer gripped my arm anxiously. "Did you tell her about the Ants?"

"No." I shook my head. "I left that part out. Unlike you and John, I trust Sarah. I just didn't write that part in the letter because I thought the fact John and Muriel have had to live for twenty years surrounded by Ants instead of their grandchildren was more than she needed to know right now.

"I wrote in Forester. That way, if the kids see the letter before Sarah does, they won't be able to read it. I'd rather they got the news from their mother than in a letter from me."

Sarah's Forester was good. I'd courted her in Forester, mostly, and in the early days of our marriage it had made a sort of secret love-language between us. The memory caused me a twinge of mental pain, now.

"You don't give yourself enough credit," Deer said.

"I give myself all the credit I deserve," I answered firmly. "Anyway, I sort of hinted that John and Muriel went with Anna and Heron and some other 'people' I didn't specify, to look for a place to establish a new kind of forest. A forest where Men and Foresters could live together. If Muriel wants to tell them the truth sometime, it'll be up to her."

"That may in fact be the truth," Deer said. "John would have liked very much to found such a forest. He was our guest in Evergreen for a time, if you'll remember, and he took to the life as though he'd been born to it." He tilted his head and regarded me gravely. "Have you considered going back to Fortress City to tell your family this in person?"

"No time," I said, adding more honestly, "and no courage. A letter will have to do, Teacher. I'll be braver when I've found Muriel."

A noise made us turn. The D&R warehouseman entered with the radio box on his shoulder.

"Time to go," said Deer sadly. "Once again, River, my wife's love, and mine. Remember that whatever news you can give us regarding our dear ones, no matter how terrible, will bring us a kind of peace nothing else can."

"You remember how to work the radio, right?"

Deer said he did, then embraced me—an embrace we both understood might be our last in this world. His cheek against mine, he murmured, "Goodbye, my son."

I answered him, with love, "Good journey, Father."

CHAPTER FOUR

I put off the day of the Muriel's departure for as long as I could, hoping for an answer to my letter to Fortress City, but when two weeks had gone by without one, I reluctantly admitted to myself it was time to give up. The only letter of thanks I got was one from Deer, brought to me by a Man who wanted a job on the Muriel.

If anybody but Deer had recommended the Man—his name was Frank—I would have refused to hire him. What the *Muriel* needed was sailors, and Frank had grown up in Foreston, a Man-town near Evergreen but far from the sea. The *Muriel* was the first ocean-going vessel he'd ever laid eyes on.

But Deer seemed eager for me to take him on, and I didn't like to refuse Deer. He wrote that Frank could work wood and sew a little, and bolstered this modest résumé with a sort of hopeful assertion that Frank had "other useful abilities which may reveal themselves to you as you get to know him." Since the Man who was presently working the *Muriel's* galley had a level of personal hygiene not much better than Captain Alcock's, I asked Frank if his "useful abilities" included cooking, and when he sort of said yes, I made Frank our new ship's cook.

As soon as I'd done that—and after making sure Captain Alcock was on deck, in the open air—I went out to tell him it was time we were off. Even Dan hadn't written to say as much as that he appreciated the effort I was making to discover the fates of his mother and stepfather, though before this, we'd managed to keep our long friendship and the failure of my marriage to his sister separate. Finding Muriel Seaborn was apparently going to have to be its own reward.

I'd come to pity our captain.

As he daily reminded me, he'd been a sailor for thirty years and knew his business as well as any man alive. "Know every rope and sail better'n you know your own privates," Captain A. would bellow, eyeing me with annoyance. "Been up and down a damn mast more times than you've trotted to the privy."

Alcock's frustration stemmed from the fact that, despite his long experience, my position meant he sometimes had to defer to me, and I was no manner of sailor at all. The captain knew his ropes and sails, but he had served on only one powered vessel in his life before the *Muriel*—a small wooden coaster whose tiny engine was considerably less efficient at propelling a ship than the wind even when it wasn't (as it usually was) out of either working order or fuel. On the *Muriel* it was the other way around. It was our masts and canvas—the captain's specialties—that were inadequate. So far, her engine had worked perfectly.

And I was the one who understood the engine. Since being hired, all Captain A. had learned about it was if he shouted, "Make her go, Mike!" down the speaking tube, sometime afterward the *Muriel* would begin making headway. He had recently also learned to shout, in panicked tones, "Mike, you whoreson bastard, make her stop!"

On Deer's recommendation I humored Captain Alcock as much as I could, so I asked him politely to prepare for an early-morning departure.

Squinting, Alcock demanded, "You coming along?"

He knew perfectly well that I was, of course. "Yes, Captain," I told him patiently.

"Expecting to use that damn engine much?"

"Yes, Captain. Every day."

Captain Alcock's reply to this was to suggest I do something unspeakable to myself.

My mind elsewhere, I wearily agreed to it. "But not now, all right? Right now I have some other things to do."

The captain was briefly startled to drop-jawed silence by this answer, then his hoarse laughter followed me to my cabin, where, despite having a million things to do, I sat down, put my feet on my desk, and stared glumly at the wall in front of me. There was no getting around it: As a husband, as a father, and as a friend, I was clearly a failure.

I must have fallen asleep. The next thing I knew, the sun was significantly farther down in the sky, and somewhere above me, Captain Alcock was shouting with even more than his usual vehemence.

I figured out from what the captain was saying that somebody was demanding to come aboard, and from the fact that only half his words were indecent, that the visitor was female. Someone's wife, I supposed, shrugging, until a familiar voice cried, "Well then, damn you too, whoever you are! We'll just see what Uncle River has to say about it!"

I leaped out of my chair and bolted for the deck.

Dan's daughter Helen was standing at the top of the gangway, staring down our captain with her hands on her hips, and she was as mad as a wasp.

I have three nieces and two nephews, but Dan's only child Helen is my favorite of the bunch. Her mother died when Helen was just a baby—a terrible shame, because Lisa was a wonderful woman and she and Dan were very happy together—and of course both Elizabeth and Sarah immediately offered to take over some or all of Helen's care for their brother. Dan wouldn't even consider it. As far as he was concerned, just because he had no legs didn't mean he couldn't raise his own child. Helen spent her first months of life playing and sleeping on a blanket under his desk at D&R, and once she could toddle, she had the run of the place. She was an engaging little girl and the boss's daughter besides; everybody looked out for her.

She was also bright and good in school, and never afraid of hard work. By the time she was eight or ten, Helen managed her papa's house all by herself, even the cooking. The older she got, the more she looked like her Aunt Sarah (and daughters of Men don't come any prettier than Sarah), a fact which had not escaped the notice of D&R's male employees. Helen had learned to fend them off by treating them all like brothers and working at the bench beside her father. Aside from Dan, she knew more about radio than anybody on the continent.

She was also stubborn. I don't remember if I mentioned that part.

I called to her, adding to Captain Alcock, "Let her aboard, will you please? It's Helen Farmer." The captain was familiar with the name of "Farmer" and stepped aside, though suspiciously. Helen threw him a glance that would have shriveled a lesser man.

Then, to my utter amazement and pleasure, she ran straight to me, flung her arms around my neck, and repeatedly kissed my cheek, announcing as she did so, "That's from Papa; this one's from Aunt Sarah; and here's one from Laura; and one from me. All you get from Bob is a manly handshake, because he's kind of at that age, you know? It doesn't mean he's not just as happy and grateful as the rest of us."

The clouds parted, the birds sang, and Captain A.'s body-odor seemed less foul than usual. My family cared. My family was grateful to me.

"No need to thank me," I said modestly, trying not to notice the captain, the dozen grinning sailors on the deck, and the usual crowd of dockside loafers, all looking on with interest. "I'm glad to do whatever I can. Come this way. After we talk, I'll show you the ship."

As soon as we got to my cabin, I told Helen I was happy to see her, of course.

"I hope you mean that," she said, cautiously trying out my bed. "Because you're going to be seeing a lot more of me. I'm coming with you. Gods, that's *hard*," she added, making a face. "How do you sleep on it?"

I immediately objected—though not to the statement about my bed, which was perfectly true. "We already discussed this. Your father can't spare you."

Helen had been conducting an intermittent campaign to secure a berth on the ship since the day we laid the *Muriel*'s keel, but her father had always been firmly against the idea—very much to my relief, since the voyage would likely be dangerous, and I had no desire to have to tell my best friend his daughter had been injured or lost in the course of it.

Helen's smile was triumphant. "He changed his mind. He can spare me after all. Aunt Sarah's going to look in on him, and I'm going to be your radio operator."

I winced at the word radio. "Navigation equipment," I corrected her. "Remember? We're not going to even say the word 'radio' for the next five years. It's special navigation equipment." Dan and I felt strongly if our competitors got so much as a hint we could broadcast radio signals over the horizon, they'd quickly make the mental leap from long- to shortwave transmission.

"I'm going to be your 'special navigation equipment' operator, then. Not all the bunks are this hard, are they? Because if this is all you've got, I'm bringing my own."

"Helen, you don't want to do this," I told her earnestly. "You smelled the captain already. The crew is worse." This was a lie—but in a good cause, I thought.

Helen gasped. "That was the captain?"

"Captain Alcock," I affirmed. "He was the best we could get."

My niece considered this.

"Suppose I pushed him overboard," she offered, "and we made him swim around a little before we rescued him? That would help, wouldn't it? In fact, we could wash the whole crew that way, one at a time."

"If we did that, they'd all quit. Then we'd have to find a new captain and crew who might smell even worse. You can't come with me, Helen."

Ignoring me, my niece rose. "Help me get my stuff aboard, and then you can show me where the 'special navigation equipment' room is. I might as well make it my cabin, right? I'm sure you've got a lock on that door."

"Helen..." I said sternly. Kind of sternly.

I got no further. "It's settled," Helen insisted.

I felt obliged to make one last attempt to dissuade her. "If you come with us, you'll live surrounded by very rough Men who smell bad, maybe for as much as a year. You won't get a bath or a good meal for months at a time, and you can't say the word 'radio,' or let anyone know we're in touch with the continent. We're just 'exploring,' using our new 'navigation equipment.'"

"I've got it, Uncle River," Helen said cheerfully. "When do we go?"

"Tomorrow morning."

"Plenty of time. I'm going ashore for my boxes. Here's a letter from Papa and Auntie to thank you."

I tried not to seem overeager to take the paper Helen offered, though I couldn't resist one quick peek. The closing was "love," and the handwriting looked like Sarah's.

"Captain Alcock isn't going to like you being aboard."

"I can take care of Captain Alcock," my niece replied grimly. "Just keep him down-wind of me, that's all."

I helped Helen aboard, then occupied the two hours she was stowing her gear away (and it was all good, practical stuff, too. I have to give her that) reading and re-reading my letter from Dan and Sarah. Though grateful and affectionate, it was short, and eventually I realized I'd memorized every word.

Just as I rose to leave, Captain Alcock and a crewman walked by the Navigation Room, talking. A particularly filthy remark of the captain's filtered through the door. Helen laughed.

"By the time I get you back to your papa," I sighed, "you're not going to be fit for decent society. I've got to go. Keep that door locked at all times, all right?"

"Of course." She was already starting up the radio set. "Uncle River?"

"Yes?"

"Thank you for making Papa so happy. You made me happy, too. I never knew my grandparents, but I still loved them."

"Thank me when I find them," I said.

CHAPTER FIVE

A s I had warned Helen he would, Captain Alcock objected to having her sail with us on the Muriel.

"Ladies distract the crew, dammit," he complained to me. "We don't need no 'navigator.' I been navigatin' ten years and never lost my way yet longer'n a couple days."

"Well, what if something happens to you?" I argued. "Or what if something happens to Mike? Not only can she navigate, Helen also knows that engine backwards."

The captain snorted. "Damn the engine! You just set me up another mast, and I'll tell you where you can stick your damn engine!"

He did tell me. He suggested several alternative locations, in fact.

Eyeing me despisingly, he said, "I thought you could run the engine. Can't you make her go? What the hell use are you, you can't make the ship go?"

I was perfectly competent to "make the ship go," but I didn't think—for Helen's sake—that I should make a point of this to Captain Alcock. "I have plenty of other things to do," I said instead. "We're not getting rid of Helen, Captain."

"Dammit!" he roared. "That woman is a woman! On a ship full of men! I know she's your niece and all, but she's a damned woman, dammit, and I want her off my boat!"

To avoid Captain Alcock, who was given to muttering darkly whenever he saw her, Helen spent the first week of our voyage locked in the Navigation Room replicating a circuit Dan had suggested might improve our radio reception. Despite the boxes of parts my niece had brought aboard, she came up short a few crucial components; a problem she "solved" by looting what she needed from our backup radio set.

"You know, that's our life-preserver you just ruined," I reminded her when she showed me what she'd done. "Without a radio, we're dead."

"We still have a radio," she countered blithely. "We have a better radio, with better reception."

"But no backup."

"That's what I love about you, Uncle River. You're never afraid to take a worthwhile risk."

"Will you still think it was worthwhile when our primary radio fails and we're sailing around hopelessly lost and starving to death?" I folded my arms. "When the food runs out, you know the crew will eat *us* first, don't you? In my case, they may not even wait until they're actually hungry."

On the other hand, thanks to Helen's new part we had really good reception. On one of my regular radio-calls to Dan, Sarah surprised me by coming to talk to me, too. She sounded great—like she was in the next room. It sure was nice to hear her voice again.

Still, I couldn't help complaining to Helen afterwards.

"You'd think Bobby could have talked, too," I grumbled. "I mean, he must have been right there in the room. How much trouble would it have been for him to say hello?"

I didn't mention Laura, because even if by some miracle my daughter had agreed to talk to me, I had no idea what I would have said to her. Bobby, on the other hand, had just started working at D&R. I could ask him a question or two about his job to get a conversation started.

"Why should he talk to you?" Helen shot back. "Have you ever asked him to talk to you?"

"Seems superfluous. I'm his papa. I'm sure he knows I'd like to talk to him."

"He doesn't know if you don't ask," declared Helen. "And another thing: You're his father, not his 'papa.' He's all grown up and manly now, remember? He doesn't call you 'Papa' anymore, and you shouldn't call him 'Bobby,' either. Nobody calls him Bobby. He's Bob."

I was about to remind Helen that she still called her father "Papa," but I stopped myself in time. She and her father, I suddenly recalled, had always been close. Dan had never let a gaping abyss develop between them.

"All right." I ran a hand through my hair. "Point taken. I will ask his mother whether *Bob*, my grown-up manly son, will do me the honor of conversing with me." I'd ask about Laura, too. It couldn't hurt to just ask about her.

"You don't have to be sarcastic," Helen sniffed.

That night, steeling myself against rejection, I asked Sarah whether Bobby and Laura could talk to me sometime.

"Is there something you want to know?" Sarah asked.

"No," I admitted. "Just—how they've been, I guess."

There was a long pause after I said this, until I blurted, "I love my children, Sarah."

"I know you do," she said quickly. "I know. You just…"

The unspoken rest of the sentence hung in the air. I thought I knew what words would probably complete it, but I didn't dare to ask, in case they were really worse ones than I was imagining. Finally, Sarah said, "Well, listen—when you do talk to them—and I'm sure they'd be happy to—don't forget to ask Laura about Tom, all right? I know you don't care for him, but he's important to her."

I had to wrack my brain for a minute to remember who "Tom" was—not unreasonable, I think, since he'd only been my son-in-law for six months or so.

"Who says I don't care for him?" I asked indignantly, when I'd placed the name. "I just don't know him, that's all."

"No, you don't know him. And you don't seem to care to." Before I could contradict this misapprehension—Tom was clearly unworthy of my daughter, but I really had nothing against him—Sarah added, "He's a good man, River, and he makes your daughter very happy. Give him a chance."

"I will. I have. Tom's fine. Anybody who makes Laura happy is fine." I ran a finger around my shirt-collar. "Will you tell Laura I asked how he was doing? It's not a lie, exactly. I'm asking right now: How's Tom doing?"

Over the crackle of static, I heard Sarah laugh. "Oh, you," she said, still laughing. "All right, I'll do that for you. Just this once, though. After this, you're on your own."

After being out of sight of land for five days—time the crew divided about equally between working the ship and anxiously scanning the horizon—we made our first stop at John Seaborn's birthplace, Big Island.

According to John, in his day Big was rugged, desolate, and half-wild, but also a paradise whose people were all handsome, intelligent, kindly, and tough. He did not except himself from this assessment. It looked to me like nothing but the desolation was left of John's paradise now. Most of the island women, their husbands and sons lost in the Final Ant War, had gone to the continent to start their lives over, and what had been a struggling but hopeful community was reduced to a fishing-camp. No one there knew the name of "Seaborn" anymore.

Nevertheless, I got the information we'd come for.

"John's island is northeast of here," I told Helen when I returned to the ship. She stared at me for a minute. "You sound pretty sure."

"I am sure," I replied. "If it was northwest, the island fishing-fleet would have found it. They're fishing all over that area. We know it's not south, because the only thing south of here is the continent, so if it's not northwest, it's northeast, right?"

"All right," Helen agreed, pulling out her (mostly blank) charts. "We'll go northeast."

"Lay out a grid," I suggested. "We'll cover the whole area."

Almost as soon as we turned eastward, the *Muriel* developed some sort of blockage in the fuel lines and we were forced to rely on our sails while Mike fixed the problem. From time to time the lookouts caught glimpses of what they thought were other sails in the distance, and since any ships so far out from the continent were almost certainly pirates, this put everyone on edge. Under power, the *Muriel* could outrun anything on the water, and even with her sails up her sheer size and steel hull would give any sensible sea-bandit second thoughts. But her guns were her best protection, because they were the newest and best afloat, so to ease the crew's mind about the pirates, Captain Alcock instituted gunnery practice.

He started by assigning everyone aboard to a gun crew—except for Helen, who was furious at being left out. Since, as I said, I'm no lover of weapons, I declined to take any part in the exercise, to the captain's annoyance, and while Helen hung around the gun deck trying to learn what she could by watching, I went down to the engine room to get away from the smell of gunpowder. Unfortunately, it clung to everyone long after gunnery drill was over, though Captain Alcock was somewhat improved by it. When I went to bed that night I was awakened repeatedly by my usual nightmare about the Valley where I'm bloody and panting and sweating and cursing and wishing I was dead. I'd wished that a lot of times in the first few years after the war—that I'd died in the Valley with my friends.

Next morning at breakfast Captain Alcock cheerfully informed me that I looked like a rotted fish belly.

He did not, however, cancel gunnery practice. After a few days of anxiety and broken sleep I was exhausted, and the captain was running out of revolting objects to compare the sight of me to.

Desperate, I waited until I saw Helen going to make sure the men wore the wax earplugs she officiously provided (and so powerful was her feminine magic that the men actually used them), and then I slipped into the Navigation Room and locked the door behind me. With trembling hands, I put in a radio call to Evergreen, and when I got through, asked in a voice I hardly recognized as my own to speak to Schoolmaster Deer.

It wasn't my usual time to call, and Deer was at the school, but I must have sounded as bad as I felt because the forest radio operator immediately went and got him and put him on. Deer and I talked for a couple of hours, and though I don't care to repeat everything we said—it was a very private conversation—I will say it helped me a lot. Over the next few days, while the captain cursed and the cannon boomed, we had more of these private chats.

They weren't just about guns and the war. In fact, what we mostly talked about was Sarah and my children. I told Deer things were maybe a little bit better between us. I'd spoken to both the kids, and though the conversations had been marked by awkward silences, I detected a surprising amount of goodwill in them, too. It seemed like they might be willing to give me a chance.

But they'd never understand me, I complained.

Years before, I told Deer, I'd tried, briefly and with no success, to teach Laura and Bob my native tongue, and taken them to Fisher's small room in the library to learn how a Forester lived. I encouraged them to stay there a night and sleep in the narrow bed and sit in a forest chair specifically designed to promote a proud, upright posture.

They hadn't seen the point. The room was cold and the chair was uncomfortable, they told me.

"They didn't understand. I was sharing my soul," I said.

Deer asked, "Do they share their souls with you?"

"If they ever did, I was probably away, or didn't notice or something. That's the real problem between us. Me."

But Deer said I hadn't convinced him there was any problem at all between me and my children. "The sharing of souls isn't always the earth-shattering event you're imagining, River. Sometimes it's no more than the steady accumulation of details about each other's lives. Just keep talking to them."

Then Deer said some other things, and by the time the engine was fixed and gunnery practice was finally discontinued, I was sleeping just fine again.

*

For a month we swept the ocean east and west, moving a few degrees north at each sweep. Then one day Captain A. called me to the bridge and pointed out a long, dark smudge off our port bow.

"An island?" I asked him, my heart in my throat.

"No." He offered a lewd alternative possibility.

"All right, dumb question," I acknowledged. "It's an island. A pretty big one, too. The darker parts would be forest, I think."

"You'd know best about trees." The captain nodded. "You want to go closer?"

"Much closer." I kept my eyes on the smudge. "I want to land."

Captain Alcock eyed me. "You're daft," he opined—although "daft" is not the word he actually used.

"It looks like a nice place."

It did look like a nice place. The closer we got, the nicer it looked, too. When Helen came out on deck, she caught my eye, and I knew she was thinking the same thing I was. The island looked just like the one John Seaborn had described to Deer. I wondered whether John himself might still be alive to greet us when we landed.

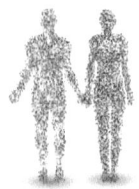

CHAPTER SIX

We approached the island from the west, but there turned out to be no harbor on that side, so we made our way slowly east, hugging the shore as closely as the captain thought prudent. Helen and I stood together at the rail, and though I continued to admire the island's leafy green beauty, as time passed I gradually lost hope it was inhabited. My niece grabbed my arm from time to time, and cried, pointing, "Look there! See?" but it never turned out to be a human form that had caught her eye. It was always the tawny hide of a browsing deer, or a stirring low in the underbrush that was probably a rabbit. I'd trained for years to be a picket of Evergreen, and I knew how high up in the bushes the leaves would rustle if a human brushed by them, and from what vantage a human lookout's face was likeliest to peer. Men said Foresters could make themselves invisible among trees, but that was only because Men didn't know where to look for them. Foresters could always see each other, no matter how thick the woods. Though I'd never fully qualified as a picket, if there had been humans on that island, sooner or later I would have seen signs of them.

But Helen remained hopeful, and part of me stayed hopeful, too.

Eventually we found a small sheltered bay, and Captain Alcock anchored the *Muriel* at the mouth of it.

"Still plannin' to go ashore, Evergreen?" he asked me.

"No reason not to. The place is deserted. There's game, though, and water. It might be a handy resupply point when traders start coming this way."

The captain stood and bellowed for a landing party to form up.

I said hurriedly, "Oh, don't bother. I'll row myself over in the dinghy, scout for water, and be back in a couple of hours."

Captain A. refused to sanction this plan. "You go ashore, you go ashore proper, with ten armed Men, like you're supposed to. You go alone and there's Ants there, they'll kill you. Then how'm I gonna get my damn dinghy back?"

The requisite number of sailors was soon mustered, headed by Mr. Jameson and including Frank, who came up on deck for some reason just at the wrong moment and was immediately "volunteered" for the job. To my dismay (though I guess I should have expected it) Captain Alcock then called for the weapons lockers to be opened and arms issued to the whole party. I sighed—probably audibly.

The sailors eagerly accepted everything they were offered—except for Frank, who refused even a pistol. Looking in confusion at the one thrust at him, he stammered, "But—there are no Ants anywhere near here."

"You don't have to take it, Frank." I added to the captain, "Do any of us need guns, in fact? Any Ants on that island—and there aren't any Ants on that island—won't have firearms. Believe me, in situations like this, the real danger is from men accidentally shooting each other."

"I'm in command here!" the captain bawled, drawing himself up stiffly.

This was true, of course, and furthermore, Deer had already suggested to me I show deference to the captain for the sake of harmony between us.

Since Deer was usually right about these things, I bowed my head slightly in capitulation. "I'm sorry. I overstepped, and I apologize. I just meant to be... offering the benefit of my experience."

My surrender was so unexpected it left Captain Alcock momentarily speechless.

When he found his tongue again, he asked doubtfully, "What experience? Ain't you a businessman?"

I'd never mentioned my army service to him. Uncomfortably, I admitted, "I fought in the Valley. And after."

"After who?"

"I mean I was in command of a Hunting Party. For two years."

Captain Alcock's tone instantly became friendlier. "You was a Hunter? Well, I'll be damned! You see much action?"

I didn't want to talk about it. "Suppose the men just shoulder their arms?"

Captain Alcock eyed me speculatively. "That the Hunter's way?" Without waiting for an answer, he thundered, "Landing party form up on the beach, then advance at the mate's orders. Arms to be shouldered except in case of attack, or further orders to the contrary. And stay away from them rocks with my longboat, damn you!"

Helen pulled me aside. "You're sure this is safe?" she asked softly.

"Completely safe. The island's uninhabited." Helen looked disappointed, so I added, "But if it's not this island, it'll be the next one. We know we're close. We've got to be."

The landing party disembarked and lined up on the beach as the captain had ordered, where Frank repeated, "No one is here."

A young sailor answered this with a nervous titter.

"Quiet, there," Mr. Jameson said calmly.

We stood ten minutes, and the only movement in the woods was of the leaves stirring in the light breeze. Then, with a mutual shrug, Jameson and I started forward, and the men trailed nervously after.

At first as we walked, they started at every chattering squirrel, and turned in jittery unison toward a pair of curious does who peeked out at us from behind a thicket. Hands slapped against wood and steel as long guns were half-lifted from shoulders. "Easy," counseled Mr. Jameson. The sailors sheepishly resettled their weapons and walked on.

But when nothing untoward occurred, the men relaxed and began to comment on what they saw.

"Nobody's to home, I guess," a gunner's mate remarked.

"Who's for rabbit stew?" another queried, spotting one in the underbrush.

"Yeah, whyn't you let us get that for the stewpot, Mr. Jameson?" a third suggested. "Frank could cook it, couldn't you, Frank?"

They were still discussing potential menus when Jameson and I both stopped at once and looked upward. Through a break in the trees we glimpsed a watchtower, looming just ahead on our right. The style of the watchtower was exactly what I had grown up with in Evergreen, and my heart beat hard in my chest.

I started toward it so quickly Mr. Jameson and the men had to hurry to keep up.

The trees ended in a clearing that was not a natural gap in the forest but had been deliberately created. It was circular, level, and at one time had been stripped bare of vegetation.

Not recently, though. New young growth, including small trees, was advancing inward from the perimeter. I gauged the trees with my eyes and reckoned the largest was about ten or twelve years old.

In the center of the clearing stood two long, low log buildings. One seemed in good repair; the other was missing most of its shingles and had started to crumble at one end.

My spirits—up and down since we'd first spotted the island—sank all the way to my boot soles this time. Everything about the place said this was John's island and that the clearing, huts, and watchtower had been built by Foresters to replicate a forest cordon and settlement.

The new growth, the ruined hut, and the oppressive silence announced that it was deserted.

We stood for a moment at the clearing's edge.

"Should we shout or something?" one sailor asked uneasily. "There might be somebody in one of them cabins."

Through stiffened lips I said curtly, "I'll look. Stay here." On the chance there were bodies of friends lying stark in one of the huts, I didn't want anyone with me.

The damaged hut was empty, with weeds growing through the floor; the second one looked sound. Its door was closed, but I pushed it open cautiously, and went in.

The hut was one long room, containing a dozen rustic bedsteads scattered about in no specific arrangement, a table, and two chairs. The beds—one still covered with a coarse blanket—were rougher than the one in my cabin on the *Muriel*, but there was no mistaking the way they were joined with wooden pins. Like the watchtower, the beds were pure forest-style. The table and one of the chairs were forest-style, too. I sat down on the chair and briefly lost myself in misery. My friends had been here. My friends were gone.

When my head cleared, I looked around more carefully. My friends had been here, yes—but someone else had been here, too. The style of the second chair in the room was strange to me, and unlike the rest of the furniture, it looked as though it had once been painted. There were pictures scratched onto the walls and the tabletop, and they weren't the work of a Forester, either. The pornographic renderings were disgusting.

Five minutes later, as I was turning over the odd chair to examine it underneath, the door opened softly behind me. Reflexively, I flung the chair aside and dived for cover, drawing my pistol as I went down.

My visitor was Frank.

"Trying to get yourself shot?" I demanded gruffly, rising and returning the weapon to my belt. "Knock next time."

"I'm sorry, sir," Frank stammered. I'd given him quite a scare. "Mr. Jameson asked me to see if you were all right."

"I'm fine." Since Frank made no move to leave, I added—sarcastically, "Anything else you want?"

I followed Frank's open-mouthed gaze to one of the pictures on the wall and had to smile.

"Yeah, it's not to my taste, either. I think Captain Alcock might like it, though."

Flushing like a boy, Frank asked, "Who made it?"

"I don't know. I'm trying to figure that out. I assume it was the same person who put this chair here, but I don't know who that was, either."

Frank came closer and looked at the chair with me. "Maybe it was a sailor."

He pointed at the only fully-clothed figure in the picture. "That man, there, is dressed like a sailor."

I agreed—and suddenly found myself wondering about the men of the *Morning Glory*. A paintjob and new name for their vessel might have been all that was necessary for them to turn their ship into one Deer's agents couldn't easily trace. Maybe the *Morning Glory's* crew had been driven to mutiny and piracy by the discovery that their captain was helping to succor Ants.

I'd have to think about it.

Putting the matter aside for the moment, I told Frank, "I want that chair over there and the table. Speak to Mr. Jameson about getting them to the ship. And by all the gods, make sure the carpenter sands the tabletop clean before my niece sees it!"

After that, while the rest of the shore party explored the clearing, I went out to look for graves. By now I'd almost convinced myself of the guilt of the *Morning Glory's* crew, but I hoped they'd granted that much at least to the people they'd been supposed to help.

But if there was a grave, I didn't find it, and after a while I went back to the *Muriel* to break the news to Helen that her grandparents were gone.

"They were there." I put a hand on her shoulder in sympathy. "It's not that we found the wrong island. So we have to assume that... I'm sorry, Helen."

She took it bravely. "We'll bear it," she said. "We have to."

Then she walked off with her shoulders straight, and if she cried when she got to her cabin—and her eyes were red later, so I think she did—she didn't mention it to me.

*

What Helen wanted most in the world was to find her grandparents, of course, but a bath was pretty high on her list, too. Captain Alcock was predictably baffled by the idea and objected to my appropriating the dinghy to row her to the island for the purpose, for reasons he bashfully refused to articulate, but which I could easily guess. When I insisted, we finally settled it between us that, as Helen's uncle, I could decently chaperone her, Frank could be trusted to row, and the rest of the crew could be confined to the ship for a couple hours. Captain A. then confiscated every spyglass on the *Muriel* and locked them in his cabin.

While Helen was off bathing and washing her clothes, I decided to climb the watchtower. From that vantage, I hoped I'd spot the grave I still wanted so much to find.

Frank immediately said he'd climb, too.

I was beginning to suspect Frank had made some secret pact with Deer to "protect" me. That morning, when he'd seen me refuse Captain A.'s offer of a firearm, Frank immediately went below and returned with a quiver and bow, saying earnestly that I mustn't go ashore completely defenseless. To the crew, it was as if Frank had equipped himself with some ancient artifact. They teased him pretty cruelly about it, but Frank just stared blankly back at them until the joke seemed like it was on them instead of him, and they finally sent him off with friendly slaps on the back.

The sailors were starting to like Frank—even the roughest ones. Initially they'd all resented the way he imposed something like Forest Discipline in the galley—no food to be taken by anyone, at any time outside of regular meals, unless by order of the captain. Then they started to appreciate his cooking and realized he was doing them a big favor. They said all the usual things sailors always say about the ship's cook—that he was supplementing the ship's dried stores with seaweed and bilge rats and so on—and for all I know, in Frank's case some of the stories might even have been true. He and his mother had known some hard times, and hungry people learn not to be picky about what they eat. But if Frank was serving us rats, he made them taste good, and his strict rules ensured everyone got a fair share. The *Muriel's* first cook had been susceptible to intimidation when apportioning his slops.

From the top of the tower there was a clear view for half a mile in every direction, and the smell of evergreens, the scent of my childhood, was carried up by the morning breeze. My already low spirits sank even lower. I'd given up my friends as lost many, many years before. I wondered how it was possible for such a brief interval of hope to make me vulnerable all over again to the same grief I'd long ago mastered. I stared into the trees, seeing nothing.

Then, almost without knowing it, I began scanning the ground.

I wasn't sure what a grave would look like from where I was—whether it would be mounded or sunken, bare or unnaturally green. I could only hope I'd know one if I saw it. I wanted to have someplace Helen and I could offer a last farewell to people we had loved where we felt like we were physically close to them. I'd always disliked going with my mother to memorialize my father at the tree in Broadleaf that grew in his name but not from his ashes.

Suddenly, my back involuntarily stiffened. Ten feet from the western base of the tower, just outside the line of trees, was an arrangement of five stones.

The stones would probably have gone unnoticed by a casual observer. They were of different sizes and placed far enough apart not to draw attention to the pattern they made. But a trained eye—a picket's eye—would detect that the outer four stones were positioned at precisely the four compass points, and that the fifth one was placed exactly in the middle. The configuration is called a quincunx.

Every Forester learns from childhood what a quincunx is. You see them everywhere in a forest, because trees planted in a quincunx grow well, with each tree getting plenty of light and air. Traveling Foresters also use a quincunx as a trailside signal to other Foresters. There are dozens of these signals—a broken branch; a cairn of pebbles—and each one means something specific. A quincunx marks a place where something important is buried. Not a grave. A quincunx specifically means something useful, like a food-cache, or letters to be retrieved and delivered.

The odds were very small, I thought to myself, that the sailors of the *Morning Glory* would assemble a quincunx for their own purposes. Someone—maybe Heron—had buried something specifically for another Forester to discover.

I was staring at the stones when Frank came and stood beside me.

I didn't want Frank to see what I saw. Growing up near Evergreen, he might have picked up enough forest-lore to know a quincunx's significance.

"We'd better go down," I said. "Helen'll be finished any minute. If she sees us up here, she'll insist on climbing this thing too."

"Helen is very brave," said Frank approvingly.

Not quite so appreciatively, I agreed with him. "Oh, she's got no nerves at all."

Once we'd climbed down, I chatted away to Frank with what I hoped was an appearance of total unconcern. But inside, I was making plans.

CHAPTER SEVEN

I would swim back to the island that night—alone—to investigate the quincunx.

Technically, a ship's like a forest in that no one's supposed to leave it without getting the captain's permission first, but since I wasn't really a member of the *Muriel's* crew, I figured I didn't need to bother Alcock about the matter. Chances were good he'd either say no or insist on sending ten nervous armed Men with me. Naturally, it wouldn't be right for me to be *seen* flouting the rules, but if I left and came back discreetly enough, no one aboard ship would ever even know I'd been gone. I doubted I'd have any trouble getting by the watch. Their attention would mostly be fixed on the horizon, looking for pirates and storms.

The *Muriel's* lighting is electric, naturally, but I knew where to get my hands on a candle, and in the bottom of my sea chest was the tinderbox I'd had with me when I rode out of Evergreen for the last time. Regulation forest-style, it was perfectly watertight. Once I'd coated the candle wick with wax to keep it dry, and stolen a little fire shovel from the galley to dig with, I had nothing more to do than wait for an opportunity to put my plan into action. After dinner, stripped down to my shirt and trousers, candle and tinderbox in a pocket and the little shovel tied to my back with a length of cord, I waited in my cabin for the ship to get quiet. When everyone was sleeping, I crept to the place in the *Muriel's* stern where a knotted rope ladder lay neatly coiled on the deck, dropped it gently over the rail, and climbed down the ship's side.

A minute later, I was swimming soundlessly toward the island.

There was a sliver of moon, and I found my way back to the quincunx by its light. Once there, I knelt, lit my candle (the center stone, moved aside, made a handy candleholder), and cautiously dug with the little spade. A curious critter or two stopped just outside the circle of light to watch, but that was fine with me. If something large and unfriendly came along, the little ones would alert me by scattering. I wasn't armed, but the watchtower was nearby, and I'd only need a few seconds to get up the ladder.

I dug without knowing what I'd find. John's library? In any danger, he'd have thought first of protecting his books. On the other hand, he'd also know a hole in the ground was the worst possible environment for them, so maybe not books after all. Something sentimental? A token of some kind? A memorial to Posthumous? It certainly wouldn't be money. A party of Foresters wouldn't regard money—even gold—as anything precious enough to bury. The one thing I felt sure of was that since it was under a quincunx, whatever was there would be of particular interest to a Forester.

Ten or so spades-full down, my shovel clinked against something hard, and putting the tool aside, I felt with my hands. The object was smooth and not large. I thrust my candle in to have a look.

Just visible was the mouth of a glass bottle, sealed with wax.

I thought for a minute it must be something of the sailors' after all, probably just some trash they'd buried. There was no reason Heron would want me to have a bottle of anything. But just to be sure, I uncovered the rest of the bottle carefully and pulled it out.

By the light of my candle, I could make out a roll of papers inside. An edge of writing was faintly visible on one of the sheets. It looked like Forester.

The only sensible thing to do was to take the bottle back—unopened—to the *Muriel,* where I could study what was inside at leisure in my cabin. After hastily smoothing the ground where I'd dug—and scattering the five stones—I hurried back down to the water and swam for the ship.

I hadn't gone many strokes before I noticed that instead of being quiet and dark, as she should have been at that hour, there were lights on the *Muriel's* deck. Looking closely, I saw movement in the rigging, too, and the next minute, I heard voices. One of them, I was pretty sure, was Helen's.

My absence, it appeared, had been noted. I stopped where I was and studied the situation.

I saw right away I had no hope of sneaking aboard unseen. The rope ladder had been pulled back up. I considered my options (few) and concluded regretfully that there wasn't any graceful way out of my predicament. Whatever the consequences of my little adventure, I'd have to take them.

On the other hand, I felt like the bottle was entirely my own private business, and nobody needed to know I'd commandeered the little shovel, either. The shovel was official ship's equipment, and Captain Alcock was sensitive about things like that. I slipped the cord from around my body and tied the bottle and shovel together with it before I swam nearer.

"There he is!" someone shouted; and against a backdrop of stars, twenty heads projected over the rail and twenty angry faces peered down at me.

The voice of my formerly loving niece hissed, "Uncle River, I am going to kill you!"

Not knowing what else to do, I agreed with the plan. "Can I come aboard first?"

A sailor silently tossed down the rope ladder, and I stealthily secured my bundle to the end of it before climbing up. How I was going to retrieve it later, I wasn't entirely sure.

Then, dripping and cold, I faced the assembled ship's company on the deck and feebly explained that, rather than having fallen overboard and drowned, as they'd imagined, I had merely gone for a midnight swim.

The captain's rage was epic. With the eager assistance of the crew, he abused my person, my intelligence, my moral character, my self-discipline, and my manners until my clothes had nearly dried. Immediately after threatening my life, Helen had begun to cry; but when I would have gone to comfort her, the captain—the same man who had never previously had a single good thing to say to or about her—prevented me. Putting a fatherly arm around her shoulders himself, he informed me in an impassioned speech, which featured many new and imaginative synonyms for the sacred act of coitus, that I had better make a "boogering good apology" to "this sweet little lady" or I would answer to him at the masthead for her tears.

I groveled to Helen; I groveled to both crew and Captain A. for the trouble I had given; and finally—after enduring a record three scathing words from Mike, who had apparently emerged from his lair in the engine room for the sole purpose of reproaching me—I was permitted to lead my sobbing niece away.

"Helen, I found something!" I whispered as we went. "Don't be mad at me. I found something on the island!"

She stopped weeping just long enough to shoot me a withering glance.

"I don't know what it is yet, but I think it may be important," I continued, looking behind us to be certain no one else was within earshot. "Only I don't know for sure, because I couldn't bring it aboard."

"Fine," Helen sniffed. "Go away." For emphasis, she added a word her father would not have approved.

I ignored this, and when we reached her cabin, I followed her in and closed the door. Whatever Helen had to say to me—and she was absolutely bursting—I didn't think the whole ship needed to hear it. "I'm sorry I scared you. I thought if I didn't tell you I was going, you wouldn't worry."

For some reason, this completely blameless remark only enraged Helen further. She told me I was hopeless.

"Why am I hopeless?" I foolishly asked.

"Because you can't learn. You did the same thing to Aunt Sarah about five million times, and where did that get you?"

"Sarah?"

"Don't you give me that innocent look," my niece warned darkly. "You know perfectly well you did. You'd go off on a job and just disappear, and then when she was an absolute wreck wondering if you were alive or dead, you'd finally telegraph that everything was just fine. Auntie told me once there were whole months where she didn't know whether she was a wife or a widow! Did you think she could live like that forever?"

"I never did that!" I protested. "I always let her know where I was! As soon as I could!" Except for that one time. I hoped Helen didn't know about that one time.

"As soon as it was convenient, you mean. And then you'd lie and say you were fine when you weren't, too, like the time you got sick and almost died. How do you think it made Aunt Sarah feel to know you'd lied to her?"

Call me stupid—and some people have—but this way of looking at things had honestly not occurred to me before.

"I didn't mean it that way!" I pleaded, hands extended. "I meant to—to protect her. Out of love. I thought I was being helpful by not telling her... certain things."

"What's helpful," Helen demanded, "about treating a strong, intelligent person like Aunt Sarah like she's a stupid weakling who can't be trusted?"

My niece went on in this strain for some time, and though it was hard for me to accept, eventually I saw her point. However lovingly I'd meant it, a lot of the times I'd imagined I was "protecting" Sarah I'd actually been hurting her instead. This made me feel bad.

I felt so bad, in fact, that by the time Helen was finished and asked, "So what was it?" I just looked at her blankly. I'd completely forgotten why I was even in my niece's cabin.

"Oh, a bottle," I said, suddenly remembering. "Full of papers. I couldn't open it, but I saw writing. Pretty sure it was Forester."

Helen brightened. "From my grandparents? No, wait; they wouldn't write in Forester, would they?"

"Well, John might," I suggested. "But so might Anna or Heron or Posthumous. I'll have to go back and get the bottle before we'll know for sure who it was."

"You mean you left it on the island?" Helen wailed. "Oh, no! It'll be *hours*—"

"No, it's all right. I tied the bottle to the ladder before I climbed up."

Helen stared at me. "But what if it's not there now? What if somebody pulled up the ladder, found the bottle, and threw it back in the water?"

I was worried about that myself. I said, "I hope not. Want to go to bed now? The sun'll be up in an hour."

"Not until I know what's in that bottle," replied Helen firmly.

I stopped at my cabin first to get my jacket before going back up on the chilly deck and—I swear I was going to do this—telling the deck watch honestly what I was there for. But luckily for me (because I really didn't want to face the deck watch right then) the first thing I saw when I opened my cabin door was the bottle itself, sitting on my desk. Under the electric light, the writing on the papers was clearer, and it was definitely Forester. But who had pulled the rope up and put the bottle in my cabin?

Where was the little shovel?

When I thought of the shovel, I thought of Frank, and when I thought of Frank, I knew I had the answer to my question. He'd have recognized the shovel immediately as belonging in the galley. The neatly coiled cord lying beside the bottle suggested Frank's work, too. Such a tidy guy. The *Muriel* could have used a whole crew of Franks.

I tucked my treasure under my arm and headed back to the Navigation Room, where Helen met me at the door. "Open it! Open it now," she whispered eagerly.

She didn't need to urge me. I was already peeling away the seal.

CHAPTER EIGHT

I recognized the handwriting as soon as I saw it. "It's from your grandfather."

Excitedly, Helen leaned in close to look. "What's it say?" she breathed. "Oh, I wish I knew Forester so I could read it for myself!"

"Pretty useless skill to have," I said. "Wow! Six pages!"

I glanced up to find Helen eyeing me severely. "What?"

"Don't say Forester's useless," she chided. "It's your native tongue."

"Yes, and outside a forest, it's pretty damn useless. Except maybe this one time." I flourished the papers in Helen's face and grinned.

My niece didn't return my smile. "Bob's learning it."

This was such an unexpected revelation that for a minute, I didn't get it. "Who? You mean Bob my *son*? Why does he want to learn Forester?"

"Isn't it obvious?"

Not to me, it wasn't. "No. The little business D&R does with the forests, it does in the Valley language. Foresters prefer to do business in Valleyspeak. That way, they can pretend they're not doing business."

"Your self-loathing is pathetic," Helen informed me coldly. "You realize when you talk about Foresters, you're talking about yourself, right? Anyway, Bob's not trying to drum up business for D&R, he's trying to understand his own heritage. He's half-Forester—in case you've forgotten."

"No, he's not," I said firmly. "Nobody's 'half Forester.' Forester's a bunch of rules, not a race, and if you only obey half the rules, you're not a Forester. As far as I know, Bobby doesn't obey any of them—which, if I may say so, is the intelligent choice. You want to know what this letter says, or not?"

Helen tried to pull off one of her special, soul-crushing "looks," but John's letter distracted her too much.

"Yes, please. Is it dated?"

I pointed. "Right here. Let's see… This was written fifteen months after the *Morning Glory* landed here. It says"—I cleared my throat— "'My dear ones: This island, which we had hoped would be a sanctuary, has proven otherwise…'"

Almost as soon as I started to read, I realized it was a good thing Helen *couldn't* read Forester, and that I was going to have to be careful about how I translated the letter or she'd be asking awkward questions. John had been as discreet as he knew how in the way he worded it, but discretion wasn't exactly John's strength. The very first thing he wrote was that by the time he and the others set sail from the continent, their party had been unexpectedly enlarged by thirty-six extra "beings," all "half-bred" (by which I knew he meant half-Ant), and they had refused to give passage to many more "of richer blood" who begged them for it.

In other words, before they'd embarked for the island, the voyagers had been besieged by Ant-soldiers—at least thirty-six half-Ants and a lot of full Ants—who'd escaped the slaughter in the Valley and come to them hoping for asylum.

In telling Helen the story, I used the word "refugees" to describe the thirty-six and left out all the references to breeding and blood altogether. She seemed satisfied with my version.

"What happened when they got here?" she asked. "Couldn't they stay? That island seems like a paradise to me!"

"Yeah, it's nice." I flipped over the page, scanned ahead, and then drew a sharp breath. "Pirates," I told her soberly.

"They made those pictures."

"What do you know about the pictures?" I demanded, aghast. "I thought I told you to stay out of that hut!"

"I did stay out! I stayed out even though you telling me to stay out was paternalistic nonsense! I heard some of the sailors talking about them, that's all."

I pretended to believe Helen when she said this. It was more bearable that way.

My niece added anxiously, "Did the pirates kill them? Is that what happened to my grandparents?"

I was still reading. "No. No, the pirates didn't hurt them. Apparently, it was all very 'friendly' on the surface. The pirates smiled a lot, ate everything they could fit into their mouths, and then took what else they wanted and left. Twice in six months."

I didn't tell Helen that the second time they came, what the pirates "wanted" included two female Ants, whom they kidnapped; a piece of savagery that, even though the females were only Ants, I sincerely hoped ultimately proved fatal to the pirates.

"After the pirates' second visit, your grandfather and the others asked the *Morning Glory's* captain to take them to another island. One farther out."

Helen and I both sat thinking this over for a moment, and then, as the implications of it dawned on us, our eyes met in astonishment.

"Another island!" Helen repeated. "Then—they're still alive!"

"Or at least, they could be," I agreed cautiously. I didn't want Helen to get her hopes too high. "John says here that except for the pirates, everything was fine. They were all well and happy and—"

As I was speaking, I turned over the last sheet of paper. It was filled on the back with drawings that were clearly Heron's work, and the picture at the top of the page was of Anna cuddling a baby.

It had to be hers. Anna had a special love for all babies and children, but the way she held this one was somehow—proprietary. I don't know how else to put it. Just the way she rested her cheek against the child's little downy head said this was her own flesh, and Heron's, who had drawn the picture.

Helen leaned over to look. "Is that Aunt Anna?"

I said slowly, "It's Anna of Evergreen, if that's what you mean. And her baby, I guess. It says 'Peregrine' underneath the picture, so that's probably the baby's name; and in Forester, that ending's male, so it's a boy."

Then I grasped what Helen had said.

Anna had lost her family—all her family—when she was very young, and because of that, I think, she had a habit of "adopting" people. Anybody who had any connection with her at all, or even none sometimes, she turned into "family." For example, John Seaborn had been her first stepfather, and then much later, he'd become Elizabeth, Sarah and Dan's stepfather, too. As far as Anna was concerned, that made them all brothers and sisters.

Actually, John had flat-out abandoned Anna (she was just a little girl at the time), and gone on to make a much better, more secure life for himself by marrying Muriel, who belonged to the rich Farmer family. But typically for Anna, far from holding that against him, she not only forgave John, but also embraced his new stepchildren—and Muriel, too, for good measure—as though they were blood kin.

"Your papa teach you to call Anna 'aunt'?"

"No. Aunt Sarah." Helen took the page of drawings from my hand and studied it closely. "The baby looks just like Aunt Anna," my niece decided, "except for being a little darker." Then she gasped and cried, "Oh, gods! That woman! Is that—is that my grandmother?"

I looked where Helen pointed.

One of a group of figures, Muriel was arm-in-arm with a fair-haired woman I didn't recognize.

"Yeah, that's her. And John's the old fellow—there—talking to the tall man with braids. The tall man's Posthumous. He was Master of Evergreen before Deer."

Helen started crying, of course.

I don't know why women have to cry when they're happy, or why, since they always do cry, they can't learn to carry a handkerchief. I fished around in my jacket pocket and pulled out mine to give my niece.

Then, excited and happy, the two of us went over the letter again, with me carefully extracting every bit of information I could from it while not letting on anything about the Ants to Helen.

Everything on the island had gone as planned, apparently—except no one had planned for pirates. The settlers organized the place like a forest and elected Posthumous its Master (no complaints from John in the letter about not being made Master himself, which surprised me). Everyone worked in the gardens, or fished, or hunted, and there was plenty to eat. John noted proudly that Muriel was having good success—and here I had to do some rewording—teaching "some" of the citizens (by which I knew John meant the Ants) to speak.

"'To speak?'" Helen repeated.

"To speak *Forester*."

"Oh. I didn't know Grandmother spoke Forester!"

I hurried on.

"We will leave this place tomorrow," I read, "proceeding initially, the sailors tell me, on a bearing of—" He listed some technical stuff about their projected course. The letter ended, "Our sailor friends will inform the Master of Evergreen Forest of the location of our new home. In the event anyone comes looking for us, please contact Master Deer for further information."

"Only the *Morning Glory* never made it back," murmured Helen, taking the page from my hand and turning it over to study the pictures again. "So the sailors never got word to Evergreen."

I couldn't keep my eyes off the pictures, either—the one of Anna, particularly. She looked somehow different from the way I remembered her.

"Uncle Heron's good," Helen commented. She pointed to another female figure and asked about her.

"Just a friend," I said, thankful Helen didn't know as much about Ants as I did. I could tell at a glance the creature wasn't human.

Helen's tone became brisk, and she rubbed her hands together. "All right, so they're alive." She added, after a quick glance at me, "that is, they *may* be alive. But they've moved to another island 'farther out.' How are we going to find them?"

"The hard way, I guess. By looking at all the islands 'father out.' We have a starting place, and we know the *Morning Glory's* initial bearing. That helps."

"Who knows what course they eventually steered, though. It's a big ocean. This isn't going to be easy."

"No."

A yawn caught me mid-sentence and prevented my saying more. Outside the porthole, it was morning.

"Bed," I sighed, getting up. "We'll call your papa in a couple of hours and tell him, and then I'll talk to Deer. He'll need to ask Snow whether we should give Anna's mother the news or not. So far, we haven't even told her we found John's Island."

"Is she worse?" Helen asked with concern.

"Not worse, but not good. On the other hand, maybe this is just the medicine she needs."

As I left, Helen was already climbing into her bunk and I'm sure she was asleep in five minutes. But when I got back to my own cabin I was too keyed up even to lie down. Instead, I cleared everything out of my desk, and as soon as the ship was awake, went down to the carpenter's shop, apologized to the carpenter for making him get up in the night to look for me when he'd rather have been sleeping—he was still mad about it—and got the table and chair I'd found in the hut on the island. I installed them in place of my desk, and between the table and chair and my bed, my cabin took on a decidedly "forest" look.

"'Little Evergreen,'" I muttered to myself as I pinned Heron's drawings up where they'd be the first thing I saw every day when I woke up. "Best thing for me. It'll keep me focused."

Then finally I slept, and dreamed I was back among the trees.

CHAPTER NINE

T he crew spent the next day filling the Muriel's water-tanks and packing the fermenter with green plant matter to make a batch of fuel—all except Frank, who asked permission from the captain to take his bow and go hunting instead. He shot a nice buck, the meat of which, being Frank, he planned to slice up very thin and smoke, serving us only the head and offal—parts that wouldn't keep—fresh for dinner. That was the sensible thing to do, of course. Smoked, the venison would last a long time.

But I couldn't bring myself to be sensible—or at least not entirely. While Frank conscientiously sliced the bulk of the meat into strips, salted them, and threaded them onto strings to hang up and smoke dry, I built a fire in a trench on the beach, and when it had burned down to coals, commandeered a few of the best cuts of venison and spitted them over it. Helen was as excited by the prospect of fresh meat as I was, and took turns with me turning the spit, and from time to time, members of the Muriel's crew wandered by to comment on our work and hint for samples.

By late afternoon, the meat had reached a state of irresistibly juicy perfection. Frank stewed up a big pot of native greens and sand cherries to eat with it, and when that was done, Captain A. passed the word to tell the salivating sailors it was dinnertime at last. The Muriel's whole company sat down with their mess kits in two facing lines on the beach to feast. It was the best food I'd eaten since Sarah's cooking, and I didn't stint myself.

We talked as we ate, of course, mostly about nautical things. I don't know if it's true of all sailors, but the ones on the *Muriel* only really seemed to have two topics of conversation, and one of them was embargoed by Helen's presence. It was the first time on the voyage everyone, officers and crew, had eaten together, and the meal had a strangely domestic ambiance. The captain held court at our head like a typical Papa; the crew bantered and squabbled among themselves like brothers; and if it's not pushing the analogy too far, Mr. Jameson and Frank between them shared a mother's role, seeing to it the platters of meat and biscuit were passed properly, and that no one took more than his share. Helen—the entire crew's secret sweetheart, though she pretended not to know it—was the honored guest, and I was the clueless outsider best known for asking stupid questions.

Not that the crewmen teased me about my ignorance, the way they teased each other. I was clueless, but I was powerful, as I continually proved by violating the ship's rules at will and answering to no one but myself.

I thought about this as I ate. Watching the Men, I tried to decide whether it would be worth it to me to give up some of my independence in order to fit in better with them. I was perfectly comfortable with being an outsider. I was used to it. I'd been one all my life. Never truly a Forester, I'd never really become a Man, either, and I'd been married and a father for twenty years without ever managing to fit into family life. I was a businessman who didn't care much for business, and now I was a sailor who didn't know anything about ships. It felt natural. I wondered whether, if I changed, and the captain and crew embraced me for it, the sensation would be welcome, or just make me uncomfortable.

I was still thinking about this when Helen spoke up and suggested that now that we had finished eating we should observe the custom of the continent by following our feast with entertainment.

The crew liked the idea. They demanded she go first, of course, so Helen opened the show by singing us a song—very nicely—which the Men cheered and applauded until she blushed. They'd have been happy for her to continue singing all evening, in fact. When she wouldn't, a couple of sailors got up instead.

The sailors' first number was inoffensive, but their second selection turned out to be a pretty typical sailor's ditty concerning the nocturnal activities of three insatiable young ladies and a willing sailor lad. When Captain Alcock figured out what the ladies and the sailor were up to, he let out a roar loud enough to split rocks in defense of what he characterized as Helen's "pure, sweet ears." The language the captain used in reprimanding the singers was forthright, and probably left Helen's ears significantly less sweet and pure, but I'm sure he had the best intentions in the world.

After that we had tunes from a gunner who played a homemade fiddle, and then a carpenter's mate did rope tricks.

Mike, who missed the rope tricks by rowing back to the *Muriel* for props, finished off the program by demonstrating (in near silence) how he could make electrical sparks leap bigger and bigger gaps. The Men were as impressed by Mike's equanimity when he singed off one eyebrow as they were by his spark-jumps, and aside from Helen with her song, he was the hit of the evening.

We ended the fun with athletic contests—foot races, long jumps, and a ridiculous relay between two teams in which the *Muriel's* two smallest crewmen functioned as the batons. Both sides would have preferred passing Helen hand to hand, of course, but she wisely refused to take any part except as starter. We all had such a good time that when Captain Alcock announced it was time for us to go back to the ship, everyone groaned.

"Get along there," ordered the captain irritably. "Anybody who ain't in the boat in five minutes can swim back." Turning to me, he added caustically, "I don't guess that would bother you none, though."

"No," I admitted. "In fact, I could use a swim. Anyone want to swim with me?"

This question led to the revelation that few of the *Muriel's* sailors knew how to swim.

They weren't joking. In fact, the few crewmen who could swim seemed regretful, rather than proud of their skill. The only times a sailor was likely to fall overboard, they informed me, was in a heavy storm or in battle, and in either case he didn't stand much chance of being rescued. Therefore, they said, a sailor suffered less by drowning sooner than later.

To my relief, Captain Alcock scorned this point of view. "I got a good mind to make you all swim back. I'm guessing somewhere betwixt here and the ship, you'd catch on."

"Can you swim, Captain?" I asked.

"Can I swim?" Captain A. puffed out his barrel chest. "Evergreen, when I get in the water, even the fishes admire my style!"

This gave me an idea.

Laughing along with the rest, I suggested slyly, "Well, what about one more race then? You and I will swim from the beach to the *Muriel*, and the first one to grab the ladder gets a deer's liver for breakfast."

Captain Alcock's eyes gleamed. He'd already hinted to Frank he wanted that liver, but the most he'd been able to get thrifty Frank to agree to was liver dumplings shared between the five of us who constituted the officer's mess.

To hoots and shouted encouragement from the crew, the captain immediately signified his acceptance of the challenge by stripping off his jacket and shirt. "Think you can beat me?" He displayed a good pair of shoulders and arms that, though dirty, had an inch on mine for length.

"Maybe not," I returned, pulling off my own shirt. "But I'm not letting that liver go without a fight!"

I grinned as I said it, meaning to make a joke, but to my surprise, instead of a laugh, the remark was answered with silence.

I seldom thought anymore about the thrust from an Ant-sword that had left a raised jagged red weal down my left shoulder and back, but it was the first time anyone on the ship had seen it.

Except Helen, of course. To everyone's relief, my niece had the wit to say quickly, "My money's on Uncle River, but a kiss for whichever of you wins!"

The tension broken, the crew roared their approval—and not only for the kiss (which I'm sure they were all coveting), but because my intention in proposing the race was beginning to dawn on them. The captain couldn't possibly swim all the way to the *Muriel* without washing off a lot of accumulated stink. A swimming contest was an answer to the sailors' prayers, in fact—though one did confide to me in an undertone that he'd regret the resulting unavoidable pollution of the cozy little bay.

Barefoot and stripped to the waist, Captain Alcock and I stood toe-to-toe at the water's edge while the rest of the crew, excited and laughing, piled into the longboat to row alongside us as we swam. At Helen's shout of "Go!" the captain and I leaped forward and the boat pushed off.

I intended from the start for the captain to win. As I'd recognized for the first time while we were feasting, a ship's company functions in many ways like a family, and I knew I had no business doing anything to undermine the authority of the *Muriel's* Papa. With no need to win, and the crew laughing and shouting like madmen in the longboat skimming along beside us, I never enjoyed a race more, and when Captain Alcock beat me fairly by a stroke, as far as I was concerned it was the perfect ending to the day. The captain bashfully claimed a chaste peck from Helen at the longboat's side, and generously declared to all that I was as fine a swimmer as he had ever seen in his life.

The only "regrettable" occurrence of the race was the loss overboard from the longboat of the captain's boots, shirt and jacket, but after a great deal of sloshing (and some surreptitious scrubbing) these were eventually recovered.

On board, as we dispersed for the night, Mr. Jameson commented, "I think we'd all benefit if the captain was to give us a weekly swimming demonstration," as though he didn't mean a thing in the world by it, and we all went off to bed snickering.

Next day, while the *Muriel* built up steam—and after asking permission first, like a good sailor—I went to John's Island for the last time. Once there, I climbed the tower and looked in the direction my friends must often have looked as they watched for the *Morning Glory* to come with supplies and letters from home, and then afterward sat awhile in the hut, trying in my mind to see Anna and Heron and John and Muriel there, instead of pirates drawing dirty pictures.

Then I sprinkled the fuel I'd brought with me from the ship all around the clearing and set everything in it ablaze. If I could have done it, I'd have turned the whole island into a desert, or sunk it altogether so pirates could never set foot again on the land from which they'd driven my friends. The most I could manage was to deny them use of the huts and watchtower.

Captain Alcock was waiting for me when I got back.

"Seems like you might just as well have let things be," he commented, nodding toward the columns of black smoke rising from the island. "When them pirates come back they'll just build everything over again anyways."

"I know," I said. "It was pointless. I don't know why I bothered."

Captain Alcock's reply to this was a snort. "Oh, you know why you bothered," he declared. "You just don't want to *say* why you bothered. There's a lot going on you don't want to say. Sailing around with no chart nor a course don't make sense. You just don't want to say to me what the sense of it is."

"We're just exploring," I lied. "It's the nature of exploration to go new places without a plan."

The captain shrugged. "Don't make no matter to me," he said, getting up and starting away. "I sail where I'm told to. You change your mind about talking to me, though, I'll still be here."

"I'll keep it in mind," I said.

An hour later, we were underway.

CHAPTER TEN

O ur strategy—such as it was—was to start off in the *Muriel* on the heading John's letter indicated they intended to sail twenty years before, note the prevailing winds and currents along the way, make corrections to our own course to allow for the effects those same winds and currents might have had on a sailing-ship like the *Morning Glory*, and from that try to calculate—and replicate—the route she eventually followed.

"You know there are too many variables in this equation for it to be solved, don't you?" I said to Helen. "As a plan for finding a specific island in a great big ocean, this is only very slightly better than no plan at all."

"You're always so gloomy," Helen complained. It was her usual remark when I tried to inject reality into a situation. "Don't forget we have Jasper. He'll keep us on track. That man reads the wind and water like a book."

"Who?"

"Jasper," Helen repeated. "Captain Alcock. That's his name: Jasper."

The captain had certainly never invited *me* to call him by his first name.

"Oh, and I got some news from Papa this morning. There's another war."

This was not a big surprise. Wars break out on the continent about every fifteen minutes.

"Who is it this time?"

Two small "nations," apparently, were each trying to grow at the other's expense.

Since the Final Ant War this kind of thing had become routine among nations of Men, but D&R didn't make weapons and had a policy of strict political neutrality, so I didn't usually care one way or the other how the fights came out. In this case, though, the *Muriel* put us right in the middle of it. One side in the conflict was backed by the Valleylands, and *Muriel* happened to be Valley-flagged. Unfortunately, the only dock big enough to accommodate her was in Coastland—and the second warring country was an ally of the Coast.

If the two countries were still at war when we got home, Helen informed me, we might not be able to land.

"Why can't Men just get along?" I complained. "You don't see Foresters fighting with other Foresters all the time."

"No, and you can thank Men for that," Helen said curtly. "Now that the Ants are gone, *Men* are the common enemy that keeps the forests united."

*

I woke next morning to rough water and gathering clouds.

As soon as I was dressed, I went up on deck, where Mr. Jameson and the captain were already discussing the situation.

"Coming right for us," Mr. Jameson was saying as I approached. "We could go west and maybe miss the worst of it."

The captain shrugged. "Get wet either way." Seeing me, he gestured to me to join them, asking genially, "What does the Hunter think?"

Mentally, I flinched at the title, but all I said was, "I think we're in for stormy weather, Captain. Three or four days of it, judging by the height of those clouds." I turned slowly, scanning the sky in all directions. "No hail, though. We should be able to stay our course. The *Muriel* was built to take this kind of thing."

Captain Alcock's face fell. "You read the weather pretty good," he admitted. Deference... harmony...

"The sky, yes," I modestly demurred. "On the other hand, I can't tell a thing from the water. Helen tells me you're an expert at that, Captain."

Captain A. immediately brightened. "I may say I know water pretty good." He nodded and threw out his chest again. "It's experience is all it is. I been on the sea since I was seven." Indicating his first officer, the captain added, "Jimmy, here—he don't know as much as I do, because he ain't got the same experience. He only started to sea when his whiskers grew. Ain't that right, Jimmy?"

"Jimmy" agreed that this was so. "I was fifteen," he said musingly. "Took a dislike to farming."

Our captain nodded wisely. "Well now, you two just listen then, and I'll learn you a little." Pointing, he began gravely, "First thing you want to do is notice the color of the water…"

Helen was right; "Jasper" knew things about water I'd never have guessed.

By midday, the first fat drops of rain were falling, and by evening it was coming down in sheets. The *Muriel* rocked like a cradle. Through the soles of my feet, I could feel her engine straining all the way up in my cabin, but her steady chugging never faltered, and we continued making headway. When I managed to stagger as far as the bridge, arms extended and tossed back and forth like a rag doll between the bulkheads, even the captain agreed that the ship was behaving well. The crew, of course, were delighted that since there were no sails to trim, there was no need for them to go on deck beyond brief tours of inspection every couple of hours. The sailors took these in rotation, and now that I knew almost none of them could swim, I worried each time one went out.

Next morning, the rain seemed less, but the winds were worse. I was as proud as ever of the way the *Muriel* dauntlessly battled on through the heavy seas, but the charm of experiencing it was wearing thin. I won't say any of us were seasick. We were all much too hardened old seadogs for seasickness now. I will say, however, that no one aboard showed any interest in eating breakfast.

But as though he'd been a ship's cook for a hundred years and knew every trick, Frank put a pot of dried-venison broth on to boil, and broth turned out to be the one thing everybody wanted. Tasty, nourishing, and comfortingly hot, it could be drunk from a cup anytime no matter how badly the *Muriel* pitched and tossed. By now the waves were occasionally dropping her so far down at the bow her propeller lifted half out of the water and spun wildly, and things the crew had tied well down earlier were continually coming loose and rattling around.

Toward evening, Mr. Jameson (who was steering at the time) shouted down that the longboat was breaking free of one of its davits and he wanted two men to secure it. The sailor due to go topside next started up immediately, and since I could swim, I went with him. At least if I went overboard, I was thinking, I'd be able to save myself.

But as soon as we started working, I understood why the men had said there was no point in a sailor being a swimmer. If at any time I had lost my hold while we were securing that davit, I would have been irretrievably gone in an instant. The sea was as black as ink, and the waves were as high as the pines of Evergreen.

Between the two of us, the sailor and I tied up the longboat again, completed our inspection of the deck sometimes by crawling, and then made our way back down the ladder to light and safety below. Frank met us at the door of the galley with blankets and cups of his broth.

Captain Alcock happened to be standing by, and taking the cups from Frank, he silently added a generous measure of something to them from a flask he produced from the depths of a trouser pocket.

Whatever was in the flask was probably responsible for my decision a short time later that since I was wet anyway, I might as well go up on deck again and see if I could make the sailors' tours of inspection safer to do. From a locker, I got the two longest lengths of rope I could find, carried them topside and made my way forward, where I secured the ends of both. Then I waited for the next time the *Muriel* went up at the bow, and clinging to one of the ropes and letting gravity do the work, slid aft, where I tied the other end of the rope near the *Muriel's* stern. I tested my work by standing and making my way back forward, hand-over-hand on the rope.

The trick worked great, so I repeated the process with the second length of rope down the other side of the *Muriel*, and finished by walking a complete circuit of the deck using the ropes to steady myself along the way. Then, colder and wetter than ever, I went back below.

In the galley, the usual off-duty gathering spot of most of the sailors, I explained what I'd done.

"I think it'll help," I told the crewmen who were there. "If you hold onto the ropes, you'll be a little safer, and I'm sure you can go faster. That's the important thing, right? The quicker you've done your inspection, the quicker you can get into dry clothes and your bunk."

In answer to this, the men stared back at me in silence.

"Anyway, pass the word," I finished lamely. "You can use the ropes or not, I guess. Your choice."

As I turned to go, somebody said, "Thanks," with no particular enthusiasm, and tired and discouraged, I went to my cabin.

Once there, I stripped off my wet clothes, threw them into a corner, and crawled stark naked between the sheets my mother wove. She'd have been scandalized.

I slept that night like I'd been pole-axed, not waking until somebody knocked at my cabin door.

"Yeah, what?" I muttered, sitting up. "All right, all right... Unless you're Helen, come in."

My visitor was—strange to say—Mike.

"What do you want? Toss me some clothes, would you? They're in that chest." Getting up, groaning, to dress, I added, "Your face says 'problem.' What is it?"

Silently, Mike tossed a piece of paper down in front of me. On it was a chart, which I studied for a moment.

"This our burn-rate?" I asked then.

"Yep."

I studied the chart some more. "This is bad."

"Yep."

"We're going to run out of fuel in—what? A few days?"

"At this rate."

"Well, shit."

"Yep."

The *Muriel* was holding her own against the storm, all right—but I hadn't considered the cost in fuel of the feeble headway we were still making on our planned course.

I thought for a minute.

"Any way we can reduce fuel consumption?"

Mike shrugged.

I answered the shrug with something wise and intellectual, like "shitshitshitshitshit," and sighed heavily. "All right. Cut the power by half, and I'll go talk to the captain."

I met a sailor along the way who greeted me with a spontaneous, "Good morning, sir!"

I did a doubletake. He didn't look like he was being sarcastic.

"Good morning, Sailor," I replied suspiciously. "Do you know if the captain's in his cabin?"

The sailor said he didn't, but offered to find out. Notwithstanding my muttered, "No need," he hurried ahead of me, and as he knocked on Captain Alcock's door, commented in an unwontedly friendly fashion that the winds of the night before had sure been bad, but the morning, by contrast, was shaping up better.

"Looks like we might be past the worst" he said, as the captain bawled from within for me to "Come in, damn you!"

Captain Alcock was also in a strangely friendly mood. As I entered, he jumped to his feet, and as soon as he could reach it, seized my hand in a crushing grip.

"Mornin', mornin', Evergreen," he said with feeling. "Mr. Evergreen, I guess I oughta be saying."

"I don't see why," I replied, mystified. "Just 'Evergreen' is fine. Captain, we've got a problem, and I need your advice."

At this point, the captain finally released my hand. I flexed my fingers cautiously to make sure none were broken.

"Sit down, sit down," the captain invited. "You all right? Damn me if you don't look like you been in a fight!"

I hadn't thought to look at my face in a mirror, but I'd noticed when I was getting dressed that my body was pretty bruised from sliding around on the deck in the dark.

"I'm fine. Just a few bumps. The problem is our fuel burn-rate, Captain. If you look at this chart…"

"You're sure no bones is broken, though, dammit?" the captain interrupted anxiously. "Banged up as bad as you are, it might be hard to tell."

"I'm fine," I repeated. "Just concerned, as I say, about our fuel situation."

When I was finally able to get his full attention, I explained what a burn-rate was, and that at our present one, the *Muriel's* tanks would be dry in three days or so.

"She ain't a good sailer," the captain remarked then.

"No," I agreed unhappily.

"I don't mean no criticism of her by saying that," Captain A. added quickly. "The *Muriel's* a fine lady. Just because she's lubberly as a blind-drunk cock-whale when her sails is up don't mean you didn't do a good job on her. Not by a damn sight."

"Thank you." I was more baffled than ever. The captain usually referred to the *Muriel*—not sparing my presence—as "this damn boogerly tin-plate piss-pot."

I said, "I apologize for getting us into this situation, Captain. I should have tracked the fuel myself and not left it to Mike to do."

Instead of swearing at me, Captain Alcock brushed my apology away. "It ain't your fault. You got a lot on your mind, is all. Now what type of help was it you wanted from me?"

I went straight from the captain's cabin to Helen's.

Helen is always unaccountably cheery in the morning, and on this morning, she was positively perky. In fact, she greeted me with a kiss.

I eyed her warily. "Is it my birthday or something?"

My niece laughed. "So," she said happily, "how does it feel to save someone's life? I've always wondered."

As a matter of fact, I had saved someone's life once—I think. It was one of my Hunters, it was almost twenty years before, and I had no idea Helen even knew the story. I'd certainly never told it to her.

"It feels all right, I guess. Better than the opposite. Anyway, there's no way to know for sure if I saved anything. He might have lived without my help. People can bleed a surprising amount sometimes and not die. Did you notice how much lighter the clouds are, by the way? Storm's starting to pass."

Helen looked at me rather oddly. "Jack didn't say there was any blood involved."

"Who's Jack?"

To shorten the story considerably over the way Helen told it, "Jack" was one of the *Muriel's* sailors. He'd gotten a little careless on his turn around the deck the night before and almost been swept overboard. Luckily for him—and for all of us, since the *Muriel* didn't carry any surplus crew—he was hanging on to one of the lines I'd rigged and managed to keep holding on to it long enough for another sailor to hear him yelling and come help him back aboard.

"Jack's alive today because of you," Helen declared. "I hope you're proud. I'm very proud *of* you!"

"Wait—" I said, confused. "Are you telling me the crew actually used those lines? My impression was they thought they were ridiculous!"

"Of course they used them!" Helen exclaimed. "They were thrilled to have them!"

I muttered something resentful to the effect that somebody might have at least said so, then.

"Oh, pooh. These are men we're talking about. When does anything male ever express gratitude or approval? Anyway, Jasper felt bad at first, because he thought he should have been the one to think of putting up safety ropes, but then Jimmy pointed out that at least someone had done it, and that was the important thing. Apparently there isn't much to hang on to on the *Muriel* compared to the kind of ship everybody's used to."

So now I knew the source of "Jasper's" extravagant affability.

"All right," I said inanely. "Fine. Glad it worked out."

"Go find Jack," Helen urged. "He wants to thank you personally."

I stared at her for a minute. "We need to talk about our fuel situation."

Then I added, "What?" because Helen was studying me with what looked like disapproval.

"You have no idea who Jack is, do you?"

Well, my niece had me there. I'm not good with names. Man-names are absurdly unmemorable anyway, and I hadn't learned many of the crews'.

"I thought they were all named 'sailor,'" I joked, and when Helen didn't smile, I amended this to, tentatively, "The little dark one?"

"No. That's Timmy. Jack is the redhead."

"Right; right. The redhead. Sure I know Jack. He's the one with… red hair."

"Learn their names," my niece said severely. "It's disrespectful of you not to know them."

Now that I thought about it, Sarah would have told me the same thing. It was disrespectful of me not to know the sailors' names.

"Can we please go back to the place where I was a big hero?" I asked sadly.

This made Helen laugh again. "You're a big hero, Uncle River, and I'm proud to be your niece. How's that?"

"Perfect. Let's have a look at your charts now and see where we are."

To myself, I was silently repeating, "Jack. Medium height, red hair, squint in one eye." I remembered the squint very clearly. "Timmy. Short, very young, dark hair, bad teeth. Nice kid, though. Always has a joke."

It wouldn't take long, I decided. With a little effort, I'd know them all in a day or two.

As she pulled out her charts, Helen asked, "Why is the engine suddenly so much quieter? And do you want me to do something for your face? It's all banged up."

"I'm fine," I said automatically. "Time signals coming through all right?"

"Of course. Why?"

"Because the engine's about to get even quieter. I'm on my way to tell Mike to shut it down completely until the sea's a lot calmer. Fighting the waves burns fuel too fast, so on Captain Alcock's advice, we're going to put out a sea-anchor and just drift for a few days. That's why I asked about the time-signal. If we lose it, we won't have any idea where we are."

I showed Helen Mike's notes, and she stared at them for a minute. "All right. If we have to, we have to. Jasper told me yesterday the current's running west, though, and we want to go east. With a sea-anchor out, we'll move in exactly the wrong direction."

"I know. I'm sorry. Track our course, and we'll head back the way we want to go as soon as we can. Your grandmother has waited twenty years for us; I guess she'll can wait a few more days."

CHAPTER ELEVEN

A couple days later, when the sea was finally calm, we fired up the *Muriel's* engine again. When they heard it chug to life, the sailors cheered.

According to Helen's chart, which was mostly blank except for a line tracing the course we'd sailed and a shape marked "John's Island" penciled in, we were weeks away from where we wanted to be.

"Damn," I said. "We need fuel bad, and from here, we have no idea where the nearest place is where we can get anything to make fuel from."

Silently, Helen put her finger on John's Island.

"Exactly." I frowned. "We're going to have to head straight back to John's Island. It's the only sure thing we have. Only we don't have enough fuel to get there. We'll have to use the sails part of the way."

"We have enough for a few days, anyway," said Helen. "And if we have any luck at all, we'll find another island before it runs out, and then we'll make more."

Then she went up on deck, and I went straight to the radio.

After the day I had to tell Sarah John's Island was deserted, I had started calling her and the kids more often, because I knew they were disappointed, and though I'm not very good at comforting people, I wanted to do what I could for them. Then I let Helen grossly exaggerate my supposed "heroism" during the storm, and when Sarah seemed impressed by the story, parlayed that into a few more calls, until, little by little, I got them used to hearing from me every day. Mostly I talked to Sarah, because the radio was at her house, but if the kids were there, I talked to them, too, and I always remembered to ask about Tom now.

This time, Bobby answered the radio and said his mother was out.

I was disappointed, but I love my son, so I gave him a hearty, "So, Bob... How are you? Job going all right?" Then I cringed, because I knew I sounded like an idiot.

As usual when I asked about his job (and I always asked about his job), Bob muttered, "Fine, fine," and immediately changed the subject.

"So, Father: How's life on a ship?"

Bob was just being polite, the same as I was being polite when I asked about D&R. As he and I both knew, Dan kept me so up to date on business matters that I knew how Bob was doing better than Bob did. And I was sure Helen kept her cousins informed about what life on a ship was like, too.

So I said my usual "fine, fine" in return, and then for some reason—I don't know why—this time I actually answered his question.

"Life on a ship is like life in a forest," I said. "It's the same routine every day, and you see the same people over and over until you all get on each other's nerves. Only despite that, you all have to get along, because you live in such close quarters that if you don't, the situation will become unbearable."

When I opened my mouth, I had no idea this is what would come out of it, but after I said it I was glad, because it made Bob laugh. My son probably laughed all the time with other people, but he hadn't laughed with *me* since he was a boy.

He asked, "Is that how you remember life in a forest?"

"Pretty much, yeah. No wonder I ran away, eh?"

It occurred to me then that all my running had, in the end, accomplished exactly nothing. Life in a forest, life in the army, and—yes—family life too, had all turned out to be, at base, the same. They were places where you spent your days among people you got to know and love so well that when you lost one of them, it was like losing an arm. You were maimed. I was becoming attached to my shipmates and involved in their lives. I didn't like it, but I couldn't help it. And in the middle of the ocean, there was no further place for me to run.

I did not say any of this to my son.

"That's not how Uncle Deer describes Evergreen," Bob told me, still chuckling.

"Yeah, Deer is different from me. When did you speak to him, by the way? Recently?"

"Yesterday," Bobby said. "We talk on the radio all the time. He's teaching me Forester."

Though Helen had already told me Bob was learning Forester, until that moment, I'd assumed he was learning it from Sarah.

I switched to Forester myself. "Are your lessons going well?" I asked in that language. "I assume they are, because I know Deer's a good teacher."

Bob was able to answer this, a little haltingly. "Yes, thank you," he said—becoming very formal, because Forester is a formal language. "My study goes well. It is difficult, but Teacher Deer is very..." A long pause, and then in Valleyspeak again, Bob said, "...patient. Sorry. I haven't learned that word yet."

It was my turn to laugh, and I did, and then I told Bob what the word "patient" was in Forester. I also told him several Forester synonyms for "patient," because patience is a quality forest-folk talk about so much they need lots of words for it so people don't get bored with "patient" all the time. Patience—or as I think of it, a large capacity for tedium—is highly valued in forests.

"You sound good, Bobby. You sound like an Evergreen native." Then, wincing again, I added, "Sorry. The 'Bobby' just slipped out. Bob, I mean. Or would you rather I called you 'Robert,' like your mother does?"

I sensed hesitation, and then to my surprise my son answered, "I'd rather you called me 'Robin.' That's what you wanted to name me in the first place, wasn't it?"

Robin was my brother, twelve years older than me. I loved him more than I loved anybody in the world, I think, and maybe even more than I loved myself.

When I was ten years old, he went to join my father fighting in the Penultimate Ant War and neither one of them came back.

"Your mother didn't care for—that name," I said, swallowing.

Even at the time we chose "Robert" instead, I knew that, deep down, it wasn't really the name "Robin" Sarah didn't like. It was the name's association with my mother. Mother could never bring herself to be more than distantly polite to her daughter-in-law, who never complained, but who deserved better.

"She's gotten over it, I guess. She calls me 'Robin' herself now."

I repeated "Robin"—in Forester, as my son had said it—speaking cautiously, in case it hurt.

It didn't hurt. It felt good. Still in Forester, I told him, "You honor my brother's name."

I'm not sure Robin knew the word "honor," but I think he understood.

We talked for quite a long time after that. It turned out that for some reason Robin was avidly curious about forest life and had a lot of questions he was shy about asking Deer. I tried to stick to funny stories, like the time when I was thirteen and decided to make myself a nice little (unauthorized) campfire that quickly got out of hand and burned up about half an acre of woods. I learned from the pickets who came running to put the fire out that, yes, the Forester language actually does have a word that essentially means "shit." I taught it to Robin, since I knew Deer never would.

"You'll find it useful," I advised him.

Robin blurted out suddenly, "Do you miss Evergreen?"

It was a question I'd been avoiding asking myself for twenty years.

"I try not to even think about Evergreen. There's no point. I can't go back."

"Think about it now," Robin urged. "Do you miss it?"

I tried to laugh the question off, but my son kept repeating, "Do you?" until it was obvious I was going to have to give him some kind of answer or he'd never drop the subject.

"Well, I don't miss all those damn rules, I can tell you that. And then, I couldn't have had Evergreen and your mother, too."

"Or D&R," Robin put in.

I knew from the way my son said it that there was more to this remark than just a simple statement of fact. He meant I'd neglected him and his sister and his mother to serve D&R's interests. That's how it looked to him.

Picking my words carefully, I said, "I like my work, yeah. But your mother and you kids came first by a long way. I'd have gone to live in the Antlands if your mother had been there!"

After that, to my relief, we moved on to safer subjects.

"Take care of yourself, Papa," Robin said when we signed off. "Get home safe."

So I was "Papa" again. That was nice.

CHAPTER TWELVE

Two days after I had my talk with Robin, the lookouts reported
something on the horizon they thought might be land, and by the
next morning it was clear what they'd spotted was a good-sized island.

"It's a little out of our way," Helen commented, squinting at it through a
spyglass.

"Hey, it's green," I answered. "What's the problem if we burn a few extra
hours' worth of fuel to get there if we get a whole fermenter full of plant
material out of the deal?"

Since Helen agreed with this, the captain steered for the island. Captain
Alcock, I was aware, respected my niece's opinion a whole lot more than he did
mine. On the other hand, so did I, so I had no real complaint.

When we anchored, I was privately all for taking a large party ashore
immediately and putting them straight to work filling the fermenter. From
what I'd seen of it, I'd already decided the island was deserted. There were no
visible structures, no obvious footpaths, no rustles in the brush that suggested
the movements of sentries. For the second time on the voyage, I told myself I'd
trained to be a picket of Evergreen, and I'd know it if the island were inhabited.

But luckily for all of us, Captain Alcock insisted on a regulation shore party
of nine sailors plus me, and Mr. Jameson to command it. As they had at John's

Island, both the captain and Jameson backed me in refusing to consider for a moment Helen's request—more of a demand, really—to be allowed to come along.

Frank wasn't with us this time, either. In anticipation of the fuel we were soon to make, he was down in the galley, using what fuel was left in the galley stove to cook the men an extra-good dinner. He promised us dried venison stew, and since we'd lived the last few days on biscuit and cold water, everyone was ecstatic about this.

When Captain Alcock had loaded us up with weapons to his satisfaction—and in the matter of weapons, he was not easily satisfied—the eleven of us rowed to shore, and I'm happy to say I knew the name of almost every sailor in the longboat.

We landed, and the shore party lined up on the beach just as we'd done on John's Island and waited ten minutes for any island inhabitants to make themselves known. The men weren't as nervous as they'd been the last time. When Mr. Jameson ordered us forward, they moved briskly, chatting in undertones about the feast on the beach they were already planning.

"You're going to race the captain again, right?" one asked me softly as we started up a gentle slope. "'Bout time old Stoney had another bath." I understood that I was being honored by being permitted to know the secret name by which his crew referred privately to Captain Alcock, and as we climbed, I was trying to think of some appropriate response to the compliment.

But when we topped the rise, anything I might have come up with to say became irrelevant. The island wasn't deserted after all. In a clearing before us stood a cluster of long, low, mud-built huts, and beyond them, tilled fields.

In an instant I had crouched down, of course, to make myself the smallest possible target, and sighted my weapon, alert for any movement, however slight. Mr. Jameson immediately did the same. The men, however, stood gap-mouthed and staring until Jameson and I simultaneously ordered, "Get down!"

I might have added, "Damn fools!" to this. I'm not sure.

The sailors crouched then too, aiming their weapons randomly wherever a leaf rattled, and sometimes at each other.

There was not the slightest sound or sign of movement from the buildings or anywhere else, so after a minute I raised my head slightly and looked around.

My first thought—hope—was that, totally unexpectedly, we'd found Anna's party after all. But almost immediately I realized that though a Forester might throw up a mud structure for a temporary shelter, he'd never live in it for long. There were trees on the island. Anna and Heron would have seen to it by now that the huts were built of wood. There were also no watchtowers, which any Forester would have built to keep a lookout for fire, if nothing else; and for a last non-forest touch, the fields beyond the huts were planted in straight, evenly spaced rows, with all one kind of plant. Foresters never farm; Foresters garden.

So—not Anna and her party. Who then? And where were they?

Cautiously, I called out, "Anybody here?" several times, in different languages.

Mr. Jameson caught my eye. "Let's have a look around."

We stood.

"Landing party advance," said Jameson, in his quiet way.

I added, "Two of you—Bertie, and, um"—the name fortunately came to me—"Lionel, keep watch to the rear."

With Bertie and Lionel walking backward, we approached the nearest hut. By means of hand gestures, I directed the men out of the line of any of the rough openings that seemed to be the building's windows.

Then we all squatted again (the sailors were catching on fast), and when there was still no movement, I shouted, "Anybody home?" a few more times.

"Whoever lives here must be hiding," I told the crewmen. "Stay here: I'm going to go look in a window and see if they're down on the floor or something."

I didn't think there was really much danger. There were several huts, each big enough for forty or fifty inhabitants, and yet whoever lived in them was apparently too timid to confront a mere eleven of us. But to be on the safe side, I stayed low as I ran, and when I reached the hut, put my back against it.

Without being asked to, Mr. Jameson joined me, nodding toward a nearby doorway to indicate he'd deal with anybody who decided to take advantage of my preoccupation at the window to come at me from that angle. As I said, I thought we were safe—but I appreciated the gesture.

When Mr. Jameson had sighted on the door, I whirled to the window, thrusting my long gun into the hut, my finger ready on the trigger. There was no response to this aggression, so I cautiously strained forward and had a good look.

"Empty," I said, surprised.

The hut was abandoned—though I suspected only recently. On the floor were mats, probably sleeping pallets, woven of some plant fiber, and a crude three-legged platform not quite well enough made to deserve the name of "table." The platform was very low, and there were no chairs or stools. Whoever used it must have sat on the floor. There were a few fire rings spaced evenly around the room (but no smoke holes in the roof), and here and there, some rough tools lying around in a way that suggested they'd been thrown down in a hurry. The tools were of bone, stone, and wood, but no metal, as far as I could see.

I wiped my forehead with my sleeve. "Looks like we've got a pretty good technological edge on whoever lives here," I commented to Jameson. "Does that mean we can look around a little more?"

Guardedly, the first mate agreed that, since we obviously didn't need to worry that we'd suddenly find ourselves facing any superior weaponry, we could look a little farther for signs of the island's inhabitants.

We checked out the rest of the huts, first.

Since coming up from the beach, the sailors had gone from being dangerously unwary to comically cautious. They advanced from hut to hut by throwing their backs bruisingly against the walls, and "covering" each other against nonexistent dangers. Still, it was good to see they'd recognized their deficiencies as commandos and wanted to do better. When the huts all proved equally empty, we wandered out to the fields.

The crop growing there was nothing any of us had ever seen on the continent. I pulled off a piece of leaf and chewed it, then quickly spat it back out.

"Bitter!" I commented. "Whoever eats this stuff has my sympathies."

Mr. Jameson, the ex-farmer, inspected the plants closely. Then he pulled one entirely out of the ground, revealing a half-dozen purple, tuberous roots.

"That's the part to eat," he said. "This is some kind of—potato, I guess."

The men, curious, forgot their exaggerated vigilance and crowded around to examine the strange purple "potatoes."

"Ugly!" one commented. "Hey, let's take some!"

Since one purpose of our voyage was to establish trading posts, I thought we might as well offer the inhabitants—when we found them—something in exchange for some tubers to get trade started, so I allowed a man or two to fill his pockets. Then we slowly moved on.

Beyond the fields were some areas of low, brushy scrub that were perfect places for an ambush, as I pointed out to the men, who would otherwise have marched straight into one. I thought I had a responsibility to mention things like ambushes since the captain had made such a point of my having been a Hunter. The paths skirting the wastes were sunken, as though countless feet had walked the exact same trails for many, many years, but since they probably led to wherever the islanders were hiding, we followed one, me leading the way. The men were relaxed. Somewhere on the island, maybe around the next corner, were the inhabitants of the huts we had seen, but they were apparently fearful beings, too shy to confront us.

I had just opened my mouth to mention to Jameson that by my reckoning, three-quarters of the time the captain had granted us to explore was gone and we should now turn back, when something—some movement off to my right— caught my eye. I stopped to look, and the others crowded up on my heels.

At that instant, a row of human-like figures rose together from behind a low ridge nearby and launched a volley of stones at us.

We had no time even to put our arms over our heads for cover. Beside me, one of the sailors—Lionel—took a hard hit from a stone on the top of his head. His legs buckled and before I could put out a hand to steady him, he went down. Someone else cried, "Ow! Hey, what's going on?" and for a minute, everything was chaos. The stone-throwers ducked behind the ridge again, and the sailors—except for a couple who stood stock-still with shock—scattered a few panicked steps in all directions.

The instant's forewarning I'd had made me less surprised than the others, and I got my wits back first.

"Run!" I shouted, as instinctively I raised my weapon and waited for the line of figures to rise again.

Mr. Jameson, no longer soft-spoken, yelled, "Back the way we came! Move, damn you!" and the sailors, roused by his voice, turned wherever they were and made for the trail, with Jameson himself and someone whose name I couldn't recall half-walking, half-carrying the stunned Lionel.

Our attackers rose again, and a second volley of stones pelted down.

A few of the stones struck me, but in spite of that I was able to shoot the first figure to fill my gunsight. As it toppled backward, the rest of the human-shapes froze for an instant, and I knew then for certain what we were dealing with.

They were Ants.

The Ants dropped back down behind the ridge again, in perfect synchrony, but I didn't move. My experience on the continent told me they'd try at least one more volley of stones before they moved on us. Except on an actual battlefield, where they line up with their swords ready in their hands, stones are always an Ant's first weapon. They're plentiful and effective: An Ant will throw stones for as long as he still thinks it may get him the result he wants.

But a barrage of stones can be deadly, so I thought before I joined the sailors I'd do what I could to persuade the Ants every volley meant certain death to one of them. I kept my gunsight on the ridge and stood my ground, bracing myself against what I knew was coming.

Jameson was still shouting orders to the men, but his voice was getting nearer. Before the Ants stood up again, he was beside me, and I had time to say, "By the gods, *don't miss*," before we were bombarded again. I got my target squarely in the chest (no more stones from him, I thought), and Jameson's went down, too. But the Ants had found their range, and we were pelted hard in return. I didn't think we could risk another round. Jameson and I started down the trail toward where the rest of the landing party was sheltering, as fast as we could run.

The men were crouched, inexpertly but determinedly sighting their long guns on the ridge.

"Forget it," I panted, as Jameson and I reached them. "They're moving to new positions. Up, up! We need to get to cover before they surround us."

Good cover was going to be hard to find. The Ants must have been living on the island since before the Ant Rebellion, which meant they'd had more than a thousand years to groom the terrain into just what they liked. Aside from the scrub and a few low hills, there was nothing to break their lines of sight.

There was one small stand of trees not too far off, but it looked like it might be difficult to reach—especially since Lionel would have to be carried all the way. Nearer, and in another direction, was a small rocky outcrop. I pointed it out to Jameson.

"What do you think?" I asked.

"Our best bet," he agreed. "Let's get to it and regroup."

"How're we gonna get back to the ship?" one of the sailors—Timmy—asked.

I pretended to have much more confidence than I felt. "Our guns'll scare them off. Then we'll make a run for it."

A thousand years alone on an island hadn't been enough time to make the Ants forget to hate Men. By the time we'd reached the rocks and lain down among them, they were already creeping up on two sides of us, picking up stones along the way as they came. Jameson shot a random stone-picker dead, and after another instant of confused paralysis, the Ants moved back a little.

This inspired some of the men to fire their weapons, too, but as far as I could see, only one hit his mark. I told them, a little sharply, to wait until they were sure of their shot. Our ammunition supply wasn't infinite, and there was no knowing how long it might take us to drive the Ants off.

Mr. Jameson's usual calm had returned.

"Richard," he asked one of the sailors thoughtfully, "didn't you tell me once you could shoot the eye out of a squirrel?"

In answer to this, Richard—the man whose name I hadn't been able to recall earlier—took quick aim and neatly dropped a squatting Ant who never knew what hit him.

"Nice!" I said admiringly.

For some minutes after that, no one spoke beyond the muttered comment from Timmy that "Lionel ain't looking too good."

The Ants began systematically to test us. Every couple of minutes, a small group stepped forward from the main body to launch a few stones at us, gauging, I presumed, both the distance and our resolve. I shot two of them, and Richard and Jameson one apiece, but instead of retreating, the Ants reshuffled their line. Older Ants and most of the females stepped aside to allow the young males through. These carried pointed sticks—crude spears—that were untipped, but black from being hardened with fire.

"This is bad," I muttered.

Over his shoulder, Jameson ordered the crew sternly, "Every one of you pick a target. I'll tell you when to fire. Stay calm, hold your breath as you squeeze the trigger, and if you can, get your Ant dead center."

"Amidships," Timmy suggested, trying to smile. Poor kid. He was all of sixteen or so—my son's age—and trying so hard to be a man.

Before Tim could say more, the Ants cocked their arms back together and launched a volley of spears at us.

Jameson, Richard, and I all fired at once, and Richard took a second shot—successfully, as far as I could see. The rest of the men fired raggedly after us, but they mostly missed their marks.

The spears, meanwhile, still fell short.

After a brief, thoughtful pause while they analyzed this, the Ants apparently resigned themselves (if "resigned" is something you can say about Ants) to taking losses. Their front line dashed five steps in our direction, heaved a second volley of spears, and retreated.

We got seven of them without taking any bad hits ourselves, but more Ants were arriving all the time, and seven dead out of a couple hundred Ants was nothing. Despite our obviously superior weapons, we were too few to strike fear into our enemy's weird, unified brain.

The Ant front line edged closer.

"We've got to get out of here," I muttered.

I ordered the men to fire. "Distract the bastards for a minute. Three rounds each and make as many of them count as you can."

While the sailors shot wildly, Jameson and I had a quick conversation.

"Should we try for the beach?" I asked.

"Not yet. Too far." He pointed out a rise of ground to our rear. "If we can get on top of that," he said, "we could shoot *down*, and they'd have to throw *up* to get us."

I looked. The rise was some way off, and moving toward it, we'd be exposed. But I didn't have anything better to offer. "What's your plan?"

Jameson grinned. "I'm a sailor. My plan is to leave the planning to you, Hunter. Tell me what you want us to do."

A few minutes later, at my signal, four sailors each seized one of the unconscious Lionel's limbs and ran toward the rise while the rest of us fired as rapidly as we could in an effort to drive the Ants back. When the first group was well away, three more men—all but Jameson, Richard, and me—jumped up and followed, ducking low, as I'd instructed them. The three of us who were left deliberately shot five Ants apiece, calling out the numbers as we fired. More than our shots, our shouted numbers confused the Ants, who stopped mid-spear-throw to listen and stare. They hadn't heard human speech for centuries.

When we'd each fired five times, the three of us turned together and ran like deer toward the rise. The Ants' stupor didn't last long, and they followed.

Halfway to our goal, we found William in our path, down on his hands and knees. He'd been struck hard in the back by a spear like a tree trunk—not sharp, but so heavy that when I reached him, he was spitting bloody foam. Between us, Richard and I got him up, but then almost immediately, Richard was hit in the left shoulder. The spear briefly stuck, and when it came away it left a bloody wound.

"Go on, go on!" Richard croaked, waving me past him.

Leaving Richard to Jameson, I got William over one of my shoulders and carried him up the rise, somehow losing my long gun in the process. The men were already firing when I reached them, using precious ammunition, but apparently accurately enough to give the Ants second thoughts about storming our position. Timmy met me and helped me to lay William down beside Lionel, while, ignoring his injury, Richard joined the fighters. Another sailor—Bertie—was also hurt, but not badly. He'd been grazed on his right hand. Despite this, he refused to give up his long gun to me, saying stubbornly he could fire perfectly well left-handed. I understood his possessiveness: Our guns were all that stood between us and a whole lot of silent, angry Ants who wanted to see us dead. But it left me with nothing but a pistol.

Jameson lay down beside me. "We're late back to the ship now, and Jake's heard the shooting for sure. I've known him twenty years. He'll likely send a relief party."

Jake, I deduced, was Captain Alcock.

"Great!" I said—not happily, but grimly. "How will they find us?"

A glance showed me the Ants' maneuvers were becoming more coordinated again, the wings of their line extending slowly to surround us. I stopped talking to Jameson long enough to order the men to pick off the leaders at either end, and as I hoped, the Ants coalesced in response. But how long before they tried again? Our ammunition was getting low.

I shoved my pistol into my belt. "I'm going for the ship. Somebody's got to guide that rescue party in or we'll be slaughtered."

Jameson laid a hand on my shoulder. His voice low, he said urgently, "Any rescue party Jake sends will be slaughtered, too. A few more long guns can't get us out of this. Jake can't spare more than five or six men, and if we're all killed—which is likely—he won't have crew enough left to sail home. And that's if he don't come with the party himself, which he might."

I shot another Ant without thinking, and then checked my ammunition bag. "Ten," I said calmly—as though it were plenty. "Gods, how did it come to this? Here I am, killing Ants again."

"Keep killing them." Jameson gave me his long gun. "I'm the one's going for the ship."

I protested.

"No, no; it can't be you," he replied. "The only way we're going to live through this is with cannon. I know them and you don't, so I'm the one has to go."

Overhearing this last, Timmy cried, "The ship's guns are gonna blow these boogers to pieces!"

The other men raised a feeble cheer at this—to the confusion of the Ants.

"How? How're the gunners supposed to hit the Ants all the way from the *Muriel*?"

"I'll tell 'em where to aim," Jameson told me. "I'll look for landmarks along the way to sight the guns on, and count my steps to get the range. Your job is to get this group as close to the beach as you can."

Deer said to me once that there are times when the hardest thing to do is not to be brave and a hero. This was looking like one of those times.

"You don't have to do this."

"Comes with the job," said Jameson. "Wish me luck, now."

Our situation was too desperate for me to argue any more. I wished our first mate luck, as he asked, and since their earlier cheer had briefly baffled the Ants, I told the men to yell and scream as loud as they could while Richard and I did some strategic killing among our enemies. Under cover of the resulting noise and death, Jameson slipped down the back of the rise. The Ants never saw him go.

To give him time to get away, we stayed where we were for as long as we dared. Then, just as I was about to order another retreat in the direction of the beach, Timmy shouted from behind me, "Somebody's coming!" adding almost immediately, "Don't shoot, nobody! It's Frank!"

As I turned to look, a horrible thing happened.

In his excitement, Timmy had raised up a little. An Ant spear caught him full in the face.

In an instant, his expression of surprise was obliterated in a spray of red, and with a scream of pain that turned to a sickening gurgle, Timmy fell backward.

The sailors yelled for real at the sight—so loudly the Ants retreated two steps in unison and stared. Frank—he was alone—was already with us, and throwing the Ant spear aside he took off his shirt to stanch the blood pouring from the place where Tim's nose had been.

As he worked, he called to me, "Sir! Sir! Now is the time! We must move!"

The shirt he had pressed to Timmy's face was soaked in red.

Frank was right, and Timmy was moaning and thrashing, clearly still alive, so I said numbly, "Right, right. Same pattern as before, everybody. Go!"

There were more wounded to carry, and fewer to carry them, but Richard stayed with me as he had the first time, firing as well as he could despite the wound to his shoulder. Somehow, we got down the rise and made for another bit of cover that beckoned.

Our retreat after that was a long and hellish nightmare. We started and stopped on Frank's commands—why his, I wasn't sure, except that (though he was as frightened as the rest of us) he seemed confident of what he was saying. He'd just come to us by the same route and probably felt he knew the ground better than we did. Bearing our wounded, we alternately ran a hundred yards or so then stopped to fight, throwing stones like Ants to save ammunition and seizing Ant spears and hurling them back at our pursuers. We weren't as good at throwing stones or spears as the Ants were, but they were briefly surprised by our efforts, and twice their surprise bought us another few precious yards.

At some point along the way, William quietly died. We didn't have any choice but to leave him where we last laid him down.

"What'll the Ants do to him?" a sailor asked me, tears in his eyes.

"Nothing," I said soberly.

Even in peacetime, even in their own colonies, the Ants never did more for—or to—the dead than to drag their bodies to some deserted place. If afterward wild dogs came around to feast on them, they sometimes killed and ate the dogs, but they never either encouraged the dogs to come or drove them away. I had seen no signs of dogs or wolves on the island. William would likely lie undisturbed where he was until his body turned to earth.

I carried Timmy, who was luckily small and light, and Frank told me in one brief lull in the fighting and fleeing that he had passed Jameson on a trail and warned him to leave it and cross the wastes instead. I couldn't see what difference it made, but we didn't have time to debate the matter. We were losing ground. After a few runs, all of us were wounded, more or less, and the Ants had overcome their fear and—while trying not to take casualties themselves—were gradually closing in.

By now I had so completely accepted the idea we were going to die that, though I automatically kept directing the men from one "surprising" move to another to confuse our enemy and buy time, my only conscious thoughts were of my family. I had made progress with my son, Robin. I hoped our recent conversation had provided him with something, some comforting thing, he could say to his sister to make her understand that, though I hadn't been a very good father, I had really loved both my children and their mother very much.

One by one, the men were losing heart, and some begged now, when we stopped, to be left behind. Lionel was deeply unconscious; Timmy, I guessed from his tormented moans, only wanted to die. At one stop, Bertie, who by then had been wounded in both legs and could only crawl, did die when an Ant stone struck him hard in the temple. On the whole, I think death came as a relief to him. Death was quickly becoming less terrible to us all. We left Bertie as we had William, lying where he fell, and after that, each time we got up to move on, Richard and I had to urge the others, pulling the most reluctant by the arm, or where that failed, like children, by an ear, or the hair.

Just when the beach was in sight, we were finally completely encircled and could go no further. I discovered then I did still want to live—but not enough to keep up the fight for the privilege. My strength was almost gone, and I lay wearily down beside the others, putting my pistol on the ground in front of my face.

Looking around me at the members of the shore party who were still alive and conscious enough to hear, I said, "There're seven shots left in this pistol. Let's do what we can with our long guns first, and then you've each earned one bullet for yourselves, if you want it."

Unlike Men—or sometimes even Foresters—Ants never showed any inclination to torture their victims, but they had no concept of mercy, either, and didn't necessarily finish them off cleanly. Like a hawk who'd injured a sparrow, Ants often simply watched from a safe distance until the death-struggles of the enemy wounded were over, unmoved by the suffering they witnessed.

The men stared at me, and Richard stammered, "You mean…?"

"I mean you get one pistol shot, and it's your choice what you do with it," I said firmly. "But first, let's take down as many of these filthy beasts as we can. Everybody got a bullet or two left?"

Stunned and silent, the men loaded what rounds they still had, now willingly sharing with less well-supplied comrades, and each deciding in his heart, probably, whether to reach for the pistol or not when his own gun was empty.

Beside me, Richard said, "Hold on! Frank ain't got a gun." He gave Frank his own long gun—given our circumstances, an act of almost unbelievable generosity.

As he was explaining to Frank how to make it fire, there was a muffled *crump* in the distance, followed by a roar and an explosion.

The first shell struck so far to our right the Ants were in no possible danger from it, but judging by their reactions, it was the loudest sound any of them had ever heard come out of a clear sky. Not all together but as individuals, like startled humans, the Ants turned this way and that and looked at each other in bewilderment.

"Mr. Jameson!" Richard exclaimed.

A second cannon fired, then a third. The gunners were shooting high, the shells throwing up earth well to our rear.

It didn't really matter where the shots struck. The Ants were as frightened by them as though whole broadsides had been landing in their midst. To heighten their confusion, the landing party spontaneously began cheering, our voices weak from weariness and thirst, but so overjoyed, where the Ants weren't expecting joy, that many of them turned from staring upward to stare open-mouthed at us instead.

Picking up my pistol again, I directed the men to fire everything they had left at those Ants who still stood, senseless with astonishment, between us and the beach. Though our enemies outnumbered us by many hundreds by now, when we fired, they moved meekly aside. As we struggled to our feet, they ran away, terrified, in every direction but toward us, and falling over each other in an uncoordinated, un-Ant-like way.

"Let's go!" I cried, and we staggered forward. Weak and in pain, all of us bleeding, we leaned on each other for support, even managing—I can't remember or imagine now how—to carry poor Timmy and the inert Lionel with us.

It was the longest hundred yards I have ever traveled.

From out of nowhere, a relief party from the ship came running to meet us. In moments they had helped us to the beach, and as they loaded us into the longboat it dawned on me that we were going to make it after all. We were going to make it home, to the *Muriel*.

CHAPTER THIRTEEN

Unlike most of the others, I was able to climb out of the longboat by myself, but that was all. I couldn't go farther. Sitting down on a hatch cover, I looked for my niece, who's usually the first one on the spot any time there's nursing to be done. But Helen wasn't there, and neither were the captain nor Mr. Jameson. It seemed to be red-haired Jack who was in charge.

By now the guns had stopped firing, and as the landing-party—what was left of it—was being brought aboard, the gun crews came up from below, talking excitedly among themselves until they saw us. Then they stopped and stared wordlessly until Jack ordered them to help us to our bunks. I waved the gunners past me to the worst cases.

"Bring water," I croaked.

Someone did, and as I was drinking I heard Mr. Jameson's name spoken.

"Where is he?" I called. "Where's Mr. Jameson?"

Frank, sitting near me, answered, "Mr. Jameson is injured."

"Injured?"

"On his way to the shore, Mr. Jameson met Ants. They pursued him and hit him with spears."

Two sailors were lifting Timmy—unaccountably still alive—from the longboat in a blanket, and I turned away from Frank long enough to tell them to put him in my cabin, rather than in his hammock below.

Then I asked, "Who told you all that, Frank?"

Frank shook his head. "I think he must be hurt very badly. He was hit with many spears."

I guessed he hadn't heard my question.

Before I could repeat it, a gunner confirmed Frank's words. "It don't look good for Mr. J.," the gunner said softly, taking my arm and helping me to stand. "The captain and Miss Farmer is with him now. You want me to put you in Tim's berth, sir? Since he's taking yours, I mean."

"Yeah, that's fine—No, wait; I'm going to see about Jameson first."

The gunner helped me to the mate's cabin, but there was nothing either of us could do there. I'm sure Mr. Jameson never knew we had come. Captain Alcock was standing beside the bed with a face like ashes, grimly watching as Helen washed blood—a lot of blood—from his friend's battered head.

My niece appraised my condition at a glance.

"Go lie down," she ordered, reaching for bandages. "I'll be with you as soon as I can." Then, looking straight at me, she added, "I really wish I could get some *advice* from a good *doctor* right now."

I'm afraid I just stared at her. I knew from the way Helen spoke there was a private message for me in her words, but I couldn't make out what it was.

She repeated deliberately, "I *said*, I'd like some *good medical advice*, Uncle River. Maybe I've got a *medical* book or something in my *cabin*."

I caught on.

"I'll find it," I mumbled, and then—with a last look at Mr. Jameson's face, from which one eye, half-open, sightlessly stared—I headed for the Navigation Room.

At the door, I sent the gunner away, and as soon as he was gone, got on the radio to Dan. While Dan was shouting to someone to get a couple doctors into his office fast, I staggered over to Helen's bunk, lay down, and was immediately enveloped in blackness.

*

The sound of the ship's engine starting woke me. Captain Alcock had evidently decided to use whatever fuel we still had to put as much distance as possible between us and Ant Island.

Cautiously, I sat up. Everything hurt, but nothing hurt unbearably. Somebody had come in while I was sleeping and, without my even being aware of it, stripped me bare and dressed my wounds. I eased myself off the bed, and by leaning against the walls along the way I managed to make it from Helen's cabin to my own, naked except for bandages and a blanket.

Timmy was in my bed, of course. Sitting beside him was the ship's carpenter, Collin, watching to see that Tim didn't need anything, or stop breathing.

"Should you be up?" Collin asked when I came in. "You don't look good."

I answered by gesturing him out of my chair and sitting down in it myself. "Get me some clothes, will you?" I asked hoarsely.

As he helped me to dress, Collin broke the news to me about Mr. Jameson.

The first mate had made it as far as the beach, Collin said, where he managed, as much by signs as words, to tell the sailors who rushed to meet him what needed to be done. Then he collapsed. Though Helen had done her best for him, after lingering for part of a day—hours during which I had been aware of nothing—Mr. Jameson slipped quietly away. He never regained consciousness or spoke a single word.

He was as good a Man as I had ever known, and I cried a little to hear he was gone, but Collin cried too, so my tears didn't seem out of place. Collin told me then that Lionel was still out but beginning to stir a little, and Richard and Frank, though bruised and bandaged, were both back on duty. Given what I already knew of Frank and what I'd seen of Richard on the island, this news did not surprise me in the least.

All the members of the shore party who'd made it back to the ship were expected to recover, in fact—excepting possibly Timmy, whose labored breaths punctuated our conversation.

When he was first brought aboard, no one expected Tim to survive the hour. Helen took one look and said his cheek was too badly torn for stitching, and she had no idea in the world what to do about the rest of his injuries. Then, secretly, she got some advice over the radio from doctors ashore, and when despite everything, Timmy continued to breathe, she went to work on him. After removing what she could of the shattered remains of his teeth, she pushed the bones of his face back into some semblance of their original arrangement with her fingers; scraped out the clotted blood from what she figured were probably supposed to be his nostrils; then wrapped Tim's whole head this way and that to hold the wreck together.

After this, Collin informed me solemnly, she staggered over to the nearest corner and vomited.

I sat where I was for a while, getting back my strength, and then I went to find Frank. There was a question or two I wanted to ask him.

Frank was in the galley, as usual, sewing something, but he jumped up when he saw me, and as he helped me to a bench, asked anxiously how I felt.

I said I was fine, which wasn't a lie. I was alive. Sometimes alive is fine enough.

"I have broth for you," Frank told me. "My stove is out of fuel now, but I made broth earlier. It's only for the wounded."

A cup of Frank's venison broth was almost worth being wounded to get.

He gave me some and I took a sip, then asked quietly, "How'd you know about Mr. Jameson, Frank?"

Frank stared at me for a minute, then looked away, unmistakably ashamed.

I knew why he was ashamed, because I already knew the answer to my question. Frank hadn't, in fact, passed and spoken to Mr. Jameson on an island trail. He'd seen him under attack by Ants. He had to have, because there was no other way he could have known about the first mate's injuries.

But just because I personally would probably have gone to help Mr. Jameson instead of continuing to where the landing party was didn't mean I thought Frank had made the wrong decision. I thought he'd done the *right* thing, in fact. Without Frank's help, the toll among the landing party would have been even higher, and there was no saying he could have helped Mr. Jameson enough to save him anyway.

That's what I wanted to tell Frank—that he'd done the right thing and had no reason to blame himself for Jameson's death. But I couldn't say it unless Frank confessed first, so I drank my broth and waited.

Instead of confessing, Frank said, "I felt them, sir."

This remark made no sense. "Felt what?" I swallowed another mouthful. "Soup's good, by the way. Just what I needed."

"Thank you, sir. I felt the Ants. I felt what they did in my... mind."

I was my turn to stare, which I did.

"When I met Mr. Jameson on the path, I warned him there were three Ant-villages on the island, and while the Ants from one were attacking the shore party, the ones from the other two were searching to see if there were any more Men in another place. I told him when he left me which way I thought was safest for him to go. But afterward some Ants saw him. They saw he was alone, and they chased him and attacked him with their spears." Frank added, looking miserable, "I thought Mr. Jameson would be safe in the wastes. That's why I told him to go that way."

I couldn't speak. I had no breath.

After a long, long minute, I managed to get out, "When did they... How far did he get?"

While we'd been fighting for our lives, Frank said, a mile or so ahead of us Mr. Jameson had been fighting for his own. The Ants had stone knives, but something in the mate's manner made them wary of venturing near enough to use them. They preferred to throw things at him from a safe distance. Despite their missiles, the first mate made it to the beach, where at the sight of the *Muriel*, the Ants who were chasing him took fright and ran away.

"I can't tell you any more," Frank said. "What the Ants didn't see, I can't see in my mind, either."

I sat for a long time rubbing my forehead. There was only one possible explanation for what Frank had just told me, and both of us knew what it was.

"You're an Ant, Frank," I said finally. "You're a damned Ant."

"No, sir," Frank corrected me. "My *father* was an Ant."

As if that made a difference. I wanted to get away from him. I *had* to get away from him. I stood up, and when Frank put out his hand to help me I said sharply, "Don't touch me!"

But I'd gotten up too quickly, and I'd have fallen if Frank hadn't grabbed my arm. He helped me to sit back down, where I closed my eyes and waited for my head to clear.

After a minute, eyes still closed, I asked, "This was Deer's idea, right?"

"Yes, sir. He was afraid you might find islands that had Ants living on them. He told me to come with you and feel for them, and if I sensed Ants in a place, to warn you not to land there."

I thought this over. In point of fact, having someone like Frank along on the *Muriel* was actually a pretty good plan.

"So—why didn't that work?" I asked, opening my eyes. "Were we too far away from them for you to—hear? Or whatever it is you do."

Frank said no, the ship had been well within range, and in fact he'd felt the Ants on the island very strongly. "But not until I went up on the deck after you were gone. When I was in the galley, I felt nothing."

This was interesting, so we talked about it, my rage and revulsion toward Frank dissipating as we spoke. Frank wasn't really an Ant, I found myself thinking. As he said himself, whatever his father had been, Frank was a Man. In fact, he was very possibly the bravest Man on the *Muriel*. He was the only one of us who'd known exactly what he'd have to deal with on the island, and he'd come anyway.

After some discussion we concluded that the ship's steel hull had prevented Frank from hearing the Ants while he was in the galley. "In future," I found myself telling him, just as though what we were having was in any way a normal conversation, "You need to be topside as soon as we get to a new place."

Getting up again—more cautiously this time—I added, "You know, I had another friend once who was the daughter of an Ant, so in a way, I'm used to this situation."

Frank put his arm under mine to support me, and this time I did not resist. "You mean Anna. I met her once. She sent me to your people."

I almost had to sit down again.

"You met Anna?"

"It was before the big battle," Frank said, leading me to poor Timmy's hammock. "My mother and I were traveling. We wanted to get away from where the battle would be." Helping me into Tim's bed, Frank studied me critically. "You looked a lot different with braids."

Frank had "seen" me before he ever met me, it turned out—in Anna's thoughts. This was such a disconcerting idea I was glad I was lying down to hear it.

He said that while Anna and the rest of her party were slowly crossing the continent, luring the Ant army to the Valley so Men could kill them, they happened to encounter ten-year-old Frank and his mother on the road. They all camped together for a night, where Anna, sensing little Frank's confusion about certain things, gently explained to him that the strange "voices" he'd heard in his head all his life meant he was a telepath who could read the thoughts of other telepaths. From the minute he met her, Frank told me, he wanted more than anything else in the world to go with Anna wherever she went.

But Anna didn't know where she was going. She couldn't be told, since that would have been the same as telling the whole Ant army. And because she didn't know, instead of taking Frank with her to who-knew-where, Anna sent him toward Evergreen. She told Frank's mother to ask at the forest cordon to speak to Master Deer and tell him privately about her son. Frank said, "In a way, my mother and I were the founders of Foreston, since other Men soon joined us there."

"Great," I muttered. I was no fan of Man-settlements at forest borders. "And then you grew up, and Deer sent you to me."

"Yes. Of course, there were other events between those two." Tucking the blanket around me like a mother, Frank said, "You should sleep now, sir."

I agreed, but as I closed my eyes, something suddenly occurred to me.

"Hey, that's why Ants don't steal helmets!" I exclaimed. "They steal body-armor any time they can get it, but never helmets. It's because they can't hear each other's thoughts through them!"

Looking back, I'm not sure whether I said this aloud, or just dreamed I did. Either way, before Frank could possibly have answered me, I was asleep.

*

We had no choice but to bury Mr. Jameson at sea.

As far as I knew, nobody had been buried at sea since ancient times. Modern continental sailors were never far from shore, and took the body of anyone who died ship-board to the nearest port town for burial. The *Muriel's* crew was uncomfortable with the idea of deliberately putting a shipmate's body into water instead of earth, and to be honest, so was I. But the nearest land we knew about was John's Island, and it was still weeks away.

Making the best of things, Captain Alcock said, "The sea were a second home to Jimmy," and when the crew had gathered at the rail—all of us who could stand—he briefly but movingly eulogized his friend of twenty years. Then he walked away quickly to avoid witnessing the moment when the rest of us lowered the weighted body over the side. I don't think anyone begrudged him his escape.

An hour later, the *Muriel's* engine sputtered and stopped, and she was a sailing ship again.

CHAPTER FOURTEEN

We had lost three shipmates and still looked likely to lose Tim, too, and pretty soon we discovered we couldn't entirely count Lionel as among the living, either. After a few days, Lionel woke up, more or less, but he seemed to have left his wits behind on Ant Island. Somebody had to urge him from his bunk every morning and help him dress, and when that was done he sat wherever he was put and looked around like he'd never seen the *Muriel* or its crew before in his life. Left to himself I think he would have sat that way until he starved to death.

Naturally, Helen wasn't going to let him starve, and whenever she had a minute, she'd go and retrieve Lionel from wherever he was and force food down him. Then she'd walk with him, talk to him, sing songs to him—whatever she could think of to engage his brain and start him thinking. I couldn't see that it was working, but Helen refused to give up.

She wouldn't give up on Timmy, either, who was mostly conscious now—though nobody was exactly happy about that for his sake, since he was in a lot of pain. His wound oozed, and after a few days his bandages stank, but Helen didn't dare remove them before the bones in his face had a chance to knit. On the advice of the doctors in Fortress (who thought they were talking to someone at a remote outpost on the continent) she wet them down with spirits—the last dribbles from the *Muriel's* fuel tanks—and then just hoped for the best. She managed to keep Tim nourished by feeding him broth Frank made by burning "non-essential" (we hoped) bits of wood from around the ship for cooking fuel (my old desk and chair were the first things to go). Though there were few hours Helen didn't worry would be Timmy's last, he hung on.

Captain Alcock, meanwhile, kept mostly to his cabin, and stood his watches wrapped in a chilly silence that warned the rest of us off.

The crew, initially subdued, reacted to the losses among them by becoming combative. Fights broke out below decks, and several times small delegations of sailors (the same few every time—and I could have named in advance which ones they'd be) stormed the captain's cabin to demand the *Muriel* turn back for the continent immediately. The captain bore with them patiently until one went too far and hinted at mutiny. Then he slowly rose in outrage from behind his desk, somehow getting bigger and bigger and angrier and angrier as he got up until he seemed twice life-size and almost smoking with barely suppressed ferocity. The chief would-be mutineer took one look and shriveled like a sunbaked snail, and we had no further trouble from any of them after that.

Finally, as if to prove that nothing is so bad it can't get worse, after a day of lying in Timmy's bunk planning exactly how I would—as my niece recommended—honestly and openly break it to Sarah that I had precipitated a battle in which I had been wounded and three good Men lost, I made a radio call home that did not go the way I hoped it would.

Before I had finished the story, Sarah was crying, saying the same old pattern was repeating itself where I threw myself into harm's way without a single thought for the people who cared about me. She said she couldn't stand it anymore. The more I tried to explain how this time was different from all the other times I'd gotten myself into tight spots, the more and harder she wept. By the time Helen finally walked into the radio room, I was almost crying myself. I turned the conversation over to my niece with relief and escaped.

So much for honesty and openness.

My initial plan after this was to stay in Tim's hammock brooding and wallowing in guilt for the rest of my life, but the ship was now desperately shorthanded, so I went to see the captain instead. He invited me into his cabin without a single oath, and when I entered, he didn't look up.

Not knowing what else to be, I was direct.

"I don't know anything at all about working a ship, Captain," I said, "but if you think I'd at least be better than nobody, I'd like to offer my services."

After a long, silent moment, Captain Alcock shrugged. "You'll do. You know your weather-signs good, and I can give you Georgie for a steersman until you get the feel of the helm yourself. Knowing you like they do, I doubt the men'll give you trouble, neither, the way they usually do a new officer. Be more likely to help you all they can."

"I'll need all the help I can get," I agreed. "But I'm not suggesting myself as an officer. I was planning to take Timmy's place. I recommend Richard for Acting Mate, unless you have somebody else in mind. Every member of the landing party will vouch for his courage and cool head."

Captain A. finally looked at me.

"Buck-seaman's brutal hard work," he said pointedly.

It wasn't news to me that I wasn't so young anymore. "I know that. But it's all I'm fit for."

The captain didn't deny this. Saying he'd had his eye on Richard for some time, he agreed to try him as mate, and me as a sailor.

We talked for a little longer, and then as I got up to leave, I asked, "What's that thing in the dish, Captain? Is it some kind of seaweed?"

The captain brightened at the question.

"No, and it ain't a tree, neither," he said, pushing the object toward me to inspect. "Though a tree's what it's meant to be in place of. Frank brung it to me. He says where he comes from, folks plant a tree for everybody who dies, for their friends and relations to remember 'em by. We don't have no trees, so he took it in his head to cut up one of them purple things from that damn island instead. He's calling the pieces Bert, Will, and Jimmy, and he wants us to plant 'em proper when we get to land somewheres.

"This one here's Jimmy," Captain A. added, poking the purple nubbin with one grubby finger. "Hope he grows good."

With the ship under sail and shorthanded, nobody had time to give me lessons in general seamanship. My position on the *Muriel* was as a pair of unskilled but available hands the men shouted for when lines needed hauling on, and sails needed reefs taken in or let out. My shipmates were surprised to discover that unlike most novice sailors, I had no problem at all with being sent up the masts. Not knowing I'd spent my childhood climbing trees and my young years going up and down radio towers, they gave me more credit for my "spine," as they called it, than I deserved.

Surprisingly, I discovered I kind of liked the life.

Being the most junior member of the ship's crew put me in the position of a Young Man Just Starting Out, and I'd never been young man just starting out before. I'd left the forest still a boy (or what forest-folk reckon is still a boy, anyway), and—skipping youth altogether—became, in rapid succession, a partner in a business, a boss, a husband, an army captain, and then a father. After a week of having nothing to do but what I was told, I discovered I wasn't in any hurry to go back to being Supercargo or anything else that came with a lot of "duty" and "accountability" attached to it.

This annoyed Helen, who thought I should have more pride.

"You know about gloves, right?" She eyed my rope-blistered hands. "I've got some ointment that'll help, if you want it, but you'd avoid burning your hands altogether if you wore gloves."

"No true sailor wears gloves," I announced. "There's probably a good reason for that, though I admit I don't know what it is. I wouldn't mind a little of your ointment, though. Jack recommended washing them in seawater to toughen them, but I tried it and I'd rank the pain of seawater on blisters as right up there with a medium-hard whack from an Ant battle-axe."

Helen's foot tapped impatiently. "You don't have to do this."

"Oh, yes I do." My jaw involuntarily tightened. "The men deserve to get to watch me suffer for messing up on that island."

"The only one blaming you for what happened on the island," Helen said coldly, "is you. Everybody else thinks you were a hero."

"If I'd been a hero, all the sailors would have made it back and I wouldn't have any blisters because the *Muriel* wouldn't be short of crew. In fact, forget the ointment, and bring me seawater, Helen."

But being my niece—and generally a loving one, when she wasn't mad at me—she brought ointment.

Then, just as quickly as things had gotten bad, they improved.

First, we passed some little islands.

The little islands were unimportant in themselves. They were useless for our purposes. There wasn't so much as a puddle or a blade of grass on any of them. But islands don't often occur singly, and with a mild but hopeful oath (his first in weeks), Captain Alcock ordered the lookouts to keep watch for something bigger.

Right after that, Helen was finally able to cut the bandages off Timmy's face, and though his face was only "improved" in comparison to what it had been when he was brought aboard, it appeared to be healing. Tim no longer had any nose to speak of. The whole center of his face was pushed in where it should have stuck out. Also, his cheek had a long, puckering scar, his jaw was broken, and most of his top teeth were gone. But as we all told him over and over, at least his eyes had been spared. Once the bandages were off his eyes, Tim could see as well as ever. No one was tactless enough to give him a mirror to see himself.

So Tim felt better, and more hopeful, and after she'd washed his face with drinking water (the rest of us were restricted to seawater for washing now), Helen tied up his broken jaw again and got someone to carry him topside for a spell in the sun.

Also, Lionel was improving. He was finally waking up mentally, a little more each day. We hoped before long he'd even talk.

But the best thing that happened was something private, just for me. Sarah radioed, and when I spoke to her, she apologized.

I know. I couldn't believe it either.

She apologized, and said she'd been completely wrong to be angry with me for just being the kind of person she already knew I was when we married.

"You'll always get yourself into risky situations," she said, sounding regretful about it—but for the first time, also resigned. "That's just the way you are. I should have stopped trying to change you years ago, and just accepted it. At least this time you told me what happened instead of leaving me to guess. I'm sorry I reacted badly. I was just surprised."

"Go ahead and get used to it, so you won't be surprised next time," I suggested. "Honesty is my new policy. Helen recommended it."

"Well, give Helen my love, then. And take some for yourself, too."

There are lots of kinds of love in the world, and the kind Sarah was offering me now wasn't the same as the kind we'd once shared between us. But that didn't mean I wasn't glad to get it.

When I saw Helen soon after, she smiled like she already knew her auntie and I had patched a few things up. I didn't care to speculate on how Helen knew this, because of course my niece was much too honorable to listen with her ear to a door. But she knew.

She said, "Sometimes you act almost like a grownup, Uncle River."

I was about to reply to this when Captain Alcock walked by with hardly a glance for either of us.

Her smile gone, Helen whispered, "He's taking Jimmy's loss very hard."

In my mind's eye I suddenly saw Bertie and William lying where we'd left them. At least Jameson had gone to his rest with his body washed and decently composed. I hadn't even closed Bertie's eyes.

"I could have done that much, at least," I muttered.

"What?"

"Nothing. Yeah, I miss him too. I miss all three of them."

After studying me for a minute, Helen went on, "He's also worried. Jasper takes his responsibility for this ship very seriously, and as far as he knows, all we've got to navigate her by are the stars. He knows we're running low on drinking water and we need to get back to John's Island as quickly as we can, but at the same time he has no real idea how fast the current is pulling us west."

"*You* know though, right?"

"I know precisely where we are. Naturally, I can't say absolutely how long it will take us to get back to John's Island. If we're delayed by bad weather or something our situation could get a little… uncomfortable. But at least I know the course I've set will get us there eventually, which Jasper doesn't."

When Helen said this, I decided not to mention a little plan I'd been working on, where we'd catch some fish and ferment them shipboard in clean—meaning, basically, drinking—water to make a batch of crude fuel. Under power, we'd get back to John's Island in half the time it would take us to sail there, and if my calculations were correct, we almost certainly wouldn't die painfully of thirst on the way, either. But it didn't sound like I could count on my niece's support for the proposal, and it might have been a bad idea.

"How about if I serenade you with a dirty song?" I suggested instead. "I'd rather see the captain angry than depressed."

"Do you know any dirty songs?"

I had to admit I didn't.

I didn't have any other ideas, either. I went back to my cabin, lay down, and stared at the pictures of my friends.

Any of them, I found myself thinking, would have come up with some way to help the captain by now. Anna had a way with people, and Posthumous was wise. So was Heron, in his own quiet way. Muriel would mother him, and John would do… something. Possibly something unfortunate, knowing John, but at least he wouldn't just lie uselessly brooding on his bed like I was. I made myself sit up and consider what, if any, comfort I could offer.

It came to me eventually that though I didn't have wisdom or warmth or whatever, I did have one thing to give to Captain Alcock that he definitely wanted. From our conversation at John's Island I knew he was aware that I was keeping things from him. He resented this, naturally. He trusted us—or at least, Helen—enough to steer the course she set even when it was contrary to his own instincts and experience. I decided I'd go to the captain now and show him he had my trust. I'd tell him honestly what the *Muriel's* real mission was, who we were looking for, and why. I'd tell him everything except about the Ants. Even Helen didn't know about the Ants.

In case trust wasn't enough to cheer up our captain, I'd also let him in on the secret of radio navigation. If I couldn't make him happier, at least I could make him less worried.

The only awkward thing about the plan was that the shippers had sworn me to secrecy about the radio. I'd sworn willingly, too. I couldn't claim to have been under any duress, the way Deer did about his vow to kill all Ants.

Luckily, the shippers were far away, and I figured what they didn't know couldn't hurt me. I'd show the captain Heron's pictures, too, I decided. Seeing the actual faces of the people he was risking his life to find could only make him feel better about what we were doing.

The captain acknowledged my revelations by saying gruffly, "I figured Miss Helen probably knew what she was doin', even with being a woman and all like she is, but I'm bound to say your damn boogery close-mouthedness ain't set right with me." He added, a little self-righteousnessly, that he'd "put it down charitable" to my being forest-born.

"I appreciate your forbearance," I told him, and promised to reform.

Captain A. was interested in Heron's drawings—particularly the female figures. "Ain't that a damn fine lady!" he exclaimed, indicating one who was almost certainly an Ant. "We find your island, you reckon she'll be on it?"

I gently reminded him the drawings had been done twenty years before.

Captain Alcock's face briefly fell, then brightened again. "She'll have daughters, though." He lifted his nose and closed his eyes for a moment. "Wind's rising," he said. "Go ask your radio what our heading's to be."

"Ask it yourself," I offered. "I'll show you how it works."

CHAPTER FIFTEEN

As I came on deck next morning, Lionel, still a little strange-eyed but definitely better, grabbed my arm and uttered his first word since the Ant-rock hit him.

Pointing vaguely west, he said, "Land!"

It was land, all right, though still too far off to be more than a hazy shape on the horizon. Captain Alcock shouted for more sail, and everybody—even Mike—crowded at the ship's rail to look.

"Island!" Mike remarked to me conversationally. "Big!"

Beside me, Helen begged, "Is it green? Please tell me it's got green things growing on it!"

Seeing Frank standing nearby, I left Helen to discuss the island's potential greenness with Mike instead—a conversation that consisted almost entirely, on his side, of admiring looks.

When I reached him, Frank answered my unspoken question with, "It's too soon to know, sir."

As we got nearer, we saw that this island was two or three times the size of Ant Island, and—yes—very green. Unfortunately, it was also obviously inhabited, and this time I didn't imagine for even a moment the occupants might be Anna and Heron's people. Heron would never have let something as big as the *Muriel* to get close enough to see the islanders without him spotting the *Muriel* first. As it was, we were watching two-legged, humanoid shapes going about their business ashore for quite a while before somebody apparently raised the alarm among them. A few of the figures climbed trees to get a better look at us and when the *Muriel's* sailors waved, hundreds of them rushed the beach.

"Don't think they're Ants," Captain Alcock muttered, suddenly beside me. "But if they are, they make a nice target for our guns standing all together that way."

Frank was still just staring, expressionless, so I said, "I guess we'll know pretty soon."

The captain steered so we'd come in parallel to the island—the better, of course, for leaving in a hurry if we had to. Though I wasn't on duty, as we changed course I automatically grabbed a line to assist in lowering a sail. This evoked a few laughs and a friendly slap on the shoulder.

"Getting to be a real sailor now," someone said approvingly. I was absurdly pleased.

The islanders tried to keep with us as we passed, running along beaches and scrambling over rocks, shouting and even singing with apparent joy. Some dove into the water as though to swim out to us, but we were too fast for them. Little boats that reminded me of forest canoes emerged from a cove, propelled by three paddlers a side. The paddlers rode the *Muriel's* wake, and like their friends on the beach, called out to us excitedly.

"Damned if they ain't glad to see us," Captain Alcock said wonderingly. "Can't be Ants, then. I never seen Ants happy like that."

Frank still wouldn't commit himself on the issue. He told me, "I feel some minds, but they're different from Ant minds. Ant minds have no words. These have words in them."

"What words?"

Frank shook his head. "I don't know them."

"I need an answer, Frank," I pressed. "If they're human, we go ashore, and if they're not, we don't. It's as simple as that."

Frank hesitated. "We can go ashore. They won't hurt us."

"So they're *not* Ants."

Frank still declined to say positively one way or the other. "All I know is they won't hurt us," he repeated. "There is no anger there."

Whatever they were, Ants or humans, hordes of them had gathered on the shore, singing and dancing, calling to us and gesturing to us to come.

It wasn't until we dropped anchor and I could study them through a spyglass that I was finally reassured. The island folk were generally brunette, not short and blonde like Ants; and though they resembled each other, they were by no means as identical as one Ant is to all other Ants.

Still, I wasn't going to take any chances. I pulled the captain aside.

"I'm going ashore without an escort this time," I informed him quietly.

"No, you ain't," he said flatly, adding a pungent obscenity for emphasis. "Shore party's ten men, same as always. Not that them boogers look dangerous, though. You could probably take the whole crew with you and no harm done except they might get loved to death."

"No, they don't look dangerous." I felt it prudent to remind him, "Ant Island didn't look populated, either—but it was."

The captain considered this point. "Well, but—you're crew now. And we're short-handed. I can't afford to lose no more crew."

I put the situation to him another way. "Do you honestly think even eleven of us could stand that mob off if they turned unfriendly? There must be two thousand people on that beach."

"Eleven men and the port-side gunners," the captain countered triumphantly. "I got 'em standing by already—just in case."

It was like Captain Alcock both to be foresightful and to think of guns as the solution to any problem.

"If anybody lays a hand on me," I said, "I hope you blow the island to pieces in my memory. But by the time those people make a hostile move, it'll already be too late for guns to save me. It's better to risk losing one than eleven, and I'm going ashore alone, Captain. As a sailor, I'm under your command, but as Supercargo of the *Muriel* I could still pull rank on you. I'd really rather not do that. Don't make me."

The captain gave his left buttock a slow, meditative scratch.

"You're a stubborn booger," he observed thoughtfully.

"You have no idea," I said.

I refused to take any weapons in case the islanders saw them as a provocation, but I said I had no objection to wearing a certain quilted linen undershirt I had, able to withstand most blades. I mentioned it was forest-made, and the word "forest" worked its usual magic. The captain stopped rummaging in the weapons locker and sent me to get it.

By my request, Timmy was still occupying my cabin. As I entered it, he was staring out the porthole at the strange scene on the island.

"Go out, why don't you?" I urged. "You could use the fresh air."

Tim shook his head. "I might scare somebody," he lisped, turning to me and forcing a smile. Having no nose gave his voice a flat, stifled quality. "I can watch from here."

I concluded he must have found his way to a mirror.

This self-inflicted isolation was worrying, but I didn't have time to address it right then. I only paused on my way out long enough to say, "Get stronger, because I'm going to want you on future shore-parties. You're somebody I know I can rely on."

By the time I got there, the men had the dinghy ready for me. Frank was in it.

"I'm going with you," he told me stonily. "You need my skills."

I wavered, then gave in. "Fine. You row."

The roar the islanders gave when they saw the dinghy being lowered made all their previous racket a whisper by comparison. As it touched the water, a dozen little canoes surrounded us, their paddlers chattering madly in some tongue I didn't recognize. When Frank started to row, though, the chatterers got suddenly quiet and stared. They'd evidently never seen anyone row with oars before.

Frank's not normally a smiley fellow, but the looks on the paddlers' faces made him positively grin. "They are more impressed with me than with you," he announced. "They see that I am the boat master!"

He struck me as preposterously relaxed, given the circumstances. Squabbles were breaking out in nearby canoes, where paddlers were trying to seize their neighbors' paddles so they could try rowing, like Frank.

"Fine," I muttered. "Row faster, 'boat master.' If one of these idiots runs into us and holes the dinghy, Captain Alcock might not let us back aboard."

As we neared shore, swarms of young males ran out into the surf and literally lifted our boat from the water and carried us in.

This was not as fun as it may sound. Carrying dinghies wasn't something the young men did regularly and were good at. Frank and I had to hold on with both hands to avoid being thrown out onto our heads. Someone got our oars and bore them triumphantly away like prizes, no doubt to the fury of the watching Captain A., but thankfully when the dinghy had been lowered to the ground we were permitted to step out by ourselves.

The singing stopped, but hundreds of islanders now crowded forward to shout directly into our faces, apparently sharing an island-wide conviction that we would understand their language if they spoke it loudly. I listened, but though I'm fluent in many continental dialects and can read both Mother Tongues the dialects derive from, I couldn't pick out a single familiar word.

Frank, on the other hand, seemed to feel he understood the islanders perfectly well—although not their words, which were unintelligible to him, too.

"They recognize that we are brothers," he said looking around, still perfectly cheery, "so they don't fear us. You see they show no weapons."

"Just because they don't show them doesn't mean they don't have them," I muttered. "Doesn't it seem a little strange to you if they don't fear us? We just sailed in out of nowhere on a boat they've never seen the likes of before in their lives. Shouldn't they be frightened?"

Before Frank could answer this, a group of older islanders started towards us. I've dealt with this kind of thing before on my travels around the continent, and I knew right away by the way the rest of the crowd parted to let them through that we were about to meet the local notables. I wanted to be in their good graces, so I did my usual thing, where I bowed low and showed them my hands were empty.

I told them I wasn't on their island to do any harm. "Water and plant matter—waste is fine—is what we mainly need," I said—not that I expected them to understand any more than my tone, of course, which was as friendly as I could make it. "Although if you've got a surplus of game—particularly some nice, fat deer—we'd be happy to take that off your hands, too. Or any other meat. We're not especially picky."

As expected, the islanders looked blank, so I raised my cupped hands to my lips and pretended to drink, a gesture I'd noticed before was pretty much universal. Sure enough, everybody on the beach said "Ah!" in unison, and hundreds of fingers helpfully pointed out the direction (I presumed) in which water could be found.

I nodded and smiled, but stayed where I was, determined not to leave the beach until I was more certain the assistance of the port-side gunners wouldn't be required.

One of the island elders detached himself from the rest of the group and stepped forward, his right hand extended. I took it tentatively, hoping the offer of one hand meant the same on the island as it did in Men's lands on the continent.

Evidently it did. Smiling broadly, the leader gripped my hand firmly and worked it like a pump handle.

"You seeing this, Frank?" I asked, trying to make it sound to leader like I was saying "pleased to meet you."

"Yes, sir," Frank said. "These people may once have shared a common culture with the Men of the continent."

The Head Leader then said something to the other leaders, and when they nodded, he reached under his leather shirt and produced an amulet on a thong. With a motion of his hand, he invited me closer to examine it.

The medallion was metal, silvery in color. From the leader's look of pride as he showed it to me I judged the disc was important to him, so I studied it carefully. I could make out what I suspected had once been letters around the edge on one side, but they were worn nearly smooth, and I couldn't read any.

In the center of the other side, however, was an unmistakable figure "10."

I showed it to Frank, and we smiled happily at each other. That and the handshake together were making it look more and more like Frank had been right to call the islanders our brothers.

"Ten!" I said to Head Leader, pointing at the figure. "That's a number '10,' right?"

He didn't get it until I held up ten fingers, and repeated, "10!"

Head Leader nodded, but seemed unimpressed. His real interest was in getting me to look again at the first side of the disc. Besides the faded writing, this side had a figure of a couple of irregular polygons, one atop the other—a shape which was, to me, meaningless.

To be polite, I said, "Yeah, I saw that. It's great."

Leader seemed confused. He pointed to the symbol again, and then at the sea, meaningfully. When I still didn't get it, he pointed again: Medallion; sea. Then he said a few sentences and waited, studying my face intently.

I looked around. Everyone else on the beach seemed to be staring at me intently, too.

"No, really," I stammered. "I mean it. It's—handsome." I touched the amulet respectfully, and tried to convey how impressed I was with it. Over my shoulder, I added, a little desperately, "Any idea what I should do here, Frank? Does this thing represent a god? Should I kneel?"

"I believe these people think the disc has some connection to the *Muriel*, sir," Frank answered. "Doesn't one of the words this man keeps saying sound like our word 'boat'?"

Leader started jabbering again, and I listened. Frank was right. A single change of letter turned one of the words the leader said into "boat."

I echoed, "boat!" the way the leader said it, and pointed toward the *Muriel*, whereupon—to my relief rather than my pleasure—he embraced me like a son.

Extracting myself, I asked Frank, "Want to scout around a little?"

"I think it's safe," he agreed.

I repeated my earlier gesture of pretending to drink from my cupped hands and looked hopefully toward the path leading off the beach.

Head Leader pointed back toward the *Muriel*.

"Yeah," I agreed. "They need water, too. How about just us for now, though? They can get theirs later."

While Head Leader was still thinking about this, one of the lesser leaders said something in an undertone.

Frank said confidently, "They've grasped your meaning now," and sure enough, Head Leader waved his hand and a bunch of people bearing crude pottery bowls of water for us to drink hurried up.

I took the water-bearers for young girls at first, because they were all small, and all wore the kind of skirted garments that are convenient for women in places where sanitary facilities are rough. A second look at them revealed they were all different ages, and some of them were males. All the other islanders wore loincloths and shirts made of scraped hides; the shirts crudely made, but elaborately painted. The dresses of the water-carriers were undecorated. Their behavior toward the leaders seemed pitifully humble. The island bosses were evidently not always as benign as they'd been so far toward Frank and me.

We drank, and then the leaders led Frank and me toward the path, a significant percentage of the rest of the island population following. I managed one quick glance back toward the *Muriel* and waved, a smile on my face broad enough, I hoped, to be visible through a spyglass from the deck. The captain and Helen were standing there together, with a third figure I hoped was Timmy. Even at the distance, Helen looked nervous.

*

It was very late when Frank and I finally climbed back aboard the *Muriel*. Captain Alcock and Helen were both there to meet us, visibly relieved to see us still in one piece.

"Gods, what kept you?" Helen moaned. "Did you have to see the whole island in one day?"

I was exhausted, dirty, and to be perfectly honest, not entirely sober. The island brew was a crude approximation of ale, and very weak, but I'd had a whole lot of it.

"I'm sorry," I said, steadying myself against a mast. "I honestly took the very first chance we had to get away. Every time we took two steps toward the beach, the island elders dragged us off to see something else. Then they insisted we eat with them. They wanted us to stay the night, but I turned that suggestion down absolutely."

"You turned it down?" Helen repeated, sounding surprised. I guess I have a reputation for saying "yes" to (potentially) bad ideas.

"I did," I assured her. "It might have been interesting, but I hated the thought of worrying you." I put my arm around her shoulders and cautiously squeezed.

Helen smiled and hugged me back. "It's all right. We're just glad you're safe."

The captain had assessed my condition by now. "You get to bed, Miss Farmer," he winked, taking my arm and starting to lead me away. "I'll see your uncle gets safe to his bunk. What's the matter you don't need no help, Frank? Never learned how to have a good time?"

Frank seemed surprised by the question. "I had a good time."

"No, no; let's talk!" Helen protested, taking my other arm and holding me back. "You're not tired, are you, Uncle River? Come on, Jasper. You want to hear all about the island, right?"

It looked like she wasn't going to take "no" for an answer. I swayed on my feet and glanced anxiously toward the rail.

"Get to my cabin, Missy," the captain abruptly ordered. "Frank, you take her. Me'n your uncle be there in a minute."

He got my head over the side just in time.

Afterward I felt better and agreed to talk.

Once we were seated in the captain's cabin, I began, "It's a nice island, and the islanders are certainly friendly. But for some reason, I just don't like this place." I shook my head, triggering another brief bout of nausea. When it subsided, I added, "There's something strange about the people here."

"Are they dangerous?" Helen asked in an urgent whisper. My niece had made it a point to get to know every Man on the ship, and her reward for it was that the deaths on Ant Island had hit her hard.

"No. They're the opposite of warlike. If you want the truth, I don't think they could be bothered to hurt anybody. I've never seen a softer, more comfort-loving bunch."

Frank spoke up. "The small people work very hard," he said softly.

"Children?" Helen asked, startled.

I explained about the water-carriers.

"It's possible they're citizens who're being punished, or something like that. We couldn't really ask about it since the only word of the island language we've figured out so far is 'boat.' Yeah, the water-carriers work hard, but they're the only ones. I saw a couple of tuber-fields that were cultivated, but everything else they served us to eat looked like it was gathered wild. Overall there seems to be enough food, because the population's not huge and the land's fertile, but nobody but the leaders—and us—got meat or fruit. With a little effort, they'd all have plenty of everything, but I don't think there's any effort being made."

"The small people got only fish and water," Frank put in.

"I can see why you didn't like it there, then," my niece said tightly. Helen is always on the side of the downtrodden and oppressed. "What about the island itself?"

"Perfect for a refueling stop. Lots of water and tons of green stuff. In fact, the place is overgrown. We'd be doing them a favor to take some now and then."

"Trade?"

I thought about this. "Well, they'll want everything we bring them, that's for sure. I don't know whether they have anything we'd want in return. They don't seem to make cloth, or pottery, or even to work wood competently. Which is funny, because from what I can tell, at the time of the Ant-Cataclysm, people here were enjoying a pretty sophisticated style of life. The patched-up wrecks of buildings from a thousand years ago are the best facilities on the island. They don't seem to have erected anything since then but mud huts."

"Maybe there used to be Ants here," Helen suggested. "Maybe it took the humans so long to get the better of the Ants they haven't had time to learn to build again yet."

I said I didn't see any signs of Ant-war. "If there were ever Ants here, there'd be some kind of defensive fortress. Weapons, too. There's nothing like that."

"Just lazy boogers, then," the captain said. "Seems like what them folks needs you to bring 'em is somebody'll make 'em work. If they try it for a while and find out they don't die, could be the making of 'em."

Hard work was our captain's sovereign remedy for every ill, including exhaustion.

"I'll suggest work," I agreed, "provided I can make them understand me. But first I need to find a way to ask for water and green waste. The sooner we make fuel, the sooner we can get out of here."

With a penetrating look, Captain Alcock demanded, "Tell me honest, Evergreen: You want to go soon because you don't *like* these folks, or because you don't *trust* these folks? Because if they ain't to be trusted, we sail on."

I already knew how I was going to answer this. I'd asked myself the same question twenty times that day.

"I trust them not to hurt us." I crossed my arms and leaned back. "At least, I trust them as much as I can trust, which isn't a lot because I don't have a trusting nature. What I don't trust is my understanding of the situation. There's more going on here than meets the eye. Did you see how they welcomed us? They had no fear at all. And besides that, they don't gesture or mime to communicate with us. They expect us to understand their language. It's like they can't grasp even the concept of 'stranger.' It's making me uncomfortable."

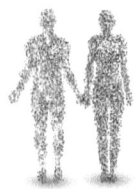

CHAPTER SIXTEEN

The four of us went on talking until I was nearly sober, which meant when I finally climbed into what I now considered "my" bunk, it was very late. Consequently, when Frank woke me not long after dawn, I wasn't pleased.

"What?" I mumbled, pulling Tim's blanket over my head. "Go away."

"Sir," Frank said, quiet but insistent. "There's something you must see."

I opened one eye and saw that he was offering me a mug of something. It was one of Frank's weird dried-leaf infusions, but as soon as I drank it, I felt better.

"I'll get up," I mumbled.

On deck, Captain Alcock was waiting for me. "What do you make of this?" He handed me his spyglass. "Must be thousands of the boogers."

I looked. From the edge of the water winding back to the highlands above—and farther, from what we could tell—the citizens of the island were standing in one long line, every one of them holding a bundle, and all staring anxiously toward the *Muriel*.

"Damn me, what'd you say to 'em yesterday?" the captain wanted to know.

I reminded him that between us, Frank and I knew exactly one word of the islanders' language. "We managed—with pantomime—to get it across that we wanted a drink. Besides a lot of nodding and smiling, that was the limit of our communication."

"Looks like you might've nodded and smiled at the wrong thing, then." Captain A. snorted. "I'm damned if I can figure out what they're up to, standing like that."

"It's just some kind of misunderstanding. I'll row over and clear it up."

Once again, Frank was waiting for me in the dinghy when I climbed in. I didn't bother to protest.

"Clearing up" turned out to be a lot easier said than done.

The islanders—all of them, apparently—wanted a tour of the *Muriel*. That much we could guess from the fact that the leaders, who were first in the line, rushed the dinghy as we landed and climbed straight in, talking and pointing eagerly toward the ship. They had "small people" carrying their bundles for them, and the Small People put the bundles into the dinghy, too. But the Small People didn't try to get into the boat themselves, which made me like them better than ever, and a whole lot more than I liked the leaders, who wouldn't get out. I tried pulling them by their arms; I tried repeating "no, no" as firmly as I could; I even mimed standing up, stepping out, and following me up the beach to talk, but this only provoked a lot of animated discussion. It didn't get them out of Captain Alcock's dinghy. In desperation, I seized a few of their bundles and threw them out onto the beach, but though the leaders looked shocked at this, Head Leader especially, they only hunkered down tighter than ever.

So, sighing in unison, Frank and I got back into the dinghy ourselves, sat down, and tried to understand with a few words and a lot of signs just exactly what was going on.

We got nowhere at first, but after a little while Frank started to pick out a word here and there, and we made some progress. The islanders, it seemed, didn't want just a tour of the *Muriel*. They wanted the *Muriel* to take the whole lot of them aboard and sail them away to...somewhere. I couldn't figure out exactly where the islanders wanted to be taken, and I wasn't sure they knew either. When I refused, Head Leader pulled the medallion out from under his shirt again, pointed at it, and spoke passionately for at least five minutes, fully half of his words the island term for "boat." I looked at the medallion again and this time I realized the image I'd thought was just a couple of irregular polygons was meant to be the silhouette of a ship. The polygons did, in fact, slightly resemble the *Muriel* in profile—but what the ship on the medallion had to do with us, I couldn't imagine.

Frank suggested thoughtfully, "I believe these people may imagine that we came here on purpose to get them. Their ancestors came here from some other place. Pete seems to be trying to tell you these people want to go 'home.'"

"Who?"

"Pete," Frank repeated. "That is the name of the man we're speaking with. I don't think Pete knows where this ancestral 'home' he speaks of is, but he imagines you have come from there."

So that was why the islanders didn't fear us. As far as they were concerned, we weren't strangers at all.

"He may be right that we're related," I said. "Whatever dialect this bunch speaks must have continental roots for you to be able to pick it up so fast. But they can't come with us, even if they're from the continent. We don't have room for them. Can you tell them that?"

Frank said he couldn't, but added that we probably wouldn't be leaving until we had made fuel, and while we were making it, he'd try hard to learn the necessary words.

"Fine," I said. "It might be better if we waited to give these people the bad news until the last minute anyway. I don't think 'Pete' is going to take it very well. In the meantime, let's get out and walk around a little and hope these people get the message that right now, at least, they're not going anywhere."

They did, eventually. After yelling awhile (I assume for us to come back), Pete and the other Leaders finally clambered back out of the boat and followed us up the trail. I heard Pete speak roughly to some of the citizens in the line as he passed them, but when he got to where Frank and I were, he was all friendly smiles.

For the next couple of hours, Frank and I made a leisurely tour of the island with Pete scurrying after us, talking, while the rest of the Leaders and the island citizens returned to what I guess was their normal daily routine of doing nothing. The Small People, meanwhile, took crude wooden tools and headed for the tuber fields.

The more I saw of the place—which Frank informed me its people called something like "Making Happy Island"—the less I respected Pete's leadership of it. It had good land and soil. With a little work, it could have been a paradise. Instead, it was wild. Everything but the actual tuber fields was overgrown, and the buildings (aside from the wrecks of ancient ones) were mud. The contrast with Ant Island was, frankly, embarrassing to me as a member of the human species.

Eventually, Frank and I returned to the dinghy, and after only one half-hearted attempt to climb into it with us, Pete let us go back to the *Muriel*.

Halfway to the ship, Frank abruptly stopped rowing.

"Sir," he said thoughtfully. "I have just realized something disturbing. I have realized why I'm able to understand the island people while you're not."

"It's because you're a better linguist than I am." I meant it sincerely, too. I was amazed at how quickly Frank had started to get the sense of what was said to us.

But Frank shook his head. "No. It's because of the Small People. It's because some of the Small People are telepaths, like me."

My stomach turned. "Gods," I breathed. "They're Ants. Is anybody ashore? We have to get out of here!"

"They won't hurt us!" Frank said quickly.

Sneering, I raised my arm to signal the *Muriel*. "Tell that to Mr. Jameson!"

Frank caught my arm and held it. "If he were here, I would do so," he said solemnly. "I would swear it by my honor."

The word "honor" made me hesitate. Frank had been educated by Foresters, who would have taught him never to use that term lightly. If Deer had sworn by his honor to kill all the Ants on the continent, he would have done it, Anna or no. Luckily for her, the Men had only required him to swear by the gods.

"All right," I said warily. "Talk fast. Why aren't they dangerous?"

"The Small People are what Ants were before the Cataclysm," Frank explained. "When Men trusted them. I believe they have Man-blood in them, too, which has a gentling effect. They don't know what humans did to them—"

"What *humans* did to *them*?"

"—or that they could resist us. They only know service and submission."

I decided—just for the moment—to put aside the issue of who had done what to whom.

"But—won't they find out?" I gestured with my hands to indicate spewing thoughts. "If they're telepaths, they know what you know, right?"

Frank reminded me—proudly—that he was a Man, and communicated a Man's point of view. "Also, the Small People and I don't read each other very well. These are not like the Ants of the continent. These speak. They have always spoken. Even among themselves, they often speak. And they mix many words in their thoughts."

So Frank hadn't actually been learning the island language at all. He'd been reading the Small People's thoughts. I found this interesting—and disturbing. "What about the rest of the islanders? Are any of them telepathic?"

Frank said he thought they weren't. "I think the Small People and I will understand each other well in time," he said. "In the meantime, we need fuel very badly, and rest, and fresh food."

He waited patiently until I'd thought everything over.

I had to concede his points about the water and fuel, at least—and fresh food would do us all good. "You'll monitor them, right? And know if they're up to anything? That's what Deer sent you to do."

"Oh, yes," Frank agreed.

He began to row again. "Sir? Can we help the Small People? They are required to work very hard or be beaten."

My private opinion was that since the Small People were Ants, I was already making a huge concession by not just killing the whole lot of them, but all I said to Frank was, "Nobody's getting a beating while I'm here to see it. That's all I'll promise."

On deck, we were greeted by Timmy, ostentatiously sporting a smear of ash down his scarred cheek. He'd been in the engine room, he informed us, helping Mike strip down the boiler.

I couldn't picture the scene. Mike, as I may have mentioned, is the silent type, while Tim talks pretty much continually.

But Tim was up and dressed and out of my cabin for a change, and that was what mattered. I said, "Fantastic!"

CHAPTER SEVENTEEN

There are times when it feels great to be right, and there are times when the last thing you want in the world is to be right. At the beginning of our voyage I'd predicted to Helen that if she raided our backup radio for parts to make our primary set better, she'd regret it, and during our third week on the island, I was proved absolutely correct about this. While Helen and I were both ashore one afternoon, there was a thunderstorm over Making Happy, and the electrical surge caused by a direct lightning strike to our radio antenna destroyed several critical components, including something—maybe several somethings—we couldn't immediately identify. We couldn't figure out what was broken and we didn't know whether we could fix it if we did figure it out. All we knew for sure was the *Muriel* was now out of touch with the continent, possibly permanently.

Up to that day, our situation on Making Happy Island had been pretty good. Frank and I were able to communicate with the islanders by keeping a Small Person nearby anytime we were ashore. When anyone spoke to us, Frank got the sense of what they'd said from the Small Person's brain and repeated it to me. Since Frank didn't really know many words in the island language, our replies always had to be made back through a Small Person, too, which seemed to irritate Pete in particular, but luckily neither he nor anybody else ever asked why we preferred to converse by means of a clumsy, three-way system. The island water was sweet, and there was plenty to eat. I tried snaring hares, only to have them confiscated by the Activity Directors (a Small Person had supplied us with their official title), but nobody could keep track of—or cared—how many fish we caught. The crabs in the coves were delicious.

The food, the water, and the island females, whose attitude toward the sailors' overtures was almost uniformly "sure, why not?" were the positive sides to the island. The big negative was Pete, who was—as I could tell without knowing a word he said to me—a natural-born tyrant and conniver.

The rest of the citizenry were pretty much like people anywhere. Given how they were raised, I wasn't surprised to find a lot of them perfectly content to spend all their time lying around letting the Small People do everything for them, but some islanders seemed like they'd have been willing to work if there'd been any profit in working—which there wasn't. As the Small People explained it to Frank, Pete and his cronies not only helped themselves to everything the Small People produced, redistributing what they didn't want personally among the other islanders, but also appropriated anything nice any other island citizen made or found.

Consequently, the women of the islands even refused the small gifts the sailors offered, aware that they would only end up in Pete's hands, and lacking any incentive to make, take, or barter for anything, the island population spent their days swimming and napping and canoeing and having sex; eating what was put in front of them by the Small People; and complaining that there wasn't more.

The Small People did all the work, but since they weren't given any real direction (which as Ants they especially needed), they worked hard, but stupidly. They cultivated the tuber fields so assiduously we ate tubers at every meal (or at least, we did until we got so sick of them that the entire ship's company swore off tubers forever), but it never occurred to them (or anybody) that with a little extra effort, luxuries like berries could be propagated in beds and turned into everyday fare.

The only initiative shown by anybody on Making Happy was that the Activity

Directors continued to press us relentlessly to allow them to come aboard the *Muriel*. Since they wanted to bring along their families and possessions, it was clear what they had in mind, and I put them off from day to day.

Helen and I were working on the radio when Frank came to the Navigation Room with news we didn't want. "Rain says the Activity Directors are gathering much more frequently than usual to talk in the Sacred Space," he said. "She thinks they are plotting."

My mind was mostly elsewhere. "What about rain?" I asked absently. "It rains every damn day here now. Helen, I think I've figured out a way to get this thing working enough to receive the time-signal, at least. Let's just hope your Papa doesn't give up when he doesn't hear from us and stop sending it."

"Papa will never give up," declared Helen fiercely.

"No. He's probably worried sick, though." Turning to Frank, I repeated, "What was that about rain?"

"Rain," Frank said. "Rain is the female of the Small People who's been helping me translate."

"Oh, that Rain. Plotting what? And what's a 'Sacred Space'?"

Frank admitted he didn't exactly know. "The 'Sacred Space' is a building, but only the Activity Directors may enter it, so Rain has never seen the inside."

I figured I could pretty much guess what the plot was: The Activity Directors wanted the *Muriel* to take them "home." The question was how far they were willing to go to make that happen. "Find out where this 'Sacred Space' is, will you? And tell Rain to keep her ears open."

Frank said he would.

*

Dan's first lucrative re-invention, before I joined his company and we renamed it "D&R," was a simple communications system that could send and receive a message a long way down a wire using patterns of long and short electrical pulses to spell out words. Dan had gotten the idea from an ancient army text he found as a boy, so we called the pulse-patterns "soldier code." This "telegraph," as the Ancients termed it, was useful everywhere, and Dan was the hero of the hour for reintroducing it on the continent.

When Helen and I finally got the radio working again—though only as a primitive receiver—the first communication we picked up was a soldier-code message from Dan.

The message was, "Helen, I love you."

Helen, who'd borne up fine until then, suddenly cried, "Oh, poor Papa! Why did I ever come on this stupid voyage?" and burst into tears.

"He's brilliant," I said—not for the first time in my life. "And he's right. We shouldn't even be trying to send voice transmissions. We should be using soldier code. Let's see if we can't find a way to generate a noise we can break into long and short beats. If we can get through even once, with even just a short message, he'll know we're all right."

While Helen went to work solving our radio problem, I went to find Frank.

He knew by now where the "Sacred Space" was, so with Captain Alcock's permission, I rowed ashore and set off on a little stroll around Making Happy, making sure my path was aimless enough that nobody would think anything of it if I just happened to wander by one specific spot.

As soon as I got near, I realized I'd seen the "Sacred" building before, on my first tour of the island. Pete hadn't taken Frank and me all the way to it, though. I'd only caught a glimpse of it through foliage. With hindsight, I realized I should have been suspicious about that. The "Sacred Space" was clearly one of the oldest buildings on Making Happy, and Pete had shown us all the other ancient buildings proudly. I stopped where I had a good view and looked it over, pretending to be interested in the bark of a trailside tree just in case anyone was watching me.

In contrast to the other ancient structures, which had been kept functional over the centuries with careless patches of whatever material came to hand, there appeared to have been an ongoing effort to keep the Sacred Space looking as it had originally. The results of that effort weren't too good. As I said, the island woodworkers weren't exactly highly skilled. The building was rectangular, with a tower-like projection at the front, and its patched roof was steeply pitched. The tower was a half-story or so higher than the rest of the building, and had its own, separate roof in the form of a ridiculously tall four-sided pyramid. Though clumsy efforts had been made to shore up the tower at the base, it had a noticeable leeward tilt.

As inconspicuously as I could, I slowly circled the whole building.

A few windows had collapsed, but the remaining ones had a distinctive peaked shape, and here and there a piece of the old glazing was still in place. I knew it had to be old glass, since I hadn't seen any evidence the islanders made glass now. Some of the glass was brightly colored. I remembered that Pete's wife wore a piece of blue glass on a thong around her neck—the only adornment I'd seen besides Pete's medallion that wasn't a shell—and guessed it was probably a Sacred Space relic. It looked to me like a poor venue for plotting, since the roof was ready to fall in, and it didn't look in any way "sacred" to me, either. But then, as a Forester, I was no judge of that. Foresters believe life is sacred, and that's about it.

After looking at it for as long as I could without giving away my interest, I wandered back toward the beach, where earlier I'd left Frank talking with Rain. Through the two of them I planned to question the whole community of Small People.

"What do the Activity Directors actually do in the Sacred Space?" I asked. "Is it for rituals?"

Rain looked thoughtful for a minute, and then Frank answered, "We don't know. Any Small People who approach the building are beaten." He added gravely, "Even very young ones."

I had no trouble imagining Pete beating a child.

"They must be happy the Small People are telepathic," I said sarcastically. "If they beat one of the Small People, it's like beating them all."

This seemed like a straightforward observation, and I expected Frank to just agree with it and move on. Instead, he hesitated for a long time before answering.

Then he said, "You have confused Rain and the others. They don't understand what you're saying."

It took a lot of discussion with Rain before Frank and I finally figured out that the difficulty with my remark was that the Small People didn't understand that non-Small People weren't telepathic. Telepathy wasn't "telepathy" to the Small People, it was just normal conversation, and despite our explanations, they couldn't seem to grasp the idea that another, totally non-telepathic way to communicate could possibly exist.

Frank—who was obviously getting more out of the conversation than I was—said, "The Small People believe the Babblers are able to let only other Babblers enter their thoughts. That's one reason they fear them."

"Babblers?" I raised my eyebrows. "They call us that?"

Frank looked embarrassed. "They would be more respectful of you if they understood."

Many years before, John Seaborn had shown me a translation he made of a letter written shortly before the Ant-Cataclysm. Assuming John translated it right (and I knew how hard it was to translate an Ancient Text) the writer was very familiar with Ants. At the time I read the letter, I didn't know Ants were telepathic. Now it struck me that the letter contained no indication the ancient writer had known it, either. It was possible, I suddenly realized, that in ancient times the two races had lived side-by-side without ever realizing they related to the world in fundamentally different ways.

"I've got to get into the 'Sacred Space,'" I said. "There might be clues in there about the Activity Directors' plot."

As soon as she understood this, Rain shook her head.

"We are watched more closely than you realize," Frank said. "The Small People see the Directors watching us."

"Do they think we're up to something?"

But of course, Frank had no idea what the Activity Directors were thinking, because neither he nor Rain could read the Activity Directors' minds. Frank's personal opinion was they were watching us because they were afraid we'd leave without them.

"What about your people?" I asked Rain. "Do they want us to take them on the *Muriel*?"

Since I'd asked Rain directly, Frank let her answer. Rain shook her head.

"You want to stay on this island?"

Rain nodded.

"They remember another place, before they came here," Frank said. "They didn't like it."

"Must have been pretty bad," I commented.

To Rain, I said, "Help me, then. Help me get into the Sacred Space. Tell Frank if anyone looks like they're going there tonight."

As Rain nodded, Frank assured me the Small People agreed to keep watch in all parts of the island that night, adding, "And I will come with you and tell you what they see."

Aboard the *Muriel*, Helen had meanwhile disabled the radio as a receiver and was concentrating all her energy and radio parts on making it transmit soldier-code, as we'd agreed.

"Guess what?" she said in greeting. "You have a cabin again. Tim's decided to sling his hammock down in the Engine Room. He says he's Engineer's Mate now, and should sleep near his work."

CHAPTER EIGHTEEN

At dusk, by prearrangement with Captain Alcock, I crossed to the island by lying in the bottom of the dinghy while someone else rowed, slipped out on the shore, then sent the dinghy back without me. Frank was already there, waiting.

"I swam over," he explained. "But I have hidden a canoe, so we don't have to swim back."

Nobody noticed Frank or I were gone—and nobody noticed that Helen had absconded from the *Muriel*, either, until Frank and I were creeping quietly up the path off the beach and were startled to hear her say in a loud whisper, "Slow down, can't you? I've got something in my shoe."

Exasperated, I waited for her to catch up. "What are you doing here?" I demanded—quietly, of course.

"What are *you* doing here?" Helen countered. "You know one of those awful 'Directors' is watching the beach, don't you? I don't think he saw us."

I suggested she stay behind to make sure.

Even by starlight, I could make out the steely glint in Helen's eye. "Not a chance."

There was nothing I could do but give in, of course—which was what she had counted on.

We headed toward the Sacred Space, meeting Rain along the way, who told us through Frank the Small People were awake and ready to alert us if any islander left a village and approached the Sacred Space.

"'Sacred Space?'" Helen asked.

"It's a building only the Activity Directors can enter," I said. "I'm going to investigate it."

Helen looked uncomfortable. "Do you think you should? I know *you* don't, but some people take things like gods very seriously. Wouldn't it be disrespectful for us to violate these peoples' holy site?"

"Helen," I told her flatly, "you're not going to violate anything, because you're going to stay outside with Frank and Rain. And—just so you know this—I'm not going to 'violate' anything either. Rain says she thinks the Activity Directors are plotting something, so I'm checking the Sacred Space to make sure they're not stockpiling weapons in it. All I plan to do is go in—respectfully—have a respectful look around, and, assuming I don't find anything bad, tiptoe respectfully right back out the way I came."

"That's all?" Helen eyed me skeptically. "All right, then."

Of course when we got there, she slipped right in behind me.

I had an electric candle, a small one that emitted a correspondingly feeble beam. I didn't dare risk anything brighter for fear a glimmer at a window or a gap in a wall would give us away. Once our eyes had adjusted, we could see that the whole room was crowded with large shadowy bulks. I pointed my candle at a low shape near us, and Helen leaned in for a close look.

"It's like—paper," she said, gingerly putting out a hand to touch the bulk's surface. "It is paper. Old paper. Old-old, like an Ancient Text. There's a whole stack of it on top of—whatever this is. A table or something."

It was a table, and some of the other bulks turned out to be things like chairs and benches. We didn't recognize the chairs at first, because they were stacked, and each chair fit with such marvelous precision into the one below it that only the top chair actually looked like a chair. They were very old, like the paper, and at this point, rusted together and probably unusable. Closely covering every other piece of furniture were smaller objects; some familiar, and some whose function—if any—we couldn't guess.

We looked at the papers first. They lay fifty or sixty sheets deep on the table Helen had first touched, and though the top layer was rotten and filthy with dust, the papers in the lower layers were smooth and shiny, and printed all over with text and colored pictures. Because of the darkness, we couldn't make the text out in any detail, except to see that the alphabet they were written in seemed to be like the one used in Men's Lands on the continent.

Helen pointed out a picture of a ship on one paper.

"If those are portholes, then this ship was a lot bigger than the *Muriel*. It's shaped like the *Muriel*, though."

"That's because we stole her design from an Ancient Text," I said, grinning. "I'm going to take one of those."

"Oh, don't do that!" Helen exclaimed. "What if somebody notices it's gone?"

"The Directors can't keep track of every single paper."

Of course, they probably could—and if the papers were "sacred," maybe they did. But when Helen turned her back, I took one from each stack. They were soft enough to slip silently into my pocket.

We explored the room slowly, looking at everything. There weren't any signs of weapons or plots, but there were stacks of dishes on the floor in one corner. Dishes were easy for us to recognize because a lot of people on the continent had ones just like them. They were often found in the ruins of ancient cities, and if they hadn't been exposed so much that the shiny finish was spoiled, they were still useful. Some large bowls among them were filled with piles of discs like the one Pete wore as an amulet. When my niece wasn't looking, I took a few of those, too. There were glass drinking beakers like ones on the continent, and knives and spoons—some metal and some made of plastic.

"Why aren't the islanders using these things?" I muttered to Helen. "These beakers are a thousand times better than those junk pots they drink from, and all the plastic could be melted down and remolded."

I knew this because recovered plastic was so widely reused on the continent that even the Foresters made things from it.

"Well, because—they're sacred, I guess," Helen ventured. "Or maybe that's one of the privileges of being an Activity Leader. You get to drink from a glass beaker sometimes. What are these, Uncle?" she asked then, showing me a tableful of strange glass cylinders with metal caps that had tiny holes drilled through them.

I didn't know.

We looked around for half an hour or so, and then, knowing we were keeping Frank and Rain and a lot of other Small People from their beds, we decided we'd seen what we'd come to see and should go.

Near the door, one last thing caught my eye. Hung on the wall was a mosaic—filthy, like everything else in the place—and made, as I discovered when I rubbed off some of the dirt from one corner, of shiny little tiles.

"What's it a picture of?" I asked Helen. "I can't make it out."

Helen cocked her head doubtfully. "Are the red and yellow parts the subject and the blue parts the background? Or is it the other way around?"

I couldn't make sense of it no matter which way I looked.

"There's a symbol down there in the corner," I said, pointing. "I've seen ones like it before—only I can't remember where."

"What does it mean?"

"I can't remember that, either."

We puzzled over the picture for a few more minutes, speculating it might be the deity to whom the Sacred Space was dedicated, then turned off our candle and went quietly out. Frank and Rain were just where we'd left them, holding hands.

"Rain is frightened," Frank explained, when he saw me looking.

The four of us headed back then, Rain leading. Frank said she would get us to the beach by paths only the Small People used.

I'd already gotten into the canoe when, on second thought, I climbed out again and offered my hand to Rain. I'd vowed to myself more than once that no Ant would ever get anything better from me than reasonably merciful death, but Rain and all her people had done us a big favor, at some risk to themselves, and I felt like it had to be acknowledged.

After a quick glance at Frank, Rain took the hand I held out.

"Thank you," I said, shaking hers firmly. "You were a big help."

As we paddled back, I said to Helen, "The captain's going to want to hear all about what we found. I think I'll let you tell him."

My niece looked at me suspiciously. "Why me?"

"Because then you'll have to confess you sneaked off and came with us, and he'll be furious, and he'll yell at you. I doubt you'll listen, but at least I won't be wasting any more of my time trying to get you to behave."

"Why don't all you overprotective men just save your breath?" Helen asked coolly. "Then nobody's time will be wasted. Fine. I'll talk to Jasper. You go to bed."

I assured her that was exactly what I had planned.

I had a cabin to myself again and a pocket full of mysterious, possibly "sacred" objects to look at. I could hardly wait to "go to bed."

The discs were like coins, except made of some light metal that—unless cheap alloys were somehow valuable in ancient times—I could hardly imagine anyone taking in exchange for merchandise. (I had to admire how nicely they were made, though.) The different sizes had different images on them—flowers, mostly—and one was like Pete's amulet, with a picture of a ship on one side, and the number "10" on the other. Unlike Pete's, the picture and words on this coin weren't worn, and I could make them out clearly. The words around the edge were "SSHOLIDAY" across the top, and "QUEEN" at the bottom, and though I didn't recognize the first word, I thought I remembered that "queen" was a name for a female king. In ancient times, there seems to have been separate names for the male and the female of just about everything—I didn't know why.

I studied the coins carefully to make sure I wasn't missing anything, then put them aside.

The papers were more interesting.

Besides more pictures of ships, the papers were illustrated with scenes of beaches (possibly including ones on Making Happy, but since they were crowded with people and lined with structures, it was hard to tell) and buildings surrounded by flowering bushes. The people in the pictures were all smiling like they'd been told to do it, and their clothes were colorful, and very brief. Their teeth were like pearls.

There was text between the pictures, and when I looked closely I saw that, as I'd already guessed, the language was one of the Ancient Mother Tongues of the continent. The papers were all folded into thirds, like little books, and one had a picture of the Sacred Space when it was new and, in big letters, three words I recognized ("*Your Island Wedding*") on the front, so I started with that one. My Mother Tongue vocabulary was fairly specialized, having mostly to do with things like engines and electricity, but between what I remembered from the schoolroom and some guesswork, I worked out quite a lot of what the papers said. I think.

When I picked up a project, I could get pretty thoroughly absorbed in it, and the next thing I was consciously aware of was my niece banging on my cabin door and yelling for me to wake up. Looking around, I found to my surprise that while I'd been translating the paper, the sun had risen. It wasn't even early anymore. It was full day.

"Come in if you want," I called, sliding the contraband under some other things. "I'm not asleep."

Helen burst in, saying excitedly, "I think I've almost got it, but I need your help." Then her eyes narrowed, and she looked back and forth meaningfully a couple of times between me and my bed.

"What?" I asked blandly. "I always make my bed."

"And I suppose you always make your eyes bloodshot, too. You stole one of those papers, didn't you?" Before I could answer this, she said, "I don't have time right now to tell you what an idiot you are, Uncle River, because right now, I need your help."

Then she dragged me off down the passage between my cabin and the Navigation Room, explaining along the way that she had gotten to the point where she could transmit a signal, but she hadn't been able break it into regular enough long and short pulses to send an intelligible message.

"You have no sense," she informed me, "but you do know radios."

A few hours later, we sent our first message since the lightning strike:

"All safe. Radio out. Please acknowledge."

Helen would have liked to say more—like "Papa, please don't worry," and "I love you too"—but our makeshift transmitter was balky and our long and short pulses were so uneven I was afraid Dan might not even realize he was hearing soldier-code if I didn't keep the message short and repeat it many times. We made the same brief transmission every few minutes for half an hour, then closed down.

"How fast do you think we can turn this back into a receiver?" I asked Helen.

The answer turned out to be about an hour, which was too long for Dan. He was already mid-transmission when we started picking it up. He went on for quite a while saying he loved us and had been very worried, obviously expecting to hear back from us, but then caught on that we were mute for some reason and said he'd take a break.

"Reply soon if you can," he telegraphed.

As I reached to cut the power so Helen and I could reconfigure the radio parts to transmit again, I was stopped dead by a touch on the key I knew better than anybody else's in the world.

"River, if you can hear this," Sarah telegraphed, "I love you."

The lightning bolt started looking like a stroke of luck to me.

CHAPTER NINETEEN

Next day we held a brief hilltop memorial for our lost friends Bertie, William, and Mr. Jameson, and planted their namesake tubers.

I was initially reluctant to take part in this, thinking it would be—at best—a parody of a Forester tree-planting ceremony, but Helen insisted, saying my absence at such a time would be inexcusable. Afterward I was glad I'd done it.

The sailors put small tokens of their shipmates into the holes dug for planting, then attended respectfully to Captain Alcock's brief exhortation to honor their friends' memories by applying themselves more conscientiously to their duties instead of "messing so damn much with them damn island women!" Helen sang a traditional continental mourning song, and we concluded by planting the strange purple nubbins, now lush and leafy. Captain Alcock's language notwithstanding, the ceremony was dignified, and I think we all left it a little comforted.

Later, Frank gave the rest of the tubers to the Small People to grow for food and asked them to look after the ones on the hill and renew them as necessary.

With a batch of fuel made, our larder replenished, and this final, sad bit of business taken care of, it was time for the *Muriel* to head for home.

At least, the shippers thought it was. The shippers had been wanting us to turn for home from the minute we left John's Island. As far as they were concerned, John's was the possible source of raw materials for continental manufacturers they sent us to find, and voyage number one should have ended right there. When I'd insisted, they'd reluctantly agreed to let me sail "a little" further, but after that all we found was Ant Island—total bad news—and Making Happy, which had potential as a market but was too far out for anyone on the continent to easily exploit. Now they wanted—really, really wanted—us to first sail the *Muriel* home, and then on a second voyage to the Southern Ocean.

The trouble was, the only thing Helen and I knew for sure about the *Morning Glory's* course when she left John's Island was that she was heading "farther out." If we went home, as the shippers demanded, it would be at least a year before we could try again to find where "farther out" had ended up being, and we'd have to do it in a wooden ship not much better than the *Morning Glory*—which sank. If we wanted to continue in the *Muriel*, we'd have to defy the shippers.

As far as Helen was concerned—and she couldn't understand how I could see it any other way—there was no decision to make. We were going to sail on in the *Muriel* and find her grandparents. But I worried that if we pushed the shippers too far, they'd punish us when we finally did come back by turning the *Muriel* over to our rivals to inspect. There was nothing about the ship that somebody else couldn't imitate once they'd seen it, and the "somebody" who did that would likely end up building the *Muriel II* (and all subsequent big ships) instead of D&R.

Deciding between my niece and my business wasn't going to be easy, and while I weighed my options, I worked on the radio. Getting the radio fixed was the one excuse for lingering on Making Happy that the shippers would accept.

Renewed voice transmission was out of the question, but I managed to turn the radio into a pretty good telegraph, at least, and reduce the time it took us to reconfigure between sending and receiving. Naturally, each little change I made had to be tested, and the easiest way to test the radio was by making calls on it. I called the family mostly, where I asked whoever was around a question or two to get them talking, and then fine-tuned while I listened. The questions I asked were inanities at first—lots about the weather—but after a few days of regular, frequent calls, a strange thing happened. I had real conversations with my family.

They were simple exchanges of information, mostly—partly because the kids weren't fast at soldier code. There still wasn't a lot of "soul sharing" between us. But especially after I discovered that it was a lot easier for me to tell them I loved them in a series of long and short electrical pulses than it had ever been for me to say it in words, our chats became warmer and more open.

I told Sarah I loved her, too. It was true; it would always be true. She could take it however she wanted.

Captain Alcock, meanwhile—whether out of boredom or for some other reason, I don't know—relented and gave Pete the tour of the *Muriel* he wanted. It had the effect we all hoped it would, of forcing Pete to acknowledge there wasn't enough room on the ship to accommodate all the islanders, and Pete was briefly discouraged. But after thinking it over, he informed us (through Frank and Rain) that he and a few friends would be traveling on the *Muriel* with us, and a bigger ship should be dispatched later to pick up the rest of the Making Happy population. He claimed my cabin for the journey. I said no.

Helen and I were discussing this a few days later, while trying for the twentieth time to improve our radio reception.

"The trouble is," I told Helen, "no one on Making Happy was originally a native of Making Happy, and the inhabitants have handed down this tradition that the island's just a temporary stopover for them."

Since Helen had never given me a chance to share what I'd learned from the "stolen" paper, I explained. "See, in ancient times, they had this strange custom where a whole bunch of people from one place would get on a ship, and then they'd—"

"A place on the continent?"

"Well, yeah. Or at least, I think the ancestors of this bunch were from the continent. Shiploads of people from other places might have come to Making Happy, too. I don't know."

"All right. Go on."

"I could read you the whole paper, if you want."

Helen's eyes blazed. "I don't even want to see that thing in your thieving paws!" she cried. It was a sore point with her.

This seemed unnecessarily harsh, so I said, "Fine," and went back to fiddling silently with the radio.

After a minute, Helen couldn't stand it. "So… what was the point of it?"

"The point of what?" I murmured vaguely, not looking up.

I sensed a short, sharp mental struggle before could Helen could force herself to say calmly, "The point of sailing all those people to Making Happy."

Laying down the tool I was using, I sighed. Pointedly.

"Look, there's nothing 'sacred' about that paper, all right? Whatever the so-called Sacred Space was originally, now it's nothing but a warehouse where the Activity Directors store the good stuff to keep it away from everybody else. Which is stupid, but we won't get into that now. Also, I didn't steal anything. I just borrowed a few things temporarily."

"A few? I thought you just took one paper!"

"A couple things," I lied.

"A couple. Great. Will you take them back?"

"Absolutely."

"You promise?"

"Don't insult me." I picked up my tool again.

Another struggle (I was enjoying this), and then Helen repeated, "What was the point of sailing people to Making Happy?"

I decided to go easy on her. "I'm not sure there was a point. Or—not a serious point. These big ships would take people on board—a lot of people, apparently—and then they'd just sail them around. From island to island. Periodically, the ship would stop for a few days at a place like Making Happy, and everybody would get off the ship and celebrate."

"Celebrate what?"

"Just—celebrate." I shrugged. "They'd 'make happy,' so to speak. Sometimes they got married. And when they were adequately happy, or married, or whatever, they'd get back on the ship and go on to another island. Or back home, depending."

"Depending on what?"

"Depending on how long the people on the ship decided they wanted to go around 'celebrating' for. The paper has a little chart on it with different numbers of days people could sail, and the number of islands the ship could stop at in that number of days. I guess the passengers picked the number of days that corresponded to how much celebrating they wanted to do. There are other choices on the chart, too, but I haven't figured out yet what the names of the categories mean."

"Did you find out anything else?" Helen asked. "Anything actually useful, for instance?"

"I thought that was useful. I thought it explained why everybody's so anxious to leave what's really a perfectly nice island. It's because nobody came here wanting to stay. Also, I think it probably explains why the A… I mean, why the Small People are here. I think the passengers brought them along as servants."

"And they're still servants," Helen said sadly. "They're worse off than servants, in fact, poor things! The islanders still believe they're just here to have fun, and the Small People still believe they're here to do all the work."

"That's what it looks like to me, too."

I'm not actually a bad uncle, and once Helen made it clear how bothered she was about me taking things from the Sacred Space, I naturally wanted to return them right away so she could be happy again. This time, I didn't tell Frank I was going, since if Frank knew, so would all the Small People, and I certainly didn't tell Helen. I slipped quietly over the *Muriel's* side at night, intending to do what I had to do, and then give my niece the good news at breakfast.

Getting away from the *Muriel* went as planned, because after a year at sea, I knew better than to repeat all the stupid mistakes I'd made sneaking ashore at John's Island. The only small complication was that I left much later than I'd intended to, because when I asked him, Frank told me the Activity Directors were in the Sacred Space again. A couple of hours later he said they were still there, and a couple of hours after that, Frank innocently went to bed.

So I waited until very late, as I said, and then went to check on the situation for myself. I swam ashore and headed inland by way of the secret paths Rain had used.

The Activity Directors were still inside the Sacred Space when I got there. Annoyed as I was by this development, I had to admire the way the light of their torches looked behind the shards of colored glass in the window-openings. When the windows were intact, they must have made quite a show. It was near dawn when Pete and his gang finally emerged, and they looked tired.

And no wonder. When I went in, I discovered the whole place had undergone a transformation. There was no possibility of returning anything I'd "stolen." The stacks of paper, piles of coins and dishes, rows of beakers, and everything else had all been made up into leather-wrapped bundles tied with strips of hide. Even the tables had been turned on their tops, and the chairs and boxes nested between their legs. Like the smaller things, the furniture had all been lashed together, convenient for carrying.

It looked to me like the Activity Directors were moving out.

Overall, I was happy about this. Little as I liked Pete and his friends, I had no wish—or, very little wish—to see them crushed to death under a falling building. Also, if they'd packed up the papers and coins without noticing a few were missing, I figured I could keep what I'd taken. That was good. Dan, Sarah, and Deer—particularly Deer—would find them fascinating. After a quick look at the parts of the room hidden by the furniture on my first visit (they were undistinguished, and as badly rotted as the rest), I turned to leave.

I took one last look at the tile mosaic, trying again to make sense of the subject. Was it the face of a deity, as Helen suggested? I turned it a little to catch a gleam from the rising sun, shining through a crack in a wall.

I realized then with a start that the image wasn't a deity at all. It wasn't even a picture. The mosaic was a map. Unless I was very much mistaken, the blue parts were the ocean; the yellow bits were islands; and the red blob in the very center (which Helen had taken for a mouth) was none other than our own Making Happy. Suddenly I remembered where I'd seen the symbol in the corner I'd told Helen looked familiar. I'd seen it on other ancient maps. Currently, the symbol was pointing at the floor, but if I turned the mosaic so the symbol pointed north, like a compass, the map would then be in its proper orientation.

I wanted to take it—or at least to copy it, but I had nothing to write with. I'd have to come back again later, better equipped.

When I climbed aboard the *Muriel*, I reported—as I was supposed to—to the deck watch. I told him I'd gone for a swim.

"You and old Stoney," the sailor said, grinning. "He swims regular every day now. Got a girl on the island, and she likes him clean."

CHAPTER TWENTY

I was half asleep when Frank put his head around the corner of my cabin door. "I'm sorry to disturb you, sir."

The look on his face brought me wide awake in an instant.

"What's going on?" I demanded. I pointed to my chair and Frank obediently sat down.

"Rain has discovered—" he began uncertainly, "—that is to say, Rain and the others—they have discovered a plan the Activity Directors have made."

I relaxed. "I know about it. They're moving the contents of the Sacred Space someplace else. I went back there last night, and everything was packed up."

Frank stopped me with an impatient gesture. "To the ship," he blurted. "They are moving it all to the ship. They want to have it when they reach the Old Land."

"What ship?" I asked. "You don't mean the *Muriel*, right?"

Frank did mean the *Muriel*.

It seemed Pete was about to turn pirate. He'd enlisted all the young island men into the enterprise, telling them to bring weapons and meet him at a certain place and time, and when they were all together he was planning to send some of them to take prisoner any sailors who were ashore. Then they would all paddle canoes to the *Muriel*, overwhelm the rest of her crew, and claim the ship—our ship—as their own.

I frowned. "I didn't know they even had weapons."

"Knives and clubs," Frank told me. "They know our knives are better than theirs, because ours are metal, but they are confident they will prevail because they will have hostages. Also, they have counted and know there are many more of them than there are of us."

The islanders' "knives" were knapped stone, not particularly well done, and their "clubs" were whatever branch they happened to pull off the nearest tree or bush when they decided a club would be handy to have. On the other hand, it was true that the *Muriel's* company was considerably outnumbered.

Of course, we had guns. We had cannon, in fact, which put the odds at about ten thousand to one in our favor no matter how many islanders we were up against. But in the first place, I didn't want to use guns against an enemy not similarly equipped (I'd done it before, and it was ugly), and in the second place, as Frank said, they'd have hostages.

I knew the Small People were hearing everything Frank heard, so I tried to seem unworried. "I've seen their knives and clubs," I remarked calmly. "I wasn't impressed. Anyway, how could Pete sail the *Muriel* if he did get her? She's not a canoe. He can't just paddle her away."

"He believes once he is aboard the ship, he can compel the crew by terror to sail her for him," Frank answered.

Pete was evidently smarter than I'd thought. "All right," I said. "Let's go talk to the captain. How long do we have before Pete and his friends put this plan into action?"

"They're already on their way."

As we headed toward the captain's cabin, Frank filled me in on a few more details.

The Small People, he assured me, weren't in on the plot. In fact, nobody'd told them a thing about it. They'd figured it out for themselves when their collective brain pieced together an unguarded word spoken to one, a hint dropped before another, and some unusual activity observed by a third. By that means they'd formed a fairly complete picture of the situation—which, of course, immediately communicated itself to Frank.

"Will they help us?" I asked.

Frank shook his head sadly. "How can they? After this, we will go, but the Activity Directors will still rule Making Happy."

Captain Alcock's reaction, when I told him what was going on, was predictable.

"Them ship-stealing boogers," he thundered, red with indignation. "Them slut-mothered, turd-fathered, dung-eating bastards."

After that, his language got bad.

His stated intention, when he calmed down enough to articulate it, was to use the ship's cannon to blow Making Happy and all its citizens to pieces.

"I'm calling up the gun-crews," he said, rising. "Unless you favor setting fire to the place instead. Wouldn't take much of that fuel you made to roast the whole whoreson lot alive. We could watch from a few miles out. Might be pretty."

Frank went white.

I may have gone a few shades paler myself. The captain had just threatened the Small People with annihilation, and from what Anna had been able to figure out years ago in Evergreen, the Ant-Cataclysm in ancient times began when the Ants of those days somehow got the idea they were threatened with annihilation. They had access to weapons, apparently—bad idea—and in response to this perceived threat, attacked every human they saw.

But what looked like self-defense to the Ants looked different to the humans, who naturally fought back. This only seemed to "confirm" the Ants' fears about the humans' intentions—and so on and so on, until the two races all but wiped each other out.

Quickly, I said, "Captain, you don't mean that. The people here don't all deserve to die. Some of them are very nice, in fact." Then I mentioned a few of the nicer ones, being sure to include in the list the female with whom Captain Alcock was said to be on *particularly friendly* terms. I had gotten her name from Frank, who learned it from Rain, who picked it out of the mind of some

Small Person unknown who had seen the female and the captain together. There is no such thing as "private business" on a small island with Ants. "And some of our sailors are ashore, too. What about them?"

The captain stopped where he was and scratched himself moodily.

"A cannon's a damn comprehensive weapon," he acknowledged. "If you got a better plan, I'll listen."

I thought quickly, then asked, "Can I go ashore myself and intercept Pete?"

"You planning to shoot a few to learn the others what a gun is? Good idea."

I'd shoot if I had to, I decided, though I answered—sincerely—"I hope it won't come to that."

Captain Alcock gave a grunt. "How many men you want?"

"I'm going alone," I said. "Unless Frank will come with me."

Actually, I needed Frank to come with me. I needed one of the Small People, too. Without Frank plus a Small Person, any conversation I had with Pete would have to be dumbshow. But it's against my principles—I do have some—to take anyone on a dangerous mission who isn't a volunteer.

"I will come," Frank said promptly.

"I'll open the arms locker for you," the captain replied. "And soon's that's done, I'll call up the gun crews, like I said. I won't use 'em if I don't have to, but I always say it's better bein' safe than boogered."

On the way to my cabin, I met Helen and asked her to get Mike to fire up the boiler with all possible speed.

"We're getting out of here. The captain sent Georgie and Collin down to the beach to get that second batch of fuel into barrels, but we can leave it if we have to. The main thing is to get the distilling apparatus aboard."

Putting a cold hand on my arm, my niece asked, "Can you get Davy and Jack back, Uncle River?"

Davy and Jack, we'd determined, were the sailors who were presently ashore.

"That's certainly the plan," I replied.

I didn't want any more volunteers than just Frank. That way, even if things went very, very wrong, Captain Alcock would lose at most four crewmen—one of them only me, who wasn't much of a sailor anyway. He could get the *Muriel* home with four fewer crew if he had to, even under sail.

But as the dinghy was being lowered, Timmy jumped in.

"Heard we was leaving here," he told me, flashing the crooked half-smile that was all the Ants had left him. "I thought I'd like a look around first. I ain't seen it yet."

I could have declined his help, I guess, but for some reason I didn't. "You ready to use that thing?" I asked instead, indicating the long gun he held. "You may have to."

"Booger," scoffed Timmy. "I don't need to shoot nobody. Folks could die from just looking at me. Whereabouts are Davy and Jack? Anybody know?"

I was sure Frank did, though he had to be discreet about it, since we didn't want anybody to know the *Muriel* was harboring a half-Ant. Sure enough, Frank stopped rowing long enough to point.

"Pete and his people are on a trail, up there. Davy is with them, but Jack ran away."

Obliquely, mindful of the presence of Timmy, Frank then let me know that though the Small People had been driven—with blows—to their own little huts and island women and boys stationed around them as guards to make sure they stayed there, a dozen or so had taken a chance and slipped away. Hidden in the brush, they were watching now as Pete and his little army passed by.

Luckily, Tim was incurious as to the source of Frank's information. "Good old Jack," was all he said.

When we landed, we found that in their haste to get off the island, Georgie and Collin had spilled fuel on the beach. I let Tim abuse them about it for a while. As Machinist's Mate, I felt he had a right. But I'd planned to confront the island force on the beach, under the *Muriel's* guns, and the spilled fuel made that impossible. One spark in the wrong place, and Captain Alcock might get to watch his fire after all. I doubted he'd find it "pretty."

I said, "We'll go up and meet Pete and his bunch on the trail. That way, we can get them before they launch any canoes."

Tim started to speak, possibly to point out that on the trail we'd be out of sight of the *Muriel's* gunners, which was true, and frightening, but then he stopped himself and only said, wistfully, "Be nice to meet up with Jack, wouldn't it? Wish I'd brought him a gun."

I wished we had, too.

We didn't meet Jack, but we didn't get far before we did meet Rain, who came scurrying out of the bushes looking scared.

"Pete and his men are just ahead," Frank said, putting a comforting arm around her.

I didn't really need him to tell me. By now, I could hear them coming. I guess it never occurred to the Activity Directors that a sneak attack should be conducted quietly.

I halted where I was. "We'll let them come to us." I added, to Rain, "You going to help translate?"

Her eyes on Frank's face, she nodded.

I spent the next few minutes giving Tim tips on handling his weapon. He listened attentively, though he pointed out, "There's a lot more of them than I got bullets for."

Before I could answer this (I wasn't planning to deny it) the first island troops came around a bend in the trail ahead.

It had obviously never crossed any of their minds we might be forewarned. The sight of us took the first islanders so much by surprise they stopped short, and a second bunch ran into the backs of them. It was funny, in a way, but I didn't feel like laughing. They all carried knives, and many had clubs or lances, too—crude weapons, but in overwhelming numbers.

I put my hand on Tim's arm to stop him from raising his gun. "Let them come to us," I repeated.

I have to give Pete credit. Without any show of fear, he walked right up to us and, according to Frank's translation, pugnaciously demanded we surrender our knives and "clubs" and step aside.

"Frank," I said, "tell these pukes I want them to give me my sailor and go home."

Rain seemed confused by the word "puke," but whatever word she used in its place made Pete's head snap back.

Then he began to yell—at Rain.

"Quiet, you!" I barked. "I said I want my sailor, and I want him fast. Bring him here."

I knew they had Davy. The Small People had already told Frank they did.

At my tone, which was unfriendly, the young men behind Pete stirred and fingered their knives.

With a sly look, Pete answered, then crossed his arms over his chest. I didn't need Frank to tell me that what he'd said was, basically, "What if I don't?"

"Bring my sailor," I repeated, "or I'll shoot you with my gun."

Again, Rain had trouble translating.

Probably the islanders' ancient ancestors had a word for "gun" in their language. Probably they had words for weapons much more terrible than guns, in fact, because we know terrible weapons existed in ancient times. But by now the islanders had forgotten them so completely they didn't even know to be grateful they could be so ignorant. When I brandished my long gun to reinforce my threat, Pete stared blankly at it.

On my left, Timmy advised tersely, "Shoot one of 'em."

Under the circumstances, it was almost a reasonable suggestion. "I'll shoot something," I agreed. "No need for it to be a man."

A gull was wheeling not far off. I shouldered my long gun and brought it down.

The islanders were so terrified by the sudden noise and smoke that some of them screamed, a few wept, and nearly all of them fell to the ground, their arms over their heads for cover. At least one lost control of his bowels, crawled off into the bushes, and—happily—didn't come back.

Pete, to his credit, merely ducked, though his mouth fell open and stayed that way for quite some time.

"Tell them it's over now, all right?" I said to Frank. "Or anyway, it's over unless one of them does something stupid."

Rain repeated what I said, and the islanders got up slowly, murmuring among themselves. When they could look, I pointed out the place where I thought the gull had fallen, and a couple of young men went after it. They brought it back a minute later—not shot as cleanly as I'd have liked, but sufficiently dead.

"I want my sailor," I repeated.

While Pete considered my request, the gull was passed from hand to hand. Fingers were stuck into the hole I'd made in it, and eventually somebody extracted the bullet. Like the bird, it was passed around and extensively commented on.

Pete wasn't giving in. His eyes narrowing craftily, he pointed out that we had only two such "clubs," while he and his friends were a thousand targets.

Even if he hadn't just all but announced it, I could tell from the way Pete's body subtly tensed that he was getting ready to run. No doubt he'd shout to his people to run, too, counting on the fact that Tim and I couldn't shoot fast enough to get them all. I had a vision of them scattering into the bushes, taking Davy with them, and after that it would be Ant Island all over again for Frank, Timmy and me. We'd have to make a run for the ship, shooting as we went, to avoid being captured ourselves.

Whether or not the three of us were caught (or would it be four? I didn't feel like we could just leave Rain), every island man, woman and child would probably join in searching for Jack. I knew from Frank that some Small People had found him (lost) on the far side of Making Happy and were guiding him back toward the ship, but after what the captain had said about firing the island, were the Small People still on our side? Or would they, in their fear, turn on all Men the way their ancestors had?

If we were captured and paraded in front of the *Muriel*, the sensible thing for Captain Alcock to do would be to sacrifice us to save the ship, or at least to risk us by ordering the gunners to open fire. Somehow, though, I didn't think he'd do either one—especially not with Helen looking on and probably crying. More likely he'd figure the least of the available evils would be to let Pete and his friends aboard and turn the ship for home.

That would be galling, but it could be borne. At some point we'd get control of the *Muriel* back from Pete; at which time I, personally, would pitch him overboard. What I couldn't stand was the thought that now that the islanders had seen Rain and other Small People helping us instead of them, they'd treat them worse than ever. If Pete was triumphant, even temporarily, there might not be anything we could do about it.

Emboldened by their leader's belligerence, the island forces fanned out.

There was still one terrible thing in the world I had never done. In keeping with Forest Principles, I had never yet turned a weapon against any human creature, but only animals and Ants. Now, with regret but without hesitation, I leaped for Pete, who was backing away, and stuck my long gun—hard—into his belly.

"In another minute, you're going to find out how that seagull felt," I said quietly. "I want my sailor, I said. Bring him."

I learned long ago—I think from Cade—that when you've got the upper hand, there's no need to shout, so if you don't shout, sometimes you can fool an opponent into thinking you've got the upper hand. Pete fell for it. His friends fell for it, too. As Pete took several more stunned steps backward, the other Activity Directors jabbered at me like frightened children. I advanced as Pete retreated, keeping my weapon tight against his gut.

Behind me, Tim cried, "I'm covering you, Mr. Evergreen!" and everybody suddenly remembered he had a "club" too. The crowd compacted again, while Pete's fellow Activity Directors, Frank informed me, were now assuring him they were one hundred percent in favor of releasing Davy.

Ants would have sacrificed Pete for the good of the race and gone on with their plan to take the *Muriel*. Luckily for us, the islanders were Men. After a long, tense moment, Pete said something, and somebody brought Davy up from the rear.

He came rubbing his wrists, which had evidently been bound.

"You all right?" I asked, not taking my eyes—or my gun—off Pete.

"Yeah," he muttered. "Fine. Shoot him, why don't you?"

Ignoring this, I said, "Let's get back to the ship now. I'm sure a couple of these Activity Directors will be happy to come with us."

Timmy and Davy were enthusiastically in favor of this plan, and even Frank slightly smiled. We headed for the shore, Pete and the Activity Leader known as "Stan" reluctantly leading the way, Rain hand-in-hand with Frank, and the two sailors watching sharply at our rear. From time to time I poked Pete with my gun barrel, just to remind him I was there.

As we walked, it occurred to me that though I'd just done something bad on Making Happy (pointing a weapon, with every intention of using it, at a human being), there was still time for me to try to do something good there, too. As we neared the beach, I steered Pete and Stan to a place on the bluffs above it, where we were far enough away from the spilled fuel to be safe.

Then I said, "Let's talk."

Once I'd handed over my long gun to Davy and sent him off a few paces, Pete and Stan nodded warily.

I won't bother to repeat everything I said to them. The main idea was that more ships like the *Muriel* would come, and when they did, they would bring many good things to the people of Making Happy. Having seen what they valued, I specified glass beakers and metal knives, adding, "Tables and chairs too, if you want them. And they'll bring other stuff you don't even know about yet, like metal shovels and hoes and nails."

"Clubs?" asked Stan hopefully, indicating mine.

"No," I said shortly. "But they'll bring cloth. I know you want cloth."

Pete and Stan both indicated they wanted cloth very much—especially, for some reason, blue cloth. With signs, Pete begged me for a pair of blue trousers.

I made a mental note to mention blue cloth to Laura, who was keeping a list for me of things to bring along on subsequent voyages. "The ships will bring you blue cloth," I promised. "But only—" I paused here to let tension build, "—only if you stop abusing the Small People. Understand? No more beating them. No more making them do all the work, either. All the people of Making Happy should work. You should all decide together what work you want to have done, and then you should divide that work equally between all the adults on the island, except very old people, the sick, and pregnant and nursing women. They should do less work than those who are strong." This was, of course, the Forest Way.

Despite their present circumstances, which were unfavorable to them, Pete and Stan argued with me about this. It was the Small People's job to grow the food and cater to the needs of everybody else, they told me.

The cloud of smoke building over the *Muriel* was dense and gray by now. Her boiler was hot, and she was ready to go. I could almost feel the sea running under her keel through the soles of my feet, and I wanted to board her and be gone.

As if idly, I pulled out my forest tinderbox. "That's not the way it's going to be from now on," I said sternly. "From now on, if you treat the Small People right, ships will come and bring you nice things." There was a dead twig lying conveniently near. I struck a spark to the straw in the box and used it to light the stick, mentally sneering at Pete and Stan's wonder in the operation. There was flint on the island. They should have had fire starters of their own. I continued ominously, "If you treat the Small People badly, the way you have been—"

I'd been planning this moment the whole time I was talking. As the last translated word left Rain's mouth, I whirled suddenly and flung the burning stick down onto the beach below, on a spot where I could see a lot of fuel had been spilled.

The resulting blaze was short-lived, but spectacular. Even Timmy and Davy stopped glaring at the Activity Directors long enough to stare.

"Damn!" breathed Davy, adding, as he looked at Tim with awe, "You *work* with that stuff?"

Tim affected unconcern. "It's safe enough, long's you know what you're doing," he said airily. "I don't recommend just anybody messing with it."

"Your choice," I told the stunned Activity Directors. "Blue trousers or burning sand. Ships will come bringing one or the other. Take your pick."

Pete and Stan seemed to indicate they had nothing further to say, and, suddenly sick of their company, I waved them away. The captain had seen the blaze too, and the dinghy, I was happy to see, was already on its way to pick us up.

There was a sudden rustling in the bushes behind us. We all turned, Tim and Davy raising their weapons together.

Our visitors were two young island men—unarmed, as far as I could see. At the sight of our "clubs," they froze.

"What do you want?" I snapped. "Speak up!" Rain softly translated.

One of the young men, looking sheepish, held out the gull I'd shot, while the other offered me the bullet with which I'd killed it.

"They have brought you your property," Frank explained.

I was so relieved I laughed out loud.

"Fine," I said, gesturing to Davy and Timmy to lower their weapons. "I don't need those, though. Why don't you keep them?"

It was the young men's turn to be surprised. A gull was meat, and, lacking weapons (or initiative) to hunt, ordinary citizens on the island didn't get much meat.

When they made no move to go, I accepted the bullet, hoping that would satisfy them.

"Keep the bird. If you don't let Pete and his bunch know about it, you can have a nice meal."

Before Rain could translate this, the young men began to chatter, both at once.

They talked too fast for Rain and Frank to keep up, but the gist of what they were saying seemed to be that their names were Jerry and Trevor, and they wanted to come with me on the *Muriel*.

No surprise there. Everybody on Making Happy wanted to come with me on the *Muriel*.

I *was* surprised, though, when Frank added, "They want to work for you, sir. They want to be sailors, like Davy and Jack."

The dinghy had landed, and Richard, who was aboard it, waved for us to come down.

"Do I look like I need more trouble?" I asked. "No, they can't come."

But even as I was saying this, it occurred to me that the young men looked strong and healthy, and the *Muriel* was short of crew.

"But no harm discussing the matter," I amended, waving back at Richard to tell him to come up, instead.

While Richard was on his way, I held out my calloused hands for Jerry and Trevor to see. The islanders in general weren't used to working hard, so it was only fair, I felt, to let them know what they'd be getting into. "On the ship, you'd have to work very, very hard," I warned.

Jerry and Trevor looked at my hands; looked at each other, and then agreed together that they would work very, very hard.

"You won't see your homes again for a long time, either."

The young men did not look devastated to hear this. They were at the age—I remember it myself—when a lot of things seem more important than home and kin. Their only question, according to Frank's translation, was, "Will we visit the Old Land?"

When I said they would, they were jubilant.

"All right," I agreed. "You can come. On one condition."

The actual condition that had to be met before they—or anybody—came aboard the *Muriel* was that Captain Alcock had to grant them permission to come aboard, and I had no right on earth to speak for the captain.

But we could sort all that out later, I told myself quickly. Right now, I had other concerns.

"I want that tile picture from the Sacred Space," I told Jerry and Trevor.

Both of their faces fell.

Through Rain, they informed me unhappily that I had asked too high a price. The Activity Directors would never consent to give me the picture or anything else from the Sacred Space, however small. A few things had somehow gone missing from the collection there just recently, and the whole island was still being combed in a so-far fruitless attempt to recover them. Such a loss made the items that were left even more precious.

I was glad Helen wasn't around.

They seemed immovable, so I told Richard I was sorry for giving him the trouble of walking up from the dinghy. "I thought I might have some candidates for new crew, but it's not working out. Might be for the best anyway."

Rain, not knowing any better, translated this, and the young men looked at each other in alarm. Then, with signs and a flood of blather, they begged me to wait a short time, pointing to the place in the sky where the sun would be in half an hour, and ran off. Jerry left the dead seagull like an offering at my feet.

Richard and I agreed there was little likelihood the young men would be back. Since we were too many for the dinghy, I said I'd wait ashore while he took the other crewmen, now including Jack, across to the ship. As usual, Frank insisted on staying with me.

When the others were gone, I said to Frank, "Overall, it's been a pretty successful day, hasn't it? We got our men back and no harm done."

There was a longish silence before Frank answered this, dully, "Yes."

"Did I tell you why I want that mosaic picture?" I continued, eyeing him. "It's a map. I'm pretty sure it is, anyway. A map of this local area. In beautiful shape, too."

"Yes."

Frank and Rain were turned slightly away from each other. They were not touching, and both were staring at the ground. Yet, oddly, anybody could have seen they were entirely engrossed in each other.

And entirely miserable, too.

I sighed and looked over at the *Muriel*. Rain was probably competent to spear fish and hoe tubers, but of course she knew nothing about working a ship. If she came aboard the *Muriel*, it could only be as virtually a non-paying passenger, and the *Muriel* was not a passenger ship.

Out of the corner of my eye I saw Rain touch Frank's arm. It was, and remains, one of the most heartrending gestures I have ever seen.

"Well, shit," I muttered to myself in Forester. It was the only Forester oath I knew, so I repeated it four or five times.

Then I switched to the Valley tongue. "Want to come with us, Rain? Frank could probably use help in the galley."

To make a long story a little shorter, I'll just say that—not immediately, but ultimately—Rain said "yes" to this. It was hard for her to leave her people. It was hard for them to let her go. But she wanted to be with Frank, so that was that.

In the meantime, while Rain and Frank were still settling their fates, Trevor and Jerry triumphantly returned after all. With them was Pete, the tile mosaic, and at least three-quarters of the rest of the young male population of Making

Happy, all of whom shouted into my face that they wanted a chance to work very hard on the *Muriel* in return for cloth clothes and the promise of a visit to the Old Land. Backing away from the mob—who seemed peaceful, really, just over-eager—I signaled to the ship.

Pete wanted concessions in return for the picture. Specifically, he wanted my knife. I refused to give it to him, offering my shirt instead, and when he still hesitated, I threw the seagull and the bullet into the bargain.

This was more wealth than Pete could resist. I did not enjoy seeing him put on my nice shirt and strut around like a rooster in it, but I hoped the mosaic would ultimately prove worth the price.

Captain Alcock arrived with the dinghy, and, delighted by the chance to fill out his scanty crew, generously overlooked the fact that I'd usurped his authority in offering positions to Jerry and Trevor. He also forgave both them and all the other candidates for Apprentice Seaman for earlier plotting to steal his ship, and appraised them all like hogs in a market.

"You got a good eye, Evergreen. These ones is fine. And how 'bout we take this one, too?" he added, assessing a third young man. "Damn, they look strong, don't they? Once we get these fellows trained, I reckon the rest of us can just take it easy."

Then he took his prizes back to the *Muriel* and left it to me to convince the rest of the applicants to go away.

"Work hard and treat the Small People kindly," I told them. "Then you can work on the *next* ship."

When Frank and Rain and I got to the ship we discovered the captain had a soft heart toward young lovers—though he denied it.

"I mean for that damn female to work damn hard, dammit, or I'll know the damn reason why," he shouted. Then he hurried to carry Rain's meager baggage below himself, while calling for Collin to come partition a corner near the galley into a cabin for "Mrs. Frank."

As the *Muriel* pulled away from the shore, I stood on the deck next to Frank and Rain and waved to the people of Making Happy. They stood in two groups, the islanders at one end of the beach, and the Small People at the other, but I hoped that would soon change. For the first time on the voyage, I found myself looking forward to going back to a place, just to see if things did change, and how much.

Jerry and his friends came up briefly to shout a last goodbye to their parents and home, but soon went below again, probably to admire each other's trousers. These had previously been the property of the late Bertie and William, but sailors are practical people, and no one objected to the transfer of ownership.

Rain and Frank, on the other hand, stayed on deck for as long as Making Happy was still in sight, and longer. I knew Rain could no longer "hear" her peoples' mental voices when she suddenly turned and buried her face in Frank's chest.

Back in the Navigation Room, I asked Helen if I had time to make one last transmission home.

"Maybe," she said, looking up from where she was digging through her sea chest to find clothes for Rain. "If you make it short. It still takes ten minutes to switch over, and we actually need the time signal tonight!"

"Not too long," I promised. "Oh, and I paid Pete for those things I took."

Helen said she was very glad to hear it.

"Hello, my darlings," my transmission began. "This will be brief, and there won't be time for me to wait for an answer to it. We're underway again. We left the island in a hurry for reasons I won't have time to tell you until tomorrow, probably, but don't worry: Everything's fine.

"In the meantime, I want you to know that I think I did a good thing today. I've done a lot of bad things in my life. Sometimes I've thought maybe bad things were all I was capable of. But I believe today I may have helped some people, and it feels pretty good.

"You probably wonder how I can be so happy about doing a good thing for relative strangers when I did so little for all of you, but believe me, I honestly don't know why I spent so many years running away from everyone I loved when it was really myself I was afraid of. If I had my life to do over, I wouldn't do that now.

"My messages home will have to be short until we can get the radio working right, but please remember that I love you all very much. Take care of yourselves and each other."

Then I said a few more things that are nobody's business, and signed off.

When I went out on deck, I found our new crewmembers getting their first lesson in setting a sail. Not that we needed a sail. The *Muriel's* engine was working just fine. But it was always possible the next time we did need sails, it would be an emergency, and we'd want them put up fast and right, which requires—I can vouch for this—lots of practice.

Trevor, I noticed, was having trouble.

"Here," I said, adding my weight on the rope to his. "Pull like this."

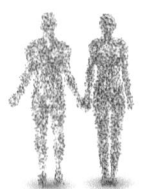

CHAPTER TWENTY-ONE

W hen Helen and I showed him the mosaic, Captain A. took one look at it and—unlike me—instantly identified it as a map.

"Is it accurate enough to use?" I asked. "Or more of a decoration?"

After intense scrutiny, and measuring this way and that by the breadth of his thumb, the captain replied confidently, "Well, it ain't no proper chart, but it ain't no piece of (unspeakable filth), neither. Sure, we can use it. Where we goin'?"

Without knowing it, he'd just settled the matter I'd been debating with myself. We had a map; we'd sail on, and the shippers be damned.

Or—pacified somehow. I'd work on that.

"Well, where should we go?" I countered. "Which of these islands might be habitable?"

"One with lots of fresh water," Helen suggested.

"Enough land folks can grow food on it," Captain A. added, nodding.

Since we were talking about Foresters, I suggested trees.

After some discussion, we concluded that none of us was entirely sure what a habitable island would look like on a map.

The bigger islands were the likeliest to have water, but we couldn't know about the land or trees until we actually saw them, so the course we finally settled on was a slow pass by every island biggish-to-big, with stops along the way at anyplace else that looked promising. It was a great plan that would take weeks to execute, and completely outrage the shippers.

Word got around the *Muriel* that we had a map now, and having a map to follow changed the whole mood of the ship. For the first time, we were able to refer to the distances we covered daily as our "progress," and to lose sight of land without wondering whether we'd ever see any again. This made everyone so happy that even the usual mutterers among the sailors stopped muttering— though whether this was because of the map itself or because the map turned Helen into a ray of pure sunshine was hard to know.

I was happy, too—about the map. Some other things were not so good.

After we left Making Happy, I put off contacting the shippers for a week, figuring the longer I could keep them from knowing that we were not actually on our way back to the continent, as they assumed, the better. I used the *Muriel's* broken radio as my excuse: I didn't call, because I couldn't. But after a few gentle hints—which I ignored—that this might be a bad idea, Dan finally broke it to me straight out that as far as the shippers were concerned, our broken radio was the strongest of several good arguments for our immediate return. I should therefore, he suggested, downplay our radio's brokenness to the maximum extent possible.

As soon as Dan said it, I saw the shipper's point. If I'd paid for the *Muriel*, the idea of her sailing blind would have scared me, too. With this in mind, I "fixed" the problem immediately, and radioed the shippers with all the reassurances I could think of. When reassurances didn't work—at all—I added a lie about how we actually *were* on the way back to the continent, though by a "somewhat circuitous route." Then I ended the transmission quickly while they were still trying to come up with better, sterner words to order me home. I hate to lie, and the episode troubled what was left of my conscience.

The next time Sarah radioed, I asked, "They're not putting pressure on you, are they? You don't have any control over where the *Muriel* goes."

While not exactly denying that there was pressure, Sarah minimized it. "I can handle them," she told me. "Just do what you need to do, River. Stay out or come home. Whichever you think is best."

The trouble was, I didn't know what I thought was best.

Part of me wanted to go back to the continent. Laura's regular sign-off when we talked on the radio now was "Miss you, Papa!" and I wanted to see whether she really did. My relationship—lack of relationship—with my daughter had been the inaugural failure of my post-war life, my first chance at redemption that I'd run away from instead of taking. I wanted to fix things between me and her. I wanted to fix things with her brother and with—other people, too. I wanted that a lot.

On the other hand, I didn't see how I could go back until I'd kept some promises I'd made. I'd told Sarah I'd find out about John and Muriel, and Deer that I'd bring Anna and Heron home. They were counting on me, and I was pretty sure they'd forgive me a lot of my previous mistakes if I came through. *I* was counting on me to keep my promises, too. I didn't know which choice to make, go or stay.

So I didn't make one.

In my experience, if I don't make a choice, the choice often makes itself. Any day now, Helen might demand to go home, or the *Muriel's* engine might fail, or the sailors could even mutiny. Decision made: We'd go home. Alternatively, we might find another letter from John on one of the islands we passed, or the shippers might relent, or some third thing I couldn't even imagine right now might happen to make it unquestionably right to sail on. All I had to do was bide my time and let things work themselves out.

I did need to keep trying to placate the shippers somehow, though. I owed that to Sarah. Since the shippers hadn't bought my lies, I tried distraction.

One of the medium-sized islands we sailed by didn't appear to ever have had a permanent settlement on it, but it did have the remains of a long dock, with a few tumbled-down ancient buildings adjacent. Captain A. reacted to the sight of the ruined dock as he would have to a venomous snake. Once a massive structure, over the centuries the dock had ruptured in a dozen places and now lay in pieces just the right size to rip out the bottom of an unwary captain's ship.

"Same stuff boogers up near every harbor on the continent," the captain complained to me. "Makes it so you can't hardly use 'em."

I knew this. It was the reason the Valley-flagged *Muriel* had to berth—at great expense—in the Coastlands, which had the only harbor clear enough for a dock to fit her.

With this in mind, next day I radioed the shippers voluntarily (they were very surprised) to suggest they might want to make their next investment a really big crane. Once their rivals had big ships too, I pointed out, clearing and controlling ship-berths might become a profitable business. They liked the suggestion (they like money), so I recommended a foundry I thought could build the crane, gave them a few ideas of my own about how it might work, and then got off the radio quick before they had time to return to their preferred topic of my immediate return.

I was indecently proud of my trick. "That'll hold them," I bragged to Helen.

Which it did—for three days. On the fourth day my niece had a regular check-in with a shipper we had both previously characterized as "the nice one," and during the call he un-nicely and unsubtly suggested that, as her father's heir, Helen might want to consider her future.

We knew what he was implying.

Like her Aunt Sarah, Helen brushed the incident off, but I felt terrible about it.

"You all right?" Captain Alcock asked me that evening at dinner. "You ain't been yourself lately."

"I'm fine," I said.

Week by week, one by one, we were ticking off the islands on the mosaic. They were all deserted. Most were so windswept and unwelcoming they had probably never even been visited, much less settled, by humans. Wherever our friends had gone, it wasn't here. We stopped for water at one island, and Frank took his bow and went hunting, but besides seabirds—and not many of those—there was no game but lizards; yellow-eyed, fearless, and unfriendly. A big one bit Jack, and even the most meat-hungry sailors declined to eat them.

The mosaic itself was turning out to be less than entirely satisfactory as a map. It was loosely accurate. The islands on it all existed, at least. The distances between the islands, though, had been compressed—probably to make them all fit neatly in the picture. More annoyingly, there were dozens of small islands in the area that weren't on the map at all. They were probably unimportant to the Ancients, who I knew from my reading had ways of seeing in the dark, but for the *Muriel*, tiny uncharted islands were navigational hazards. On dark nights we could only crawl along at low speed, lookouts straining, to ensure we didn't end our voyage fatally aground on something not much bigger than D&R's warehouse. It was taking us days longer than we had anticipated to travel between islands, and every island we reached was just another disappointment.

Helen remained determinedly cheerful, though I noticed she didn't go singing around the ship anymore. She told me one day she had letters for her grandparents. "Every year, Papa wrote a letter to Grandmother on her birthday," she confided. "I can't wait to see her read them!"

I stopped myself from reminding her that having a bundle of letters for somebody does not in any way increase the chance you will soon be in a position to deliver them. What would have been the point? Helen already knew it.

"You all right?" Helen asked me then. "You don't seem like yourself."

I said I was fine.

On what should have been the plus side, the shippers were no longer speaking to me. I say, "should have been," because it turned out to feel different to be the one who chooses to cut off communication and goes off to put up a radio tower or something versus the one whose radio calls are not returned. I got hints that they were still talking to Sarah and Dan, however—and apparently in strong terms. Neither Dan nor Sarah complained to me about it, but that only made me feel worse. Pressure was mounting on all sides, and I had no escape. No obvious go-or-stay choice had made itself yet; I had no big, preferably physical, job to distract me; and the farthest I could travel away from my troubles was to the top of the *Muriel's* tallest mast. That wasn't far enough. Every time I climbed a mast seeking silence and mental oblivion, I was joined within five minutes by a bored sailor wanting to chat.

Eventually, only the island the captain habitually referred to as "the big bastard" was left for us to visit.

Strangely, at this point my much-commented-upon low spirits finally rose a little bit. Reaching the final island would mean we were out of other options, and single options are my favorite kind. Helen, for her part, seemed to have no doubt that when we reached Big Bastard, her grandparents would be waiting on the shore. "After all we've been through," she asserted, "we deserve it. It's only fair."

"Fair is fair," I agreed.

A Forester axiom says that nothing in life is fair, or pretends to be. Big Bastard was deserted.

Even from far out we could see it was the kind of island no one with any sense would choose to settle. There were a few ancient ruins there—the remains of a short line of buildings ranged along a beach on its lee side. But whoever built the buildings not only would have needed to import the building materials, they'd also have had to be continually supplied from other sources afterward. Like many of the smaller islands we'd passed, Big Bastard was low and flat and scoured by sea winds; its few trees stunted and bent. Beyond water and a fringe of vegetation around the perimeter, it had no resources of its own.

Her sunshine extinguished, Helen asked to go ashore.

"I'll take a look," I offered. "You stay here."

But when the landing party formed up, Helen joined it, and this time nobody denied her.

As soon as we got ashore, the sailors renamed the place "Dead Island." They had good reason to.

There were no signs of any game at all on this island, not even seabirds, and the lizards that darted away at our approach were tiny. There was nothing in the way of native fruits or tubers, either. But the detritus of human occupation—all ancient, to my relief—lay everywhere. The sailors, who had begun fanning out to explore, unconsciously drew together again.

"Creepy, ain't it?" Timmy murmured, staring with Helen and me at the naked remains of a steel-framed building, its girders rusted to lace. "It's like a house for ghosts. It's like the building's still there, only all the walls and windows and furniture and stuff's invisible."

"Looks like you could push it over with a finger," added Georgie.

He didn't try it, though. In fact, nobody wanted to touch anything. I'd seen plenty of abandoned ancient sites on the continent—even spent nights in them if they offered shelter. But if ever there was a place on earth that was haunted, it was Dead Island, and I wasn't the only one of the landing party who kept looking uneasily over his shoulder.

The large structures we'd spotted from the ship hadn't fallen apart naturally. They'd been stripped, and pieces of them fashioned into low structures along the shore that Helen identified as fish traps, and, further inland, water tanks, and crude irrigation works. Whoever had made the bad decision to settle Dead Island in the first place had apparently made the even worse decision afterwards to try to farm it. Given island weather conditions, gardens might not have thrived, exactly, but crops would frequently have failed outright.

Besides the fish traps and so forth, salvaged elements of the large structures had also been assembled into small shelters. Judging by their varying conditions, these had fallen into disuse gradually. The population, too small to sustain itself, had dwindled away.

"How long do you think people lived here?" Helen asked listlessly.

"I don't know. A few hundred years, maybe."

"Were they marooned here by the Ant-Cataclysm?"

"I guess. Yes."

Taking her arm, I steered her away from one of the shelters I'd looked into earlier—one in good condition; still upright; with a shred of its woven-kelp door-cover still in place. Inside, the bones of its last occupant showed beneath a light covering of blown sand. With no animals to scatter them, they still lay in a sleeping posture. I didn't think Helen needed to see that. I wished I hadn't seen it myself. What had it been like for these people, I found myself wondering, to find themselves separated without warning from everything they knew—forever? What had they left undone behind them, and what words unsaid? Did they ever know, as the people of Making Happy apparently did not, why the ships that brought them here hadn't come back?

Suddenly, I was tired beyond endurance of dirt, salt-water, boredom, cramped quarters, and my shipmates' company.

"It's time to go home," I said.

Helen turned to glare at me, and when I didn't look away or relent, asked coldly, "Are you saying you want to just leave my grandparents to die alone somewhere?"

I lacked the will to explain myself or argue. Sitting down where I was, I drew up my knees and rested my elbows on them. It was late afternoon, and the sun and clouds were beginning to arrange themselves into a beautiful sunset. I'd seen too many beautiful sunsets on the voyage. I didn't care for them anymore. "We'll come back," I said dully.

"Come back?" my niece repeated, dropping down beside me. "What do you mean, come back? This isn't the right island, maybe, but we're certainly closer to the right island here than we would be at home! Let's keep going until we finish the job we came out here to do!"

I closed my eyes. "We'll come back," I said again. "We'll… go find a new map first, maybe."

Helen's subsequent arguments—pleas—prayers—commands—went on for some time, a distant buzzing in my ears. The only clear thought I had was that, if we started for home now, I might at least be able to pull D&R from the wreckage of the previous fifteen months. I owned a third of the company, and I didn't care about my third. But Dan and Sarah owned the other two-thirds, and the shippers could destroy us if they really, really wanted to.

I've failed so many times in my life you'd think I'd be used to it by now.

The next time I listened, Helen was saying angrily, "A ship can only go one direction at a time. If you decide we go home, *mister big all-powerful Supercargo*, then we all have to go home. Are you really selfish enough to want that? Are you?"

"Not selfish," I said wearily. "It's time."

"It's time to find my grandparents, you mean!"

My niece was silent for a minute, like she expected something from me.

When she didn't get it, she said, teeth gritted, "Fine. We'll go home then. And you can go sleep in a bed, or whatever it is you want. I can't say I won't ever speak to you again because I'll have to. But I won't forgive you for this, Uncle. I won't *ever* forgive you!"

Then she got up, hissed "Booger!" at me, and stormed off.

I knew I should follow her and apologize. Instead, I went back to the ship and my bunk. I felt old and tired, and like the only thing I wanted in the world was to be home—wherever home was. I lay down and put my arm over my eyes so I couldn't see the picture of Anna with her baby in her arms.

I couldn't sleep. I was boiling inside. Aside from the "booger" part, which was purely comic, Helen's attack had been bruising. Before long I'd convinced myself it was totally unfair, too. I wasn't selfish, I told myself. I just lived life by my own law. Everybody knew that about me. I wasn't the kind—I knew plenty who were—to stay in a forest, grumbling about Forest Law while nominally submitting to it, or to take orders from so-called generals I didn't respect. I wasn't the kind to stay home tormenting my family during times I wasn't fit to live with, either. My niece should have been grateful for that, at least.

And anyway, it wasn't my—or anyone's—"decision" to go home. It was a legal imperative. Our contract with the shippers was for two years and two voyages, and we had passed the one-year mark. By my reckoning, I wasn't actually breaking the contract—yet—by extending voyage number one, but the shippers were clearly of a different opinion on the matter. They wanted us home first, and then in the South Ocean, and they could punish D&R if I refused to go along with the plan. Maybe Helen wanted to deal with the shippers herself, since she was so smart.

I got that far, and then reality obtruded. Helen wasn't wrong; I was. The only thing I'd done right in my life so far was to build a successful business, and now I was in danger of losing it. I let time and circumstances make decisions for me, and this time the outcome was bad. The only way to save the business on which my family and a lot of other people depended was by going home, but if I went home without John and Muriel and Anna and Heron, those same people who depended on D&R—including myself—would never forgive me.

There was no possible happy ending to this story. The world would be a better place without me in it.

At this point I sat up so abruptly that I hit my head. My mind was running in circles, which it does sometimes. But the "better place without me" circle was one I'd promised Deer I'd stay strictly away from.

I needed advice, or at least comfort, fast.

Deer would have been my first choice for advice, followed by Sarah for comfort, but they were both a radio-call away, and the radio was in Helen's cabin, where Helen herself was probably lying in her bunk raging and pounding her pillow and not ever forgiving me.

I rubbed the bump rising on the side of my head.

The captain had given me good advice a couple times, too; but after thinking things over carefully I decided my present situation was much too humiliating for me to reveal to the captain. He'd probably say—perfectly correctly—that I was in trouble because I'd tried to avoid a storm instead of steering boldly through it. The only concession Captain A ever made to bad weather was to raise his voice enough to ensure that his curses could be heard over it.

On the chance Helen had left her cabin by now, I tiptoed down the passageway and listened at her door. She was still in there, though; and flinging things at the wall, judging by what I could hear. I stood listening long enough to catch my name coupled a few times with words my niece was going to have to get out of the habit of saying before she went home, and then, sighing again, I decided to go see Captain Alcock after all. He'd already seen me drunk, and he'd seen me sick, and he'd seen me get slapped repeatedly in the face by the flapping sail I was attempting to secure in a squall. In regard to the captain, I really had no dignity left to lose.

I knocked on his door, and he bawled out his usual obscene welcome.

"Take a chair, take a chair, Evergreen," he said more affably, when he saw it was me. "This a friendly call, or something you got on your mind?"

My sense of shame made me—touchy. "Can't anybody on this ship call me by my actual name?" I complained. "It's River. Just River. 'Evergreen' is… Well, it's not my name."

"Ain't it?" asked the captain, not taking offense. "Damn me, thought it was. Mine's Jasper, by the way. I'd'a said so earlier, only I know you Foresters is real proper about things like names. It's Jasper, and my friends call me Jake. I'd be honored did you do the same. What's on your mind, River?"

His friendly tone disarmed me. I confessed everything, including what my niece had said.

"The shippers are badgering my people, and if they decide to, they can do a lot worse than just badger. What am I supposed to do? Helen says she won't forgive me if we go home without her grandparents."

"She don't mean that," Jake soothed. "She'll forgive you. I used to talk that same way to my old dad. Even marked my words with a fist to his jaw once or twice. It didn't mean nothing. I was just young, is all."

I wanted to hear more of this interesting story, but Jake continued, "Don't you have nothing you can give them fellows will make 'em shut up? Damn me, I don't want to go back now, neither, just when we finally got a idea where we're goin'."

This remark confused me. "Come again? We've got a decorative map, of questionable precision, and we're about to sail off the end of it. We have no idea where we're going, Jake."

The captain scratched his chin thoughtfully. "Ain't we?" he asked. "Look here." Reaching into a drawer, he produced his personal set of nautical charts, which—naturally—he'd been keeping since the beginning of the voyage. He unrolled them in front of me.

They were beautiful.

All the information common to a chart—distances, water-depths, anchorages, and so forth—was included, and in addition the captain had added a border of colorful sea-creatures and decorated the various islands where we'd landed with tiny representations of the kinds of vegetation they offered. The image of Ant Island, along with a terse, obscene warning concerning the danger there, contained a well-drawn image of a purple potato-plant.

"These make Helen's and mine look like scribbles," I told Jake admiringly.

Jake, who was now rummaging in his sea chest, agreed with this assessment—though modestly.

"His charts is the measure of a captain. It's the facts they got on 'em that's important, but it don't hurt to make 'em pretty, too, and I like doing it. Here: Have some of this horse-piss and I'll show you a few things."

He handed me a small cup, which I sniffed cautiously. "Where'd you get this?"

"Mike," the captain replied, winking. I should have guessed, of course. Mike had charge of the distilling apparatus. "I flavored this batch up with something Frank give me to calm my bowels. Tastes pretty good, don't it?"

Once the burning subsided, it did taste pretty good. "As bowel tonics go," I said honestly, "I've never had better."

"Now then," said Jake, "take a damn look at this." He tapped the chart before me. "See this here line? That's how we sailed so far."

I recognized the shape of our path from Helen's chart and nodded.

"These lines here is the winds," the captain explained, pointing. "And then these lines here that's dotted is the currents we met up with on the way."

Helen and I hadn't noted the currents on our charts. Under power, we were hardly aware of them, unless they caused a noticeable spike in our fuel consumption. "How do you recognize them so well?"

The captain explained his system (incomprehensible to me), then suggested, "Let's talk about this current right here."

A warm glow was beginning to shroud my brain. "All right," I agreed genially. "Let's."

Jake retraced the long, looping path we'd sailed. "This is where we been so far, and this here is the current we was followin' early on when we hit that big storm. Remember?" He became reminiscent. "Big, big storm," he mused. "Ever one of the damn crew scared to death. You strung up them ropes for 'em."

The ropes were regularly deployed in bad weather now. The crew called them "Jack-ropes," in honor of the first sailor saved by their use.

"We was pulled off that there current when the storm hit, but if the *Morning Glory* had better luck, she might have rode it quite a while. She'd make damn good time that way, too, if the winds was right."

Since the days when I was too stupid to know to keep close track of our fuel burn-rate, I hadn't given another thought to the course Helen and I had so naively plotted from John's Island to where we thought the *Morning Glory* might have landed. Now I remembered we'd assumed the ship would have followed a route favored by the prevailing winds and currents.

"Never knew none of the *Glory's* crew," Jake was saying. "Never heard they was fools, though."

"You think the *Morning Glory's* captain would have followed that current?" I pointed.

Jake said he did.

"But—we can't be sure."

The captain leaned back in his chair. "You ain't willing to chance being wrong?"

Part of me was. Part of me was hopeful and excited.

But another part was tired. "Every day takes us farther from the continent."

Jake nodded. "That's a fact. But look here."

The captain leaned forward again, and with his two grubby index fingers, simultaneously extended the line of the *Muriel's* present route and the line representing the current in question. The fingers met at a place not impossibly far from where we were at that moment.

"A week's sailing," Jake coaxed. "Maybe a little more, if the weather don't hold good. Then we just follow the current to—wherever it goes."

I stared at the chart, tempted.

"But for how long?" I asked. "I can't keep the shippers believing we're on our way back forever." Not that they actually believed we were anyway.

"Folks hate to be lied to," Jake informed me—as though I didn't already know it. "Better to make a deal instead."

"What kind of a deal? I don't have anything to offer."

The captain reached for the bottle again. "Let's talk about that. Only how about another little one, first?"

I held out my cup.

CHAPTER TWENTY-TWO

The deal we came up with was for two years, *one* voyage, and to my surprise, the shippers took it. They probably figured it was already happening anyway, so why not? There wouldn't be any extensions, they warned.

"This means we start for home in four months, no arguments," I told Helen sternly. She'd had some time to think by then and seemed penitent, so I risked taking a firm tone with her. "This deadline we can't miss."

When my niece meekly nodded, I gave her a tentative hug. It was returned.

Despite having to navigate around more tiny islands—there seemed to be no end to them—it took us exactly the week the captain had predicted to reach our target current and steer into it. I was at the wheel, and for the first time I felt the change a current made in the way the *Muriel* handled.

Jake grinned. "You can call yourself a Seaman now."

I returned his smile—with interest. "Seaman River". It had a nice sound.

We'd had clear sailing until then, but within hours of changing course, a light fog blew up. I thought it looked pretty, like a shimmering veil hovering above the water—until I saw Jake's sharp look.

"What's wrong? Is this bad?"

"Likely not." He scanned the sky. "We'll keep an eye on it is all. And double the watch."

Double watches meant double work for the sailors. I went to the duty roster and added my name.

As night came on, the fog rose higher, no longer skimming the waves, but topping the masts.

Jake said, "Long as the breeze holds up, it won't get no worse."

The breeze didn't hold up, and it did get worse. By midnight, the fog was a solid wall of clammy gray that briefly swirled as the *Muriel* passed through it, then recoalesced behind her.

As I came off watch, I asked Richard, "When will it lift?"

"When it damn well wants to!" he snapped, looking anxious, and as I walked to my cabin, a voice out of the fog added, eloquently, "Booger."

I woke up with a start a few hours later. The *Muriel's* engine was shutting down. Outside, the fog was as thick as ever, but now it was pink. Somewhere— presumably in the east, as usual—a red sun was rising.

I dressed and went to the bridge.

"Why are we still moving?" I asked. "I want to *find* an island, not run aground on one."

There was a time when Jake wouldn't have borne patiently with such an ignorant remark on my part. Now he took the time to explain kindly, "We can't stop. There ain't no bottom here to drop anchor. The sails we got up is to steer by."

I stared out into a void. "We could pass the island we want and never see it."

Jake shrugged. "I got lots of lookouts posted. Ain't no more I can do."

Pushed by the current, we continued slowly, a dozen nervous sailors posted all around the ship, looking for a glimpse of anything that might alert us land was near. I hung over the stern of the *Muriel*, looking for any trace of vegetation churned up by our wake, and tried to avoid seeing where Helen and Tim were riding the bowsprit. Helen insisted they could see "for miles" from that vantage, but I didn't like to think what might happen to them if we struck a reef.

The fog turned from pink back to gray and then to white as a pale disk faintly visible aft announced midmorning. Frank and Rain brought cups of broth to the crew at their stations.

"Is there an island near?" Frank wanted to know.

"Maybe. But unless this fog lifts, we may not see any."

"When the fog is gone, will we turn around and go back to look again?"

I shook my head. "That would take too much fuel. Going the other way, the current—and the winds, if they ever pick up again—would be against us."

Frank nodded gravely. Then, without even looking in Rain's direction, he said, "Rain says the captain wants more broth. I'll bring it," and went below.

I went back to staring down at our wake, drinking my broth and thinking about Sarah. The shippers had backed off, she'd told me. They were drawing up plans for a crane.

"Thanks for suggesting that," she said. "A little hint we might pass the idea along to their competitors has made them more respectful." Then she added that if four more months weren't enough to find John and Muriel, she wanted us to give up the search. "I don't like the idea of you going back out there in some little wooden boat."

I countered that going in a wooden boat might actually be an advantage in tracking the *Morning Glory*. "The *Morning Glory* was wood."

"The *Morning Glory* sank," Sarah reminded me.

I was thinking about this when Rain suddenly let out a shriek and ran toward the rail, pointing and calling out something I couldn't understand.

"What'd you say to her?" I shouted to the captain, but he shook his head, as bewildered as I was.

I recognized a few of Rain's words from our time on Making Happy.

"There! There!" she was saying, followed by more words I didn't understand. "Go there!"

Frank rushed up on deck, followed by most of the rest of the crew, who had heard Rain scream. Seeing my confusion, Frank called to me, "Rain says our friends are there!" Then, like her, he pointed into the fog, where as far as I could see there was absolutely nothing.

"Friends?" My heart jumped in my chest. "Do you mean—Anna?" I'd have preferred to be a little more discreet, but there was no time to pull Frank aside for a private conversation. "Do you… Are you positive it's… Can you hear her?" I blurted. All we needed, I thought, was to stumble by mistake into another nest of Ants.

"I can't," Frank replied. "But Rain can, and she says we must stop now! She says she is just there! There!" He pointed again, and if his points were anything to go by, the place where Anna was standing was slipping behind us.

"Captain," I shouted up to Jake, on the bridge, "can we bring the ship about?"

Like me, Jake looked into the blank white where Rain was pointing, and asked, doubtfully, "You say there's land there?"

I sensed that if I wavered at all in my answer, we'd sail on. What I was asking him to do would take the concerted efforts of all hands, and, given the strong current, a lot of fuel.

It would also give Frank and Rain away as Ants.

With all eyes on me, I said firmly, "Yes."

After a volley of obscenities, some of them new to me, the captain turned to business.

"Get them lookouts in from the bow!" he bellowed. "Prepare to bring her about! And get that damn boiler hot, Mike! I want power, so's I can maneuver!"

Nothing happens quickly on a large vessel. It was a long time before the engine coughed to life and the *Muriel* began to turn in a wide circle back toward the island Rain had "heard" through the fog. It was plenty of time not just for Captain Alcock, but for the whole crew to begin formulating questions as to where Rain was getting her information.

Near noon, we made our second approach, just as the fog was finally lifting enough to reveal a dark bulk of land exactly where Rain, unsuspicious of any danger to herself, was again pointing excitedly.

"They are there!" she told Helen, who was standing beside her.

Helen's forehead wrinkled. "Who? And how do you know? I mean, how did you know before you could see it?"

"She heard voices from shore," I lied.

Rain, a little offended, turned questioningly to Frank. He shook his head.

I'm not telepathic, but I knew exactly what Frank was thinking right then. He was thinking if Jake and the crew figured out he and Rain were Ants, there'd be trouble. The captain was shouting now for the anchor to be readied, but in another ten minutes the men would have time and leisure to ask how Rain knew without seeing it where an island lay, and that it was inhabited.

"You and Rain go stand next to the dinghy," I ordered Frank quietly. "If I give you the signal, we'll launch it together, and then you two jump in and row like hell for shore."

He didn't need to be told twice. Before Helen had even finished asking me what on earth I thought I was up to, he was leading his wife away.

Apparently, the only part of this exchange Helen had heard clearly was "row for shore." She burst out indignantly, "Well, if they're going ashore, I'm certainly going, too!" and started after Frank.

I caught her arm. "Move slowly. Don't draw attention to yourself." Some of the sailors seemed to be whispering to each other, which I took for a bad sign. "If you're determined to go, then when we get to the dinghy, be ready to jump when Frank does."

"Uncle, you have lost your mind," my niece informed me. "Gods! This could be exactly the island we've been looking for! You're supposed to be happy!"

I knew I was spoiling the moment for her, and I was sorry. The business with Rain had come up at a bad time.

"I'll be happy in a minute," I promised. "Get ready to jump."

The captain was coming toward us now, shouldering his way through the crew.

"What do you think?" he called, gesturing toward the shadowy island. "Is this the place we been looking for? There's people on it, anyway. A bunch of 'em is lining up on the shore like they was expecting us."

"Yes, this is the island, Captain," I said. "And they are expecting us. Keep back, please."

Jake's response to this was to laugh.

"I won't get in your way," he assured me cheerfully. Then he said aside to the crew, "The folks here is Mr. River's kin."

"Oh, forest-folk!" said Timmy brightly.

Stupid with surprise, I responded, "Huh?"

Jake then proceeded to share an anecdote about a party of Foresters he'd encountered in his young days, who, having inadvertently arrived in a Mantown during a festival, instantly produced musical instruments and played to accompany the dancing. "Foresters is real musical," he said. "You musical, River?"

It was a nice story, but not very much to the point. The point was that by now, Jake and the entire crew of the *Muriel* had all the information they needed to understand clearly that Frank and Rain were telepathic, and therefore Ants.

"Uh—I play the flute," I stammered. "I mean, I used to."

The situation was getting away from me. Hardening my tone, I said, "Look here, Captain: I'm sending Frank and Rain ashore. Let them go, and then we'll talk."

"Them first?" Jake asked. "Damn me, I woulda thought…"

Before he could finish, Helen jumped into the dinghy and ordered me to "Get in this minute, you idiot, we're going," and in the resulting confusion, the sailors rushed us. They were on me before I could react—although to be honest, I don't think I could have brought myself to fight them anyway.

"I think those folks on the shore are waiting for you, Mr. River," Richard said, patting my shoulder. "Look at 'em waving! You'd best get along."

I'd missed something.

"Well, but… You must have guessed about Rain and Frank by now, right?" I faltered. "I mean, that they're…"

I couldn't say it. I didn't have to.

"If you mean that Frank's part Ant," Helen spoke up sharply, "of course we've 'guessed.' We're not blind, you know. And Rain must be, too, since she was the one who knew where the island was." She added to Rain, in a sisterly tone, "You read Aunt Anna's thoughts, didn't you, Rain?"

The looks on the sailors' faces suggested that, despite what Helen had just said, the information that Frank and Rain were Ants was new to quite a few of them. Jake's mouth absolutely gaped.

But when Helen added, "Look, Uncle River: If you want to come with me in the boat, get in now. Otherwise you'll have to swim over," everyone just laughed, and the sailors nearest it prepared to launch the dinghy.

Frank and Rain were Ants, and they didn't care.

After a long, witless silence I said awkwardly, "I guess we'll go ashore now."

Jake pulled me aside, and taking the pistol from his own waist, thrust it into mine, under my coat at the back.

"You get into any trouble on that island," he said gravely, an arm around my shoulders, "you just fire this here piece, see? I know they're your kin, so you don't want to aim *at* nobody, but you just shoot in the air. I'll have men standing by here, and they'll have you and Miss Helen out of there before you know it."

The offer of an instrument of violent death can be, under certain circumstances, a token of friendship. I quietly transferred the pistol from my belt to Frank's without letting Jake see.

"Uncle, come on!" Helen cried.

As the dinghy hit the water, I heard the captain saying to Frank, in a perfectly amiable tone, "Whatcha got in the galley, Frank? Booger me if I ain't starved!"

"At least tell me *you* understood what I was saying," I sighed as I rowed. "Frank and Rain are Ants, Helen. Not pure Ants, but Ants. I don't think anybody else got it."

"Frank and Rain are Frank and Rain," Helen answered indifferently. "Anyway, back home everybody's said for years the reason Aunt Anna could read the Ants' minds was because she was part Ant herself, and everybody admires her. Will I be allowed to come ashore, Uncle River? This is a forest, sort of, and I'm not a Forester."

The Foresters, it may be needless for me to say, had never confirmed the rumors about Anna.

"Neither am I," I pointed out. "Don't worry. All forests have a place where Men and Foresters can meet if they need to."

"Oh good. Who are all those people?" Helen begged, straining to see through the lightening fog. "Do you recognize any of them? Tell me who you recognize!"

I turned for a quick look. "Nobody. Just to be clear, Helen, it's not only Frank and Rain and your Aunt Anna who are part Ant. A lot of the people who came here with your grandparents were Ants, too."

"Fine, fine," she said without interest. "Oh, I wish Papa was here!"

CHAPTER TWENTY-THREE

As we got closer, the waiting islanders arranged themselves, as if casually, into a formation I recognized as subtly defensive in nature. There were ten in the welcoming party, some males and some females, and mostly young, but I'd have put money on it that there were at least ten more forest pickets—armed—concealed nearby.

I stopped for a moment to study the group.

"Why do they do that?" I complained, beginning to row again. "That's just the kind of thing that makes Men say they're cold fish."

"What kind of thing?" Helen asked, not turning her eyes from the beach. "Do you recognize anybody yet, Uncle? Anybody at all?"

"No. I'm talking about that impenetrable forest 'dignity' they put on," I said. "It's like being greeted by ten stones. I felt more welcome on Making Happy."

"Where everybody went insane at the sight of us?" Helen sniffed. "Well, if that's your taste... Still," she added regretfully, "I wish these people would at least wave again or something. I'm starting to think they don't want us here."

I'd been a member of a few Forester welcome parties myself. "Take my word for it, inside, they're going insane, too. They're just not supposed to let on about it."

Uneasily, Helen said, "I don't see anyone old enough to be my grandfather."

I reminded her John would be over eighty. "I think as far as he goes, we have to be prepared for the worst."

Before Helen could answer this, we touched bottom.

At a word from someone on the shore, two pickets dashed into the surf to drag the dinghy in. I noted uncomfortably they were both short and blonde.

The leader of the welcoming party stepped forward to greet us.

I knew him immediately from his father's drawing. Still the image of Anna, now Peregrine had his father's height and smile. I managed to respond to his traditional "thousand welcomes" with only a slight crack in my voice, but then my self-possession deserted me. I put my arms around him and pulled him close.

He didn't seem to mind.

"You're Peregrine," I stated, and when he nodded, I turned to Helen and told her in Valleyspeak, "Come and meet your cousin."

Peregrine apparently didn't speak Valley. I heard someone softly translate my words for him. Helen had taken a few lessons from Robin and in response to Peregrine's greeting managed a breathless "thousand thanks!" in a pretty fair forest accent before adding in Valley, "I don't really speak your language," and blushing.

Everyone smiled. Peregrine gestured another of the welcoming party forward and introduced his younger, shyer brother, whose name was Loyal.

"You will meet our two sisters soon," Peregrine said. "They're with our mother, who is waiting for you."

From behind me, Helen whispered urgently, "Ask about my grandparents! Is Grandfather alive?"

Before I could say anything, the same quiet voice from the background translated this, too. Peregrine's face changed. His eyes on Helen, he gravely informed us that John had died ten years before. "Your grandmother lived four years after him, but then she died, too," he said. "I'm very sorry. I'll take you to see their trees."

This information was tactfully left to me to translate, which I did, and then I put an arm around Helen as she leaned against me for a minute, her eyes closed. I closed my eyes briefly, too. I'd told myself a thousand times I wouldn't get my hopes up about John and Muriel, but of course I had. Muriel's kindliness, so unlike my mother's reserve, had meant a lot to me at one time in my life, and I'd never thought to tell her so.

While Helen was recovering, Peregrine told me Posthumous was also dead. "Master Posthumous lived three years after John," he said, adding with visible pride, "My mother was then acclaimed Master of this forest."

While I was processing all of this, Peregrine mentioned a few more names I guess he thought I'd know. A couple were slightly familiar, but I think they were names that had been given to Ants—friends of Anna's—rather than of people I really had any curiosity about. I nodded and tried to appear interested, but what I was really thinking was how much I would regret breaking bad news to Sarah and Dan by means of a clumsy soldier-code message.

I was brought back to the present by a change in Peregrine's voice. He seemed to choke a little as he said, "And my father died last year. He was killed in a fall."

His father. Heron.

I wasn't prepared for it. I couldn't take it in.

I remember repeating, "Heron?" a few times, disbelieving, and hearing Helen, who recognized the name even in Forester, saying first, "Where is he?" and then, though nobody answered her, "Oh!" I was aware that Loyal turned suddenly away, and saw Peregrine put a hand on his brother's shoulder while the other members of the welcome party tactfully withdrew a few paces. I saw and heard it all, but I couldn't make myself speak.

It was only when Peregrine asked—and it might not have been the first time he said it—"Will you come to my mother now?" that I managed to pull myself together.

Nodding, I started toward the woods above the beach. I stumbled, and Peregrine took my arm.

"How's she doing?" My voice was like a rasp. Helen took my other arm and squeezed it.

"My mother is—well," Peregrine responded. The little hesitation told me everything.

The news sank in slowly as we walked. Heron, my friend, was dead. I felt sick.

We didn't talk much as we walked to where Anna—Master Anna—was waiting for us. Along the way, some part of my brain that wasn't connected to the part that ached noticed the island was very well-kept. I didn't see any buildings. They were probably clustered as they would be in any forest, in the place farthest from all borders. But there were extensive tidy gardens and groves where trees were planted in the traditional quincunx arrangement, pruned to grow tall and straight to provide building material. I had an impression people were working in the gardens and among the trees, but I didn't turn my head to look at them.

When the path narrowed, Helen left me on Peregrine's arm and dropped back to walk with Loyal, who was clearly taking his father's death very hard. She couldn't say much to him in Forester beyond, "I'm sorry," but her sympathy was obvious, and I hoped it would help.

After what seemed like miles, I caught sight of Anna sitting between two young women on a wooden bench in a bower like the ones in Evergreen, where in our young days she and Heron and I had spent hours laughing and talking together—and in Heron's case, endlessly sketching.

Hardly aware of what I was doing, I pulled away from Peregrine and ran the last few steps to her. Anna was slow to rise, because instead of a jointed metal brace, her crippled leg was supported by a stiff wooden collar, and she needed two crutches to stand. I reached her before she had gotten all the way up and I lifted her off her feet. Eyes closed, I held her to me for a long moment while she breathed in my ear, "I knew you would come."

When I released her, Anna sat down again, pulling me down next to her. Then, laying her hand against my cheek, she studied me closely.

"Don't wake me if I'm dreaming," I said.

This made her smile, and we began to talk eagerly.

She introduced the two young women as her daughters, Margaret and Pearl.

Unlike their brothers, they spoke Valley. I presented Helen, and told her about my own children, and gave her Elizabeth and Dan and Sarah's loves without mentioning that Sarah and I had parted. I was thankful not to have to break the news of her foster-father Cade's death. She'd heard it years ago from the captain of the *Morning Glory*. I said her foster-mother May was "pretty well"—which was a lie, but kindly meant.

As I caught her up on the news of friends and family in Evergreen, Pearl considerately translating in an undertone for Helen, I noticed her children were hanging on every word I said. The people I was telling their mother about were ones she had mentioned, and missed, for twenty years. A lot of what I said wasn't even important news, and could have waited until later, but maybe we were both reluctant to deal with more difficult topics until we'd gotten to know each other again.

Finally, I told her about the radio, apologizing for the fact that she'd be able to send and receive messages but not actually talk to her mother and Deer.

"You ought to be able to talk." I pounded my leg with my fist. "We—that is, Dan and Helen and I—have made radios that can be used for talking on. But ours got broken on the way here."

After so many years of no communication at all, a message that would be received as she sent it and answered almost as quickly was as good as a miracle to Anna, and her eyes lit up.

"Oh, when?" she begged. "Can we send a message tomorrow? Is that too soon?"

As soon as Pearl translated this, Helen jumped up. "Of course it's not too soon!" she exclaimed. "We can do it tonight! I'll go get the radio right now. You two stay here and talk. It won't take long."

When I pointed out that the radio was heavy, and that if we were going to use it on the island, she'd need to set up an antenna, too, Loyal and Peregrine offered to go along and help. The three of them left together, and at the same time, Anna's daughters went back to the village. There was only one on the island, where everybody lived. Margaret was going to arrange for a suitable room to put the radio equipment in, and Pearl was going to rest. She was weeks away from delivering a child—her first—and everybody agreed it was time she put her feet up.

Anna and I were left alone.

As she watched her children go, I watched her.

I thought she hadn't changed as much as I had over the years. Her hair, like mine, was shot with gray now, and there were a few lines around her eyes. But she still looked a lot like the girl who'd married my best forest-friend, Heron, on my very last night in Evergreen. She was more confident than she'd been in those days—no more blushes or downcast glances. She held her chin up now, like a proud Forester.

She dressed as she always had, too, in the traditional shirt and trousers that all Foresters wore, though the fabric of the shirt wasn't forest linen but some yellowish material I'd never encountered before. It didn't surprise me that after twenty years the clothes the islanders had brought with them were worn out, but apparently they'd learned to make do. There were even hummingbirds embroidered on Anna's shirt, as in the old days. I wondered if they were Heron's work.

The only really striking difference between the old Anna and the new was that the new Anna wore her hair loose around her shoulders. Her hair was curly and inclined to be wild, and in the old days she'd always kept it tightly braided.

When she turned and looked at me, I said, "I like your hair like that. Is that style the custom in your forest?"

Anna looked away again.

"No," she whispered. "Heron liked it."

Hard as it was going to be, we had to talk about him.

Steeling myself, I asked, "What happened? Peregrine told me he fell."

A pause—and then Anna began softly, "There was a storm…"

Her voice caught, but she forced herself to go on.

She said storms weren't uncommon on the island, and this one wasn't by any means the worst they'd weathered. It caused some flooding in the gardens, though, which were naturally an important source of food. "A dozen of us went out in the rain to dig a drainage ditch," she told me. "Heron liked that kind of work, so he went. And I went because I liked to be with Heron."

The job was done, she said, and the tools being packed up when Heron slipped in the mud and fell.

"He didn't fall very hard," Anna told me, beginning to cry a little. "But he hit his head on a stone and was knocked out. He came to right away, and said he was fine. He laughed about falling." Miserably, she added, "We all laughed."

"You don't have to tell me any more if you don't want to."

"I think you should hear everything." Anna wiped her eyes. "Of course, the boys wanted to get a litter from the infirmary to carry him home. They'd have carried him in their arms if he'd let them. But Heron kept saying he was fine; it was just a bump. He seemed fine. We all thought he was. But as we were walking back toward the village, he—he collapsed."

"Collapsed?"

"Yes. He just collapsed. He fell down. He was laughing about the knot on his head, and then he just fell down unconscious. No one knew anything to do for him, and in a few hours, he was gone. That's all that happened." Anna sobbed, crying in earnest, now. "Heron fell down unconscious and never woke up. It was so sudden that for days I couldn't believe he was gone. Sometimes I still can't believe it."

I couldn't believe it either.

Anna added, "He was our infirmarian. He'd never trained to be one, but we needed somebody, and he'd learned a lot from watching his mother. He took care of all of us, but when he was hurt, there was no one to take care of *him*."

Something occurred to me. "A storm," I repeated numbly. "When was that?"

I suspected I already knew the answer to my question.

"Fourteen months ago. Fourteen months and two days."

Fourteen months and two days before, the *Muriel* had been fighting her way through the same storm, trying to reach the island where Anna and I sat now. The winds had blown us off course and we'd taken more than a year to make our way back.

I groaned. "Gods, why did we stay on John's Island so long? If we'd left there earlier, we might have gotten here before the storm hit!"

But Anna said, "River, no. Don't torment yourself. Even if you'd been here, Heron would have fallen just the same."

I was about to argue the point, when a second's reflection told me anything I said might make Anna feel worse, and nothing I said could bring Heron back.

Anna and I sat silently for a long time.

"What took you so long to find us?" she asked suddenly.

I guessed she'd been wondering that for at least nineteen of the past twenty years.

I said flatly, "Well, we didn't forget you, if that's what you're imagining. Not for one single minute of a single day that's passed. The voyage that brought you here was the *Morning Glory*'s last, Master. On her way back to the continent, she was lost with her captain and all her crew. No one knew where John's Island was, or that you'd left it and come here."

I went on from there to tell the whole story, and by the end of it, Anna was in my arms with her head on my shoulder. There was a time in my young days when I'd have given everything I owned plus ten years off my life to have held her like that; now our embrace was just that of two old friends, united in grief.

"Heron always knew you'd be the one to come for us," Anna murmured. "He said it a thousand times. 'River will find us. River will never give up.'"

"It was Deer, really," I said. "He was the one who told me where to look."

"You needed Uncle Deer's help," Anna acknowledged, "but you're the one who came. It's all just as Heron knew it would be."

All just as Heron knew it would be—only twenty years late.

Anna started to say something else, then straightened up and looked in the direction her daughters had gone. "Helen says she needs your help," she advised me.

I must have looked shocked, because Anna laughed.

"Don't worry." She reached for her crutches. "I can't hear Helen. She told Margaret she wished you were there to answer a question, and I heard Margaret."

I laughed too—from sheer relief. "I guess you don't have many secrets on this island," I said, getting up and helping Anna to her feet. I took one of her crutches, and in its place offered her my arm for support.

"No secrets at all." She looped a hand around my arm. "In fact, 'no secrets' is a rule here. It should always be a rule where Men and Hybrids live together."

"Hybrids?"

"Part Man and part Ant, like me." She added, "We don't have any full Ants here. All my Ant-friends turned out to be Hybrids in some degree or other. That's why they came to get me at my village, and stayed near me all those years. Full Ants wouldn't have done that. When we were leaving the continent and more Ants came to us for help, Papa said he thought full Ants might be dangerous, so we didn't bring any full Ants on the ship."

I smiled grimly to myself. John *thought* they might be dangerous. John had a crippled foot and a million bad memories, courtesy of the Ants.

Anna continued, "But what we found when we were still on the first island was that even though we shared the same space, and did the same work, and ate the same food, Men and Hybrids still lived as though they were two separate groups. The telepaths couldn't help being together mentally, of course, and when Muriel taught them words—she was such a good teacher, River! I'll tell you about it later—they only used them for practical things, like asking Men for things they needed. When the Men wanted conversation, they could only get it with other Men. That left me in the middle, going back and forth all the time trying to explain each group to the other."

"Doesn't sound too pleasant for you," I commented.

"It was tiring," Anna agreed. "Anyway, we finally we got the idea of making it a rule that any thoughts anybody shared, whether mentally or aloud, they had to share with all. It was hard at first. In fact, some of the older Hybrids still rely on the younger ones to do most of their talking for them. But once the rule was made and the two groups began to open their minds to each other, it drew us together, just as we'd hoped."

Forgetting Anna's background, I said tactlessly, "Well, if a certain member of our crew is anything to go by, Hybrids are very good about obeying rules."

"Frank," stated Anna, nodding. "I'm sure I never consciously broke a rule. It's the Ant in us. That's how we were made."

I flushed.

"We'll soon have another citizen who isn't telepathic," Anna added. "My grandchild, Pearl's child, won't be. Quite a few of our young people aren't, in fact—including my sons."

Which explained why they didn't know Valleyspeak, while their sisters did.

"I guess I was imagining with Heron…gone…there were nothing but telepaths here now."

Anna shook her head. "When Men and Ants mate, their offspring become more like Men with each generation. Unless they're at least half-Ant, the males aren't telepathic, even though their parents may have daughters who are. So far, only one of our young female Hybrids isn't telepathic, but many of the males are not. My daughter's child is probably male."

Then she pointed, and when I looked, I could see the village in the distance.

If I squinted, I could almost imagine it was Evergreen, and that the citizens who were beginning to come forward to welcome us were the friends of my youth.

Quickly, while the illusion lasted, I said, "I'm not sure I can promise to always remember the rule about secrets, Master. If I was good at remembering rules, I might still live in a forest. But while I'm here, I'll try to be good."

"Just be River." Anna smiled. "Anything else would disappoint us all."

*

At first, as I worked with Helen to finish setting up the radio, Master Anna was happily imagining sending and receiving messages to her mother May, who was a grandmother four times over and didn't even know it. But by the time the work was done, Anna had changed her mind. After some discussion between her and her children, she had decided her first message had to be to Snow, instead. Her reasoning—all carefully articulated in words, as per the rule, for the benefit of the non-telepaths—was that the fact that she was sending a message at all would tell her mother she was alive, but Snow had to know immediately that her son was dead.

This meant Anna's first transmission to Evergreen wasn't the happy reunion I'd promised Deer more than a year before. Soldier-code turned out to be just as terrible a way to communicate bad news as I'd feared it would be, and on the Evergreen end, it meant there was a long delay after my initial communication ("Anna is found") while Deer summoned an Evergreen telegraph operator who knew soldier-code. Deer had been working hard to learn soldier-code himself ever since the *Muriel's* radio had been crippled, but thought (rightly) that for this exchange, we needed someone faster at the key. While we waited, and as unobtrusively as I could, I sent the message—at a beginner's speed, so Deer would be sure to understand it—"bad news for Snow," so when Snow came, he'd be ready to help her.

With Snow came Rumor, Anna's foster brother, who was a forest infirmarian now, and was going to help Snow judge when and how May should be told about her daughter. I pictured them gathered excitedly around the Evergreen telegraph key as Anna began to dictate the news about Heron and felt terrible.

Of course, like good Foresters they all took it bravely, offering comfort to Anna and her children in their return message instead of speaking of their own grief. But Heron was Snow's only child, Deer's closest blood relative, and Rumor's cousin and brother-in-law. Whatever courageous, kind things they said, I knew they were devastated.

They wanted to know everything, of course, so even though a primitive form of telegraph is a poor medium for long stories, I stayed at my key, sending and receiving, until my hand cramped. There was no one to help me, since Helen only knew a few words of Forester, and neither Snow nor Rumor could understand Valley.

Luckily, not all the news was bad. Once Snow got past the worst of her first grief over Heron, she started to take an interest in the fact that she had four grandchildren. Not only that, but she was about to become a great-grandmother, too. It was almost more than she could take in. Pearl was only seventeen and not married long, but she'd evidently taken after her mother

Anna—and her unknown Ant grandfather—in fertility. One quality the Ants had never lacked was fertility. When they wanted to, they could breed faster than we could kill them. Naturally, I didn't mention this.

By the time I'd finished relaying messages from each of Anna's children, it was well after midnight. After a last, private message from Deer promising he'd see to it Snow was not left alone, we signed off for the night. By then, Helen was already asleep on a pallet in the corner, and I woke up on one myself a few hours later with only a faint memory of being led to it after dozing off in my chair. I lay where I was, listening with my eyes closed to the old, loved sounds of a forest gently waking, until Helen blurted out one of Captain Alcock's milder oaths.

"What is that?" she gasped.

We'd been joined in the night by a small furry creature of some sort—a hazard of forest living. I'd never seen an animal like this one before, but it looked reasonably inoffensive.

"Dunno," I said, yawning. "Ready to get up? If we don't report to the ship soon, the captain might start opening the gun ports."

Helen preferred to stay. She'd heard the village had baths.

Back at the ship, I was relieved to find Jake had already heard the news from the island—from Frank, I guess. He met me as I came aboard, saying quietly, "I'm real sorry about your kin-folk, River. Your friend, too. Losin' friends is real hard."

I didn't want to talk about it. "I'm only back for a few minutes. I've got more radio messages to send. Can somebody give this to Mike for me?"

Jake took the skin-wrapped bundle I was carrying. "What's in it?"

It was the leg brace Anna had been wearing when she left the continent, the last in a series of braces designed and made for her over the years in Evergreen. In a transparent attempt to demonstrate to me that engineering had its place in a forest, too, Deer and Roar had asked for my help with it. I'd left the forest anyway, of course—but I was proud of the brace.

I explained some of this to the captain. "It's broken," I told him. "I don't know whether it can be repaired or not. See what Mike thinks."

Jake said he would, and then, as I started away, called after me, "Think there's any chance we could get shore leave here, River?"

I'd forgotten to ask.

"Talk to Frank," I called back. "He'll know."

CHAPTER TWENTY-FOUR

I spent the rest of the morning on the radio again, breaking bad news to my family, who I knew had gathered around the radio set hoping for something better. There'd been the compensation of grandchildren to help Snow the day before, but now I had to tell grandchildren they'd never know their grandparents. This time, since everyone spoke Valley, Helen took over the telegraph key from time to time, and we got through the ordeal together.

Sarah stayed on after the others to thank me for persevering in finding out about John and Muriel. "I know it wasn't easy. You've never been one to take the easy way. I admire you for that."

"I owed it to you," I said. "I owe you more than I can ever repay."

"I think there's debt on both sides," Sarah answered.

As soon as I came out of the hut that was now the Island Forest's "radio room," Master Anna met me. She looked worried.

"Would it be possible for you to bring Rain ashore?" she asked me. "Will the Shipmaster permit it?"

For a minute, I just stared. I had no idea who she was talking about.

"You mean Captain Alcock?" I asked finally. "I don't think he has any say in what Rain does."

Anna blushed. "Captain," she repeated. "That's right. I remember that word now. It's been a long time."

When I realized she'd just equated the captain of a ship with the master of a forest, I laughed so hard my eyes watered. "Jake can only dream about having the authority you do," I gasped. "Sure, Rain can come, if you want her to. What's up? You look like there might be a problem."

There was a problem, though Master Anna seemed reluctant to call it that.

"The Ants of Making Happy never knew about the Ant-Cataclysm," she told me. "They left the continent before it occurred. Rain has just learned the story, and she's upset. I think it would help her to visit with us."

Anna said on Making Happy, the only name Rain knew for humans meant "creators," which was the name the Ants had given to men originally. She picked up the word "Men" for them from Frank, but it came with no negative connotations. Frank had nothing against Men.

But from the minds of the Hybrids of the Island Forest, some of whom had escaped slaughter in the Battle in the Valley, she'd gotten another picture of Men. I could easily imagine it wasn't a very nice one.

"We've reassured her," Master Anna said. "But I thought seeing the two races living here, side by side, would be the best reassurance. Do you want to talk with her?"

I almost blurted out that I was the very last person on earth anybody should expect to reassure an Ant before I remembered every telepath on the island—or in other words, most of the population—was hearing every word I said. So instead I said sure, I'd love to, only I had to check the radio or something right now, and stumbled away.

The fact was that anybody who wanted Rain to believe Ants and Men could live peacefully together needed to keep her away from me. I'd spent two years of my life—and most of my dreams since—hunting Ants like rabbits and killing them like dogs.

And now I was on a small island full of them. I looked around myself and muttered, "Gods, what am I doing here?"

I wanted to talk to Deer, but when I got to the radio hut, Helen, Peregrine, and Pearl were already there, "talking" to May and Rumor. Peregrine was dictating a message in Forester that Pearl was translating into Valleyspeak so Helen could send it, and at the Evergreen end the telegrapher could translate the message back into Forester for May. This involved a lot of laughter, for some reason.

"Something wrong?" Helen asked when she saw me.

I said "no," and went out again.

I walked around the island for a while, but it didn't make me feel any better. Every time an island citizen hailed me with a respectful, "Greetings, friend!" I wondered how many of his family I'd killed. Eventually I came to the beach where Frank and Rain had left the dinghy, and it occurred to me with them ashore, the *Muriel* was one place I could go where I wouldn't be surrounded by Ants. I gave the dinghy a shove toward the water and jumped in.

I had hardly lain down in my bunk, wondering how a few months ago could feel like the distant past while twenty years ago was always yesterday, when somebody knocked at my door.

I stopped myself from saying, "Go away and don't come back," but managed not to make my invitation to come in sound welcoming.

It was the captain. I scrambled to my feet.

"Shit," I said in Forester, happy to know he wouldn't understand me. "What can I do for you, Jake?"

"Got a little something," he said, holding up a bottle.

It looked legitimate—not raw spirits and bowel-tonic this time. I gestured the captain to the chair and sat back down myself on the edge of my bed.

As he produced cups from the depths of a pocket, Jake explained, "Been saving this to open the day we turned our bow towards home, but when I saw you come aboard I thought I wouldn't wait. You looked to me like a man needs a drink *now*."

"Why would I need a drink?" The cup he handed me was brim-full.

"Because you was a Hunter," said Jake flatly. "And these folks here is Ants. I'm guessing you ain't too comfortable right now."

I stared into my drink for a minute, not speaking.

"They're Hybrids," I said finally. "A mix of Man and Ant. Trust me. They're harmless."

"I know they're harmless. I seen that."

A long silence followed this. I had nothing to say.

Finally, Jake inquired, "Who mixed 'em?"

I looked up. "What?"

"I said, who *made* the mix of Man and Ant?" Jake leaned back. "You don't need to answer me. I already know what the answer is. It's the same one as if I asked, 'who slaughtered all them children?'"

I emptied my cup at a gulp.

"What do you know about the children?" I demanded harshly.

"I don't know nothing about no particular ones." Jake tipped the bottle into his cup again. "I know Ants killed children, and I know they savaged women. And I know you and the rest of the Hunters saw it all. Here: Have another."

This drink was smaller, and I sipped it.

"You have no idea what I did in those days," I muttered.

"I know you done what you had to do. It's a soldier's job to kill the enemy. That don't have nothing to do with these folks."

I leaned back wearily. "You ever fight Ants, Jake?"

"Me? No. I got friends who did, though. I fought plenty in my time, but only Men, and never in no war. War's a harder business than what I done. In war, soldiers got to fight Men they got nothing personal against, and then afterwards, they got to be friends with 'em again. Or when it was the Ants Men was warring with, soldiers didn't even get no choice whether to kill the enemy or maybe just hurt him bad enough to teach a lesson. They had to kill. And if their blood wasn't up for killing, they had to kill anyway."

"I wonder sometimes if we were wrong about that. Look at Frank and the people on this island. Maybe we did have a choice not to kill."

Captain Alcock snorted. "Don't look to *these* folks to know if we done the right thing killing Ants," he said firmly. "Look to them boogers on Ant Island! Frank was right there with you, wasn't he? And you know he was talking in their minds the same way they talk to each other, saying, 'Don't kill these people. You don't need to kill these people; they won't hurt you.' But they didn't listen because they was Ants. All Ant. Not no—whatevers."

"Hybrids. Ants decide by consensus. Frank's mind was outnumbered."

I'm not sure Jake knew the word "consensus," but his reply was to the point. "Ants ain't reasonable. The folks on this island has got the light of reason in 'em. Makes all the difference."

He gestured toward the bottle again, but I shook my head.

"Trouble was," he continued, "you was too young for a job like war. It should be older Men go as soldiers. Ones who's seen a thing or two. It's bad how by the time Men get to know enough to handle war, they're too old and broke down to fight."

Before I could answer this, Jake rose to go. "You'll feel better after you get some sleep," he advised.

Idly, I wondered why the captain would imagine I could sleep in the middle of the afternoon. That was the last conscious thought I had for several hours, and when I woke up, I did feel better.

The next day, with the forest master's permission, shore leave was granted for the crew, though only for three sailors at a time and only during daylight hours. This was on Captain Alcock's advice. Before anyone was allowed off the ship, I assembled the crew and explained telepathy to them. Jerry and his friends' Valleyspeak—the ship's principle language—was still a little weak, but I knew they'd caught on to what I was saying when they turned together to stare with their mouths open at Frank and Rain.

I concluded, "So, what I'm saying is that you'd better behave yourselves on the island, because anything you do or say to one of the islanders, all the rest of them will know. Any questions?"

Jerry and his friends were the only ones to ask any, all of them variations on "The Small People? Are you kidding?" but by the time the crew dispersed, I was reasonably certain none of the sailors would give the Island Forest pickets any trouble.

Officers were welcome on the island anytime, of course, which Helen interpreted as an invitation to move ashore. The Island Forest had baths, a laundry, good food, and young people her own age. Once her cousin Peregrine had overseen the construction of an addition to the radio room for her use, she virtually never stepped aboard the *Muriel*.

I spent most of my time on the island, too. Even though my exile from Evergreen was official and absolute—and, since I had married and produced a non-forest family, also irrevocable—Master Anna exercised her prerogative to treat me as one of her own citizens. I ate at the master's table in the Hall, attended meetings of her council, and accompanied the forest pickets on patrol. I think if I'd shown any interest in having one, Anna would have awarded me the sword I'd never won in Evergreen. I didn't tell her how much things had changed since she'd left the continent. Even in the forests, a long gun was bestowed on newly qualified pickets in place of a sword.

I'd never lived in a forest as an adult, and I was astonished to discover from that vantage how much went on in one that I hadn't noticed as a boy.

After accompanying Peregrine on just one picket-patrol, for example, I knew the pickets who'd rushed in to help me put out the fire I'd started almost thirty years before in Evergreen had been watching me from the moment I kindled it, waiting to intervene until it became clear—to me—that I'd lost control of the situation. The Island Forest pickets, trained by Heron in the ways of Evergreen, spent far more of their time keeping an eye on the island's children than in looking out for pirates or other potential enemies.

Which made sense, when I thought about it. A single picket in a watchtower could observe a lot of coastline or cordon, whereas the children were scattered, roaming freely, as I had.

I also learned I'd been wrong, when I was growing up, to believe my mother when she said that I was the only citizen of Evergreen who didn't willingly embrace Forest Principles even when it was a personal sacrifice. The "no secrets" rule meant the Island Forest citizens didn't hide what was in their hearts, and surprisingly often, it turned out what was in their hearts was the same simmering rebellion against Forest Principles I'd sometimes felt. I'd been a better—or at least, more typical—Son of the Forest than I'd ever realized.

The experience of being a full citizen of a forest brought other surprises, too. Some of them weren't easy to accept.

At my first dinner in the Hall, as we waited for Master Anna to enter, the other diners formed themselves into a line and filed past my place at the table, each taking my hands in turn to bid me welcome. I was uncomfortable with the ceremony. Some of the citizens looked normal, but some were so Ant-like that I was glad the table was between us, so I only had to touch their hands and not put my face against theirs.

One older woman presented her son to me—a good-looking boy of about thirteen, much taller than his mother.

"This is Masterson," she said proudly.

Now, "Masterson" isn't a common forest name, and when it occurs, it can only mean one thing. A male of that name is always a son born to a forest master during his tenure. For a minute I couldn't say anything. Then I mumbled something idiotic—I have no idea what—and turned to greet the next citizen in the line.

"This 'Masterson,'" I asked Anna later, pitching my voice below the hum of surrounding conversations. "He's—?"

"Posthumous's son," she confirmed. "His mother is Bird, one of my first Ant-friends. You'll like Masterson. He's very bright."

"But—Posthumous?" I repeated, shaken.

The master laid a gentle hand on my arm. "It was a good marriage," she said gravely.

There were happier events, though. A few days after that dinner, Pearl had her baby. It was, as Anna had predicted, a male, and though Forester babies aren't officially named until they're three months old, I knew he'd be called "Heron."

After saying initially that Anna's leg brace was beyond repair, Mike met Anna, and immediately decided he might be able to fix it after all. He set up a forge on the beach and got to work with his tools and the secret stash of metals he'd previously denied having, and, naturally, the island metalworkers came down to see what he was up to. Before long, Mike had them making brace parts, too.

After twenty years' isolation, the Islanders had run short of a lot of things, though unlike the people on Making Happy, they'd found local substitutes for the most part. They had no paper, so they wrote with a stone stylus on thin sheets of bark that they first beat to toughen—a bulky but adequate alternative to the handmade paper used in Evergreen. For small tools and cups, they made clever use of wood and shells; and their pottery, though unglazed, was handsome and strong. Cloth was woven on simple handlooms from the pounded dried fibers of an island plant—although island cloth was coarse and scratchy, and I pitied even the most Ant-like islanders for having to wear it. Life on the island was a lesson in make-do, but for the most part, no more primitive than the forest life of my childhood.

But there was no island substitute for metal, and the metalworkers' only job since arriving there had been to repurpose the metal objects they had brought with them into things that met their greatest needs. They were delighted to have a chance to use good tools on good material, and the brace was finished in no time and worked perfectly.

I took no part in the work. I was off playing picket captain in the forest.

Anna's younger son, Loyal, wasn't recovering very well from the loss of his father, and Peregrine had the idea some new activity might help to revive his spirits. The radio was new, and Loyal seemed interested in it. Peregrine came to me privately, offered me his sword, and asked whether I'd mind taking over his duties for a few days while he and Helen introduced Loyal to radio communication.

Would I mind? It was all I could do to keep myself from snatching the sword from Peregrine's hand and running off into the woods that minute.

It turned out that picketing was another of those things I'd misunderstood as a boy in Evergreen—although to be fair to Anna's foster father Cade, who'd trained me, the reality of picketing was exactly what he'd warned me it would be. There was always a *chance* of danger from animals, accidents, or the sudden arrival of enemies—pirates here, instead of Ants—but for the most part, it was quiet work. After a couple days of it, it even got boring.

On the other hand, picketing did give me lots of time to think. As I stared from a watchtower out over an empty ocean one day, I worked out a partial fix for the radio, and as soon as my watch was over, I went to the radio hut.

When I told Helen my idea, she said immediately, "That won't work. We won't be able to transmit."

"We'll still be able to transmit soldier-code," I answered. "We can do that as long as we can generate any noise at all. But I'm almost positive we're wasting our time trying to transmit voice. We just don't have the equipment to do it. It's a lot easier to make a receiver than a transmitter, and I think if we put everything we've got into it, we can make this thing receive voice, at least."

"If it's only going to work one way," Helen objected, "I'd rather we put everything we've got into *sending* voice so May can hear Aunt Anna again."

We tried that, since it was important to my niece, but as it happened, I was right; I am sometimes. After several futile days of work, we abandoned the idea of voice transmission and configured the parts we had available into the best receiver we could manage. Then we summoned the master and her family into the radio hut to where May was calling through the crackle of static, "Anna? Anna, my darling, are you there?"

At the sound of her mother's voice, Anna cried, and so did everybody else in the room—including Mike, who later denied it.

"Grit in my eye," he claimed—unconvincingly.

Communication with the continent after that was much, much easier. Helen and I could send soldier-code almost as fast as we could talk anyway, and on the Evergreen end, Deer and the forest telegraphers got better at reading it until, after a while, we hardly even noticed what we had wasn't "normal" conversation.

It wasn't just forest voices I was happy to hear, naturally. I talked with my family as often as I could—usually late at night, when the islanders were in bed. As in Evergreen in the old days, the island citizens went to bed early because they had no source of artificial light that didn't smoke and smell and consume resources—a feature of my young years I'd conveniently forgotten. My children laughed and joked with me easily now, just the way they did with each other, and told me about themselves and their lives in a way they'd never done before.

I told them about my life, too—the parts I wasn't ashamed of. Maybe one day I'd share the rest of it, too. Maybe.

One night when we were talking alone, Sarah told me, "It's like you've finally come back from the war."

I told her it seemed like that to me, too. "I'll never love Ants, but I've made peace with the ones here. It's like making peace with them all." I didn't mention it, but I hadn't had a nightmare for a long time.

"Sleep well, sweetheart," Sarah said when we signed off. No one had called me "sweetheart" for a long time, either.

When I turned around, I found Helen standing behind me, smiling like a cat.

"How long have you been here?" I grumbled. "And where were you before that? It's late." I was embarrassed, and my tone came out rougher than I meant it to be.

"Oh, pooh," Helen said, still smiling. "I'm not a child, you know. Peregrine and I were out looking at the stars. I keep forgetting how far north we are. The sky looks different here."

Then she said abruptly, "Uncle, you should talk to Robin. He hates working at D&R. He's afraid to tell you because he thinks you'll be disappointed, but it's not what he wants to do for the rest of his life."

This was news—and yet in a way, it wasn't. And I *was* disappointed.

"All right. What does he want to do for the rest of his life?"

"I don't know." Helen shrugged. "I'm not sure if he knows. Just—something else. Anything."

"Fine. Let him do anything, then." When Helen's look turned steely, I added, "What I mean is, it's his life."

"He needs to hear that from you."

I stifled a sigh. "I'll talk to him."

"Tell him you'll love him no matter what he does," Helen urged. "Try to say it like you mean it."

"I'll tell him I'll love him no matter what he does, and I'll sound like I mean it because I do mean it."

Mollified, Helen put her arms around me and kissed my cheek. "On the other hand," she said comfortingly, "Laura likes working at D&R just fine. Of course, she'd like it even better if Tom worked there, too."

"Is that a hint?"

"Give him a job, Uncle River."

After thinking for a minute, I agreed with my niece that if Tom was good enough for Laura, he was good enough for D&R, and then we said goodnight.

The next day, as I'd promised, I called Robin to tell him he could leave D&R anytime, adding that if he knew of something else he wanted to do, I'd help him in any way I could.

My son didn't have to take even a minute to think about it. Because of our broken equipment, radio "conversations" had to take the form of alternating monologues, and when it was his turn to talk, he said instantly, "I might— teach school, then. Maybe." For politeness' sake, he tried to sound tentative about it, but I could tell that in his mind, the choice was already final. "I know it's not something you would have picked for me, Papa, but Uncle Deer says they could use me at the Evergreen school."

He talked about the school then, and it was clear he'd discussed the whole project pretty thoroughly with Deer already. "I'd live in Foreston, naturally, but since the school's in Evergreen, I'd be there all day," and then he was silent for a minute before saying, "That's all, I guess. I want to be a teacher."

Then he added, "Your turn, Papa," which was the signal for me to switch the radio over to transmit my answer back to him.

I didn't do it right away. I felt like I hadn't really taken in what he'd said yet. I sat back, folded my arms across my chest, and waited for the hurt to break.

Because it was definitely going to hurt. How could it not hurt to hear that my son planned to leave a business I was proud to have helped to build to go to a place from which I'd been exiled? And that he'd made the decision with the very person who'd exiled me?

Brutal.

So, I waited.

It took me a few minutes to realize it didn't hurt at all.

My son didn't like working at D&R. I could understand that. There was a lot about working at D&R I didn't like either. The things I did like—travel and periods of absolutely unfettered independence—had no appeal to my homebody son.

As for making the decision with Deer's counsel—well, Deer was ten times smarter than I was, and until I met Sarah, the first person I'd always gone to for advice, too.

I finished reconfiguring the radio, pulled the key over, and telegraphed back, "Great idea, 'Robin of Evergreen'. When do you think you'll start?"

Later I talked to Dan about hiring Tom. Dan blithely suggested training him to replace me.

"You're pushing me aside?" I asked, wounded.

"Not aside," Dan said. "In the right direction."

*

I was coming in from a picket-watch that night when Helen met me.

"I want you to hear something," she said. "Can you come?"

I was tired. Picketing was starting to seem like a young man's game. "Can it wait?"

"It could, but you don't want to wait," Helen informed me. "You want to hear it *now*."

Experience had taught me there was no point in arguing with my niece. I followed her to the radio hut where she sat down in front of the radio set and fiddled with the knobs.

"You know how I was experimenting with different radio frequencies trying to get better reception?" she asked. "Well, I found something interesting."

We'd been doing everything on the radio, transmitting and receiving, in the upper midrange of shortwave frequencies—basically because those frequencies worked.

Helen shoved a chair in my direction.

"You find something better?" I asked, grateful to sit down.

"I don't know whether I'd call the lower-range frequencies better, exactly, but I found something there I think you'll be interested to hear. Listen!"

I listened—then hitched my chair closer.

"What is that?" I murmured.

"Keep listening!"

I reached past my niece and twiddled the tuner knob myself—to her annoyance.

After a minute I shrugged. "It's just some—weird anomaly, probably. Does it always happen on this same frequency?"

"No. That's one of the interesting things about it. It moves up and down the dial. I pick it up on this frequency at night and in a couple different places during the day. Here: Listen some more."

I listened again then repeated, "What *is* that?"

Helen looked at me and smiled broadly. "What does it sound like?"

"Static."

"No, it doesn't!" she said indignantly. "Well, all right, it's kind of static-y. But what does it sound like besides static? What does it remind you of?"

I would have felt stupid saying what it reminded me of. I repeated that it was some unfamiliar kind of static.

"You're not even trying!" Helen cried. "Imagine it without the crackling and the distortion, and tell me what it sounds like. If you were listening to that from the other side of a thick door, what would you say was going on in the room?"

"It has some—unusual low notes, for static," I ventured cautiously.

"Yes, *and*?" she demanded. "What does it sound like? Just say it."

There is a cadence to human conversation that is unmistakable, whatever the language. Helen's "static" had that cadence.

"Talking," I admitted.

Helen leaned back in her chair. "Oh, doesn't it just?" She sighed happily, linking her hands behind her head.

"You're picking up somebody in the shop or something." Dan's workshop in Fortress was customarily full of radio sets in varying stages of assembly. It was conceivable that one was picking up and broadcasting someone's idle chatter.

"No." Her smirk turned superior. "That was the first thing Papa and I thought of, too. But we checked. That's not it."

"The men out at the antenna, then." Our shortwave antenna was stashed in a tumbledown shack on the bleakest, least inviting stretch of coast the continent offered, and operated by men who were well paid to be discreet.

"Nope."

I named the one of our closest competitors in the radio business. "She's figured out shortwave, damn her."

"Ha!" Helen snorted. "Papa talked to her. They're a million miles from shortwave."

"I don't know what you've picked up, then," I said, "but I'm sure it's not talking."

"Why? Why isn't it talking?"

"Because there's no one out there to talk. Unless you're suggesting that in some other part of the world, Ants have figured out shortwave broadcasting. Take it from me, Helen. They're not that smart."

"Who said anything about Ants?" Helen exclaimed. "Uncle, *we* survived. Humans in other parts of the world could have survived, too, and if they did, they probably have access to all the same Ancient Texts we do. By now, they could have re-invented radio just like we did."

I hesitated. She had a point.

On the other hand, I didn't like to see her getting her hopes up too high. I said firmly, "It's static. But keep listening. If it still sounds like talking after you've listened for a while, we'll discuss it some more."

*

Our four months were nearly up. It was time for us to head back to the continent.

The sailors weren't sorry. They all liked the place, which Jake designated *Annasland* on his charts, but it was too tame to make them forget their homesickness. They complained the females weren't as accommodating as the ones on Making Happy had been, and since they were telepathic, there was no way to be "private" with them anyway. Most of the crew had eighteen month's salary on the *Muriel's* books, and I was disconcerted to discover how many of them planned to spend it injudiciously. And, naturally, they missed their families.

I missed my family, too. I wanted as much as ever to see Sarah and my children again, and to make things right between us. But as for home— in some ways I felt like I was home already. The Island Forest had the same cleanliness, good manners, and order I remembered from Evergreen, with the advantage over Evergreen that its inhabitants subscribed to Forest Principles— still the only principles that made sense to me—but were…flexible…in their observance of them. Master Anna was more willing than other forest masters to make allowances for her citizens' individual quirks. She had to be. There was no place to exile anybody. Also, with Posthumous and Heron both gone, there wasn't a whole lot of "Forester blood" on the island anymore—except for mine. That gave me a little celebrity. I enjoyed it.

On the other hand, the place was full of Ants. Or rather, Hybrids. It was more their land than mine, so I kept a smile on my face when I was around them, but also a wary eye on every move they made. I couldn't help myself. I was alive because I'd never trusted an Ant an inch, and I couldn't seem to lose the habit.

Frank and Rain, on the other hand, were right at home among them.

Mornings, the two foraged, and being in perfect, uninterrupted communication with Island Foresters who'd been foraging there for twenty years meant they knew instantly what was plentiful and tasty to gather each day. Afterward, aboard the *Muriel*, they fed the sailors and lent an uncomplaining hand with whatever needed doing. In the evening they went ashore to visit with the friends they'd made on the island, which included just about everybody. Their habits were so quiet and regular I was sorry my mother had never had a chance to meet Frank. She'd have loved him. He was everything she'd hoped I'd turn out to be.

Frank surprised me one day by telling me he and Rain were hoping to go back to Making Happy.

I asked, "Why Making Happy? I thought you'd probably want to stay here, to be honest."

"It's very nice on this island," Frank agreed, while Rain nodded. "But Rain is lonely for her people. And we can do a lot of good on Making Happy. We have learned many useful things here."

I asked what kind of "good" they thought they could do. I didn't want to discourage them, but I figured if Frank was imagining he could reason Pete into being more like Master Anna, the kindest thing to do would be to disabuse him of the notion right away.

Frank answered that he was sure the people of Making Happy would like to have the nice things people on Annasland had. "They are simple to make. Rain and I could teach them how."

Frank and Rain, of course, had learned pretty much instantaneously how to make anything any telepathic islander knew how to make, though Frank admitted that their hands were much slower than their brains at mastering a skill.

"You *could* teach them," I said cautiously, "if they wanted to learn. From what I saw, though, most of the people of Making Happy would rather watch you make 'nice things,' and then take them away from you."

Frank's jaw went out with uncharacteristic pugnacity.

I mean, it was a mild pugnacity. More of a slight degree of forcefulness, really. But even that much was a side of him I hadn't seen before.

"We will not let them. They must make things for themselves." Then, relapsing into his more usual self, he added, "We will help them, of course."

I looked at Rain. "What about you, Rain? Do you think this plan will work?"

I could see immediately where Frank's suddenly steeliness emanated from. Rain said stoutly, "Small People are many. We will not let Babblers take nice things!"

I'd have laughed out loud if I hadn't been afraid they'd misunderstand.

"That's great," I said sincerely. "And if that's what you want to do, you should go back."

"You will take us on the ship?" Frank asked.

"Sure." I grasped his shoulder, like a friend's. "I'll take you wherever you want."

We talked a little more, and then, as I was starting away, Frank called after me. "Sir, are you able to help? A citizen of this place is hurt, and no island medicine is helping her. I feel the master wondering whether, if we have anything useful on the ship, it would deplete our supplies too much if she were to borrow a little."

Dan and I had seen to it the *Muriel* was supplied with all the best medicines we could get, of course—although what Frank was intimating was true; they weren't in unlimited supply.

"What kind of sickness are we talking about?" I frowned.

"The weaving master hurt herself here." Frank made a cutting motion across his calf. "It has been some time, but the wound will not heal."

How could I refuse? My own mother had been a weaving master.

"Let's see what we can do," I said.

I sent Frank to retrieve the medical supplies from the ship, advising him to stop by the radio hut on the way to let Helen know the situation, and asked Rain to guide me to the sick woman's cabin. After standing still for a minute, a look of intense concentration on her face, Rain pointed and said "Here!" and led the way.

Anna met us at the door of the single-roomed house where the sick woman lay in bed, one of her legs raised on a cushion and a damp cloth on her forehead. The woman's face was flushed and her eyes were much too bright, but when I approached her, she exerted herself to be polite.

"Greetings, friend," she whispered, putting out her hands.

Her speech was good, but there was a thickness to her voice I recognized as characteristic of Ants—excuse me: Hybrids—who learned to speak late in life. Her hands, when I took them, were very hot.

Anna told me the injury had happened more than a week before, and the wound seemed minor at first. "Then it got red," she said worriedly. "And now there is fever."

"All right. I'm not an infirmarian, but I've dealt with wounds before. Let's have a look."

With help from Anna, the woman rolled onto her side to allow me to remove the bandage on her calf. I didn't like what I saw.

"What have you done for it so far?" I asked.

The standard island remedy for open sores, Master Anna told me, was scrupulous cleanliness and not much else. "I've applied some salve we make from clean fat and the juice of a kind of leaf that grows here. But it's only for the pain. The plants Aunt Snow used to heal wounds in Evergreen don't grow here. Heron tried everything, but he never found any native plants that worked the same. We have infusions for stomachaches and that sort of thing, but nothing that really works against infection."

"Well, cleanliness is the best thing anyway." Trying to be honest, but still hopeful, I said, "It's pretty bad, but I think the stuff we've got on the ship will help. As soon as Helen gets here—"

I got just that far before Helen bustled in, all cheer and confidence as usual. Also as usual, my niece was more up on everything than I was. She even knew the sick woman's name.

"Greetings, Doe," she said in Forester. "I will help you." Pulling a bowl of wound-salve out of the medical box she was carrying, she took off the lid and showed it to the sick woman, who sniffed it and seemed reassured.

"Uncle River and I will clean this up," Helen went on—in Valley, since Anna was there to interpret—"and then you'll get well."

My niece looked at me, and I knew we were thinking the same thing. The "cleaning" of the leg would have to be brutally thorough if we expected to get the better of the infection.

"This is going to hurt," I warned; I was already wincing myself in anticipation. "But try to be as still as you can."

For such a tiny, elderly female, our patient was tough. I'd been thinking we might need to call somebody in to help hold her down, but clinging to Anna, she managed all by herself to be still, and she hardly made a sound. Once the leg was clean and rebandaged, she dropped off to sleep almost instantly.

"I can't promise anything," I whispered, as Master Anna tenderly covered the sick woman. "An infection like that's dangerous."

"I know it is," Anna replied sadly. "We've lost others the same way. We lost a child last year to what seemed barely a scratch at first."

"That won't happen with wound-salve," Helen put in quickly. "We'll leave ours for you when we sail. Apply it right away, before an infection gets started."

To Helen's surprise, the master refused to take the gift. She wouldn't risk one set of lives to safeguard another, she said.

"The men on your ship—and you yourself—might need that salve," she pointed out.

Helen was surprised, but I knew there was no point in arguing. What the master had just said was a basic Forester axiom. All lives being equal, one couldn't be saved at the cost of another. Before my niece could argue the point, I took her arm and pulled her gently away.

"We'll bring medicine next trip," I promised Anna as I maneuvered Helen out the door. "Helen and I will go radio Dan about it right now." I'd radio Evergreen for medicine, too, I decided. The forests still made the best kinds on the continent, and they'd be generous with a fellow forest.

Midway to the radio hut, I finally placed the name "Doe."

"That woman is one of the main reasons you grew up in a world without Ants," I told my niece. "She was the first Ant ever brought into Evergreen. Posthumous wanted Deer to study her, your aunt wanted to help her Uncle Deer, and that's how we found out that Ants—and your Aunt Anna—are telepaths."

"That's the Ant?"

"That's her. Luckily, she was really a Hybrid all along or the plan probably wouldn't have worked."

I remembered I'd disliked—no, hated—Doe back in those days. She was an Ant and an interloper; dirty, mute, and savage.

"Poor Auntie," Helen said. "Doe must be the oldest friend she has on the island. I hope we can save her, but I admit I'm not entirely confident about it."

I wasn't, either. "How would you feel about amputating that leg if you had to? Do you think you'd be up to that? We could get a doctor from the continent on the radio to talk you through it."

Helen gulped, "Are you crazy?" She wasn't the first person who ever asked me that. But a minute later, she said, "If it's her leg or her life, I guess I'd be willing to try."

CHAPTER TWENTY-FIVE

Once I'd talked to Dan and told him we'd be leaving Annasland soon, I needed to let the master know, too.

I was starting to appreciate a few things about living among telepaths. I asked the first Forester I saw if Master Anna was available, and after looking briefly thoughtful, he replied, "She says if you want to talk to her, she will meet you at the Grove. May I direct you there?"

I already knew where the Island Forest's Memorial Grove was, so I said no.

In traditional fashion, the Island Foresters had logged a pretty valley for material to build their homes, and now they were replanting it with Memorial Trees. Two pines standing near each other, one just a little younger than the other, honored my mother- and father-in-law; and nearby was another pine tree for Posthumous. The first time I'd visited the grove and realized other young trees must mark the graves of Hybrids, I remembered my father's tree, and my brother's, and my mother's, and thought it was wrong—monstrous, even—to honor an Ant with an equivalent tree to theirs. Standing in the Grove now, I suddenly realized this was not only right, but represented the Island Forest's distinguishing virtue. Other forests believed in the concept of "forest blood"—that the blood of other races was somehow different from their own. Anna's people rejected that prejudice. To them, blood was blood. A Forester was anyone who believed in, and obeyed, Forest Principles.

There were a few broadleaf trees in the grove, too—a kind I knew from the continent, that produced tiny reddish-brown flowers in spring. I didn't need to be told that these trees marked the graves of babies or children. The forest way to memorialize those who died before reaching maturity was with fruit trees, and since there weren't any real fruit trees on the island, the fleshy seeds these trees made, food for birds, were the best the Island Foresters could do. Looking around now, I thought pears might do all right on the island and made a mental note to ask Dan if it was too late for him to get some cuttings from Evergreen for the *Muriel* to bring when she came back.

I walked in turn to John's tree, Muriel's, Posthumous's, and lastly Heron's, taking a moment at each to remember my friends. I'm not ashamed to say I shed a few tears at Heron's tree. As boys, we'd been like brothers.

When I looked up, Anna was standing not far off, watching me.

Embarrassed, I called, "I'm sorry. Did I keep you waiting? I have some news."

There were benches here and there. Master Anna took my arm and I led her to one, where I remembered to remain respectfully standing until she had seated herself.

I told her the *Muriel* would sail as soon as we could get her ready. "She'll come back with all the things I promised, including a new, better radio, and a backup radio. You won't ever need to worry again about losing touch with your people on the continent."

"The radio will be nice." Anna patted the bench for me to sit next to her. "Tell my brother not to send too many other things, though. We have most of what we need here already."

This was a typical forest attitude. "Most of what we need" to a Forester was something to eat, something to wear, and a dry place to sleep—plus maybe a hot bath. Foresters were divided on whether hot baths were necessities or luxuries. Frank's plan to help the people of Making Happy by teaching them to make do with what they had would likelier turn them into a bunch of Foresters than good—meaning, insatiable—trading partners of the kind I was supposed to be looking for, but I'd already decided I could live with that.

After a short silence, Anna asked, "Will *you* sail with the *Muriel*?"

I hoped there was more to the question than a desire on Anna's part to know whether to arrange a leave-taking ceremony.

"I don't have to," I said guardedly. "Would you like it if I stayed?"

Anna didn't answer immediately, but her intense expression suddenly reminded me our present "private" conversation was three-sided—me, Anna, and—no secrets—every other citizen of the island. I wondered if I would ever get used to that.

Turning to me with a smile, the Master finally said, "You would be very welcome to stay. You will always be welcome here!"

That was Consensus. It would have meant a lot more to me if it had been just Anna who wanted me.

She stood up, then, and reached for my hand. "Come and look at something. I haven't been able to look at it myself for more than a year, but now I think I'd like to show it to you."

At the edge of the Grove was a little one-roomed building, a typical forest-style structure I'd assumed was somebody's house. Anna led me into it and started opening the rain shutters. As I hurried to take over the job, I made another mental note: The islanders needed window glass, too.

The room was tiny, and completely unfurnished, but as I looked around I was astonished to see that the walls were thickly hung with forest scenes, landscapes, seascapes and portraits—all molded in clay. They were Heron's work, of course.

"By all gods, Master!" I gasped as I looked. "These are wonderful! I didn't know Heron modeled clay!"

The pictures were all good. They were better than good. But the portraits were *fantastic*. I stood in front of one of Deer looking just as he had on the day I'd left Evergreen for the last time, and half-expected it to talk to me.

"How did he do it? These are alive!"

Anna smiled. "Well, he practiced, naturally," she said wryly. "Our paper ran out pretty quickly. That was hard for all of us, but it was terrible for Heron. We used everything we had—even pages out of books, but at last it was gone. We tried making paper, but the only things we found to use that made *good* paper were rags, and those ran out, too. Papa suggested woodcarving, but by then we'd guessed the *Morning Glory* wasn't coming back, and Heron didn't feel he could use knives we weren't sure we could ever replace. Art was so necessary to him that when he didn't have anything else, he went down to the beach and drew in the sand. I'd send the children to call him home before the tide turned. I couldn't bear to think of him watching as the water took his pictures, day after day."

Anna looked so sad at the memory that I asked quickly, "What finally made you think of clay?"

The distraction worked. "Cook pots," she said, brightening again. "We were running out of cook pots. None of us knew how to make them, but we'd all seen potters working at one time or another. We put together the little information each of us could contribute and experimented. Heron was in charge of making the actual clay to use, and we made a dozen different kinds of kilns—all failures but one."

"Well, one's enough. You make good pots. I've been admiring them." I was circling the room slowly as I said this, closely examining every modeled scene.

"Yes." Anna leaned on her walking stick, watching me. "We don't have any glazes, but the clay itself is handsome, isn't it?"

"It's wonderful," I agreed fervently. "Don't let anything happen to these. Gods, it's Duck, the old kitchen master! Looking at this, I can almost smell venison cooking!"

Then I stopped dead in my circuit of the room and looked into my mother's face.

Heron had captured her perfectly, from her features and hair to the slightly haughty expression she often assumed. Even more, he'd put in things I'd never recognized before; my mother's innate shyness, and her feelings of—what? Of incomprehension; of not fitting in, I think—that were the reason she wore that proud mask. She'd shown a different face to people like me, people she wasn't afraid of. In Heron's portrait I saw that other face peeking out, fearfully, hopefully, as though she wanted to trust the viewer but was unsure. All this in unpainted, unglazed clay. It was more than a work of art; it was a masterpiece.

I'd cried a little before, now I wept in earnest. Strangely, though, at the same time the portrait made me happy. It reminded me that the wariness that had kept my mother from freely trusting others was gone now, wherever—whatever—she was.

Anna came and lifted the portrait from the wall, where it hung by a leather thong, and gave it to me.

"A gift," she said. "From Heron and me."

"This?" I asked, wiping my eyes and smiling at the same time. "Of course I'll accept it. I probably shouldn't. It's too much. But if you can bear to part with it, I'll absolutely take it."

"It's one gift." Anna smiled. "And there aren't any strings attached. You can take this gift and still refuse another I'm about to offer."

"Another gift?" I cradled my mother's face in my hands. I couldn't take my eyes away from it. "What is it?"

"It's my son," Anna said gravely. "My son Loyal."

I was so startled I almost dropped the portrait. "Loyal?" I blinked. "You're giving me *Loyal*?"

"Not permanently," Anna said. "More of a loan than a gift. I want you to foster him. You can say no to this, remember. He might be more responsibility than you want."

Heron's son *was* more responsibility than I wanted. Anybody's son was more responsibility than I wanted.

"Master," I began; then stopped. Near us on the wall was a sculpted forest scene—two young pickets at their posts. I thought one of them might be me.

"I haven't said I'd stay," I reminded her.

"Whether you stay or not." Anna looked into my eyes. "Loyal isn't happy, and it's not just the loss of his father. It's hard being a non-telepath among telepaths. But where Heron was content, and Peregrine, and Masterson, and Valiant, and all the other non-telepaths on this island are content, Loyal is not. We've talked about it, of course. He doesn't have any specific complaints.

He just feels like he's adrift, he says; like he doesn't belong."

I thought Robin might know that feeling. I knew it myself.

"You can work it out," I urged.

"Until you came, I thought we'd have to. I thought we'd all be confined to this island forever, and we'd have to work it out. But now ships will come. Yours is only the first." I heard fear in her voice as Anna admitted, "I'm afraid Loyal will go away on a ship. I'd rather he went on your ship, with you, than any other."

I glanced down at my mother's sculpted features again. Anna had gotten me in a soft spot. She'd probably intended to. My mother never felt like she fit in either. Had she ever known an entirely happy day in her life?

As I looked aimlessly around the room, wondering what to answer, a mask of Posthumous caught my eye.

"*Help him,*" the mask's eyes said to mine. "*For your mother's sake.*"

"Master…" I pressed my lips together. After a moment, I tried again. "Let me call you just 'Anna' this time," I suggested. "I can't tell this to my master, only to a friend. Anna, I have two children. I was a terrible father, and it's to their credit—and their mother's—that they still speak to me at all. If I go and you send Loyal with me, there's a good chance you'll be sorry for it."

Maybe it was because I'd called her my friend, I don't know. All I know is that for the first time since I'd arrived, Anna smiled her *old* smile. Seeing it made it easy for me to remember why I'd once been in love with her.

She said, still smiling, "I'm not a fool, you know—and Deer's not a fool, and my sisters and brother aren't fools, and your children aren't fools. All of us think you're the best possible choice of someone to foster a fatherless boy who doesn't feel like he belongs where he lives. We know you better than you know yourself, River. You're not what you think you are. When we look at you, we don't see the darkness you imagine is inside you. We see the real you."

She'd been discussing me with—everybody, apparently.

"Most of the time, the people I love don't see me at all," I said bluntly. "I'm gone."

"But not because you don't love them. They know this. They understand."

While I was thinking this over, she added, "Your children told me that though you traveled a great deal in their childhood, wherever you went you always brought gifts home to them."

"Oh, gods, yes," I agreed, shaking my head—but smiling, too. "The kids would crawl all over me the minute I walked in the door, looking for loot. I fooled them once by hiding something in my shoe, and after that they'd almost strip me naked on the threshold to make sure they didn't miss anything. I can remember Sarah just watching and laughing…"

I stopped myself. "Sorry," I said awkwardly. "Happy memories."

"For them, too." Anna put her hand on my arm. "Foster my son, River, please. He has happy memories of his father, too, but he's at a crossroads in his life and he needs guidance I can't give him. Help him to be happy here, or take him to another place that would be better for him."

Thinking of Robin, I asked, "Have you thought about sending him to Evergreen? There's no reason they wouldn't take him. You and Heron weren't Exiles."

"If Loyal doesn't stay here, I hope that's where he'll go. I hope he'll decide it's not forest life that's the problem but only that this forest has so many telepaths in it. But the important thing is that he's happy, as I said. Help him to be happy, like you."

It sounds stupid to say it, but I hadn't thought of myself before as being "happy." My mother taught me good people are happy because they're conscious of being good. I had no such consciousness.

On the other hand, now that I thought about it, I *was* happy.

"I'll do my best for Loyal, Master. I still think you might be making a mistake to pick me to foster him, but I guess it's your mistake to make."

"Thank you." Anna looked pleased. She put her hands on my shoulders, and, her walking stick dangling from her wrist by a thong, pulled herself up on tiptoe to kiss my cheek.

Impulsively, I put my arms around her.

"I missed you," I whispered hoarsely. "Did you ever miss me?"

Anna slipped her arm around my neck and drew me closer. Her body was warm against mine. Her hair smelled of wood smoke and pine.

"I missed you every day," she said softly.

She released me, and stepping back, took my hands in a formal salute.

"I hope you will decide to stay with us, River," she said in her proper forest master voice. "But stay or go, I trust you with my son."

We looked a while longer at Heron's pictures after that, his presence almost palpably between us, and then, after closing the little hut tightly against wind and rain, we walked back toward the village together.

We talked as we walked. Silence would have been unbearable.

"How's Doe?" I thought to ask.

Doe had been sick out of her mind for a few days. Helen and I cleaned her wound several more times, applying wound salve each time, but the stuff isn't magic, and sometimes a patient's strength gives out before the salve has a chance to work on the infection. All we could do in Doe's case was wait and hope she could hang on.

She did. On the fourth day her fever broke, and on the fifth day, she wanted to eat.

"She's sitting up in bed today," Master Anna told me. "All of us are so grateful to you and Helen for saving her. Doe is our oldest citizen, you know. Our young ones think of her as a sort of grandmother."

I said I was glad to help, not thinking I could possibly mean it, since Doe was an Ant. But once the words were out of my mouth, I discovered I actually *was* glad.

"I'll come see her later," I promised.

CHAPTER TWENTY-SIX

A s soon as I left the master, I went looking for Loyal. Might as well get
started with the "fostering" thing right away, I decided.

He wasn't with Pearl and the baby at her place, and he wasn't
at any of the picket-shelters—which on second thought didn't surprise me,
because although Loyal was supposedly training to be a picket, according to
his brother he didn't show much interest in the job. He wasn't in the library
or the Hall, either. Nobody seemed to have seen him for hours. That left a
lot of island to search, and I wandered around aimlessly until it suddenly
occurred to me there was a certain kind of place an unhappy fifteen-year-
old male would probably seek out. Sure enough, I found Loyal sitting at the
furthest edge of a sea-cliff, legs dangling over the edge, staring down at the
breakers.

I couldn't just walk up to him. A little more weight on the ledge might be
all it took to bring the whole cliff face down. I studied the situation for a few
minutes, and then circled cautiously around behind.

"Nice view," I said calmly. "Do you come up here a lot?"

Loyal hadn't heard me coming—inexcusable in even a trainee picket—and
he started.

Turning, he stammered, "No. I mean, *yes*. I like it here."

I found a safe spot—I hoped—and sat down. "There's a place in Evergreen kind of like this," I told him. "At one time in my life I spent so much time there people called it 'River's Chair.'"

If Loyal caught the hint that other people in the world were sad and lonely sometimes, he didn't give any sign of it.

"My mother told you to talk to me, didn't she?" he said, sounding resentful.

I couldn't see any point in lying to him. I couldn't think of a good lie anyway. "She told me you aren't happy because you don't feel like you fit in very well. She thought maybe I could do something about that."

"Well, you can't," Loyal declared. "Nobody can."

"No, probably not," I agreed.

Loyal must not have liked this answer. He muttered something under his breath to the effect that I could at least try.

Ignoring this, I continued, "As a matter of fact, I've got the same problem, and I've never figured out what to do about it in my own case, either. I mean, besides just putting up with it, which is what I do."

Loyal didn't say anything, so I rambled on about myself for a while, always my favorite topic, finishing up by saying, "I left the forest because I didn't feel like I made a very good Forester, and then it turned out I didn't make a very good Man, either. Don't get me wrong," I added. "I like Men. I just don't understand them. Which is fair enough, I guess, since they find me pretty inscrutable, too."

Loyal finally spoke. "It's the same with me," he said gloomily. "It's worse. No one sees that I'm different from them."

"I guess you are." I pitched a small stone over the edge. "I guess the reason you feel like you don't fit in is because you don't fit in. Here you are, living on a small island with a bunch of other people who are in each other's minds all the time, sharing everything, and you're not a telepath. I can see where that would be tough. You seem smart, though. I'm sure you can think of better ways to deal with the situation than by jumping off a cliff."

"I'm not going to jump," Loyal said, looking guilty.

"No," I agreed. "You're planning to let the cliff decide the matter. But if it gave way and you fell, halfway down you might discover you didn't want to die after all, so don't do that."

Time for a change of subject.

I said, "Hey, I need to go out to the ship. Want to come along and keep me company? I need somebody to talk to. Out loud, because I'm not a telepath, either."

Loyal's smile, which I was seeing for the first time, was like his mother's.

Along the way to the *Muriel*, we stopped at the armorers to get Peregrine's sword, and then at the radio hut, where I knew I'd find Helen. I could hear her laughter—and Peregrine's—before I even opened the door.

My niece and her cousin were sitting opposite each other at the radio table, Peregrine with the telegraph key in front of him. Helen had rigged it for teaching, so it made an audible sound when depressed but wasn't connected to the radio, and was evidently drilling her cousin in soldier-code. As I opened the door, she leaned across the table to swat Peregrine's hand.

"No!" she said in Forester. "That's not right. Do again!"

Then the two of them looked up and saw me.

Peregrine stood up immediately, of course. I was senior to him in age, and a guest, besides.

"You're embarrassing me, Helen," I said in Valleyspeak. "Get up." To her cousins, I added in Forester, "Has my niece been giving you lessons? Let's give her one."

Winking broadly at Loyal, I put out my hands to his brother. "This is how it's done, Fair-face," I informed her.

Evidently no one had told Helen what the Island Foresters privately called her.

"Who?" she asked, getting reluctantly to her feet.

I repeated the name, and she looked pleased.

"Peregrine is the oldest," I explained, "so I greet him first, see? If Loyal was the picket captain, and Peregrine didn't have a title yet, I'd go to Loyal first even though he's younger, but that's nuance. You can learn that later."

Though I was speaking Valley, Peregrine had caught on by now and assumed a formal stance. "Greetings, River of Evergreen," he said, taking my hands. "Are you well?"

We touched cheeks as I replied, "I'm very well, thank you. And you?"

"Very well also," Peregrine answered.

Helen rolled her eyes when I looked at her, but she was paying close attention.

I released Peregrine's hands. "Your turn," I told Helen, putting out my hands to her.

Helen jumped. "Me? I'm not a Forester!"

"Believe me, that is abundantly obvious," I told her—then repeated the remark in the forest tongue, so her cousins could enjoy it. Peregrine's guffaw earned him a sniffy look from Helen.

"Put your hands out," I instructed her, "and when we embrace, step forward on your right foot, and put your right cheek to mine. Right-right; got it? It's very bad form to step on the other person's toes." We exchanged ritual forest greetings, with Helen getting all the words right, but stammering from nervousness.

I turned to Loyal then—who surprised me with a little joke.

"Please forgive my cousin's lack of manners," he said gravely as he took my hands. "She is young, and very ignorant."

We were all the way to the cheek-pressing part before Helen worked out what he'd said.

"That's not very nice," she chided.

I was starting to like my foster son. "Don't quibble," I said, pressing Loyal's cheek warmly. "You could use a little polish."

I gave Peregrine his sword then, and apologized that I wouldn't be able to stand my assigned picket-watch.

"Something's come up," I explained. "I have to go talk to Captain Alcock."

Helen and Peregrine had been isolated in the radio hut all morning and were probably the only people on the entire island who didn't know already that the *Muriel* would soon be leaving Annasland. I told them, and Loyal and I left the two staring at each other like I'd said the world was about to end.

After a passerby ascertained for us that Master Anna had no objection to Loyal accompanying me to the ship, we walked down to where the dinghy was moored.

"You row," I ordered Loyal.

Timmy met us as we climbed aboard.

"You here to visit?" he asked Loyal eagerly. "I'll show you around. Can I, Mr. River?"

I said I was willing and sent them off together, Tim already chatting away happily even though neither one of the boys knew much of the other's language. As long as there were plenty of Tims around, I thought, "fostering" would be a breeze.

Captain Alcock was also in an excellent mood. At my knock, he bellowed out a cheerful invitation to come right in and perform an act better left unspecified. He'd already caught the rumor we were leaving Annasland, and was at his desk, surveying his charts.

"Sit down, sit down!" he roared. "Fine sailing weather, ain't it? When we goin'?"

"Well, when can we be ready?" I asked in return.

Jake suggested that two or three days would be time enough to provision, and we spent the next hour discussing what supplies we'd need.

"Where we gonna make fuel, though?" Jake asked then.

The Coast was now officially at war with the Valley, and we no longer had the option of not making fuel. With her Valley flag, the *Muriel* would have to sail to a neutral port all the way on the far side of the continent, and be ready the whole distance to run (my personal choice) or to fight. The Coastlands had an extensive merchant navy, and in wartime their vessels traveled in armed squadrons, eagerly seizing—legally—anything they could catch.

"Men lose more than they gain every time they go to war," I grumbled. "Why do they fight so much?"

"It's different ones doing the losin' and gainin'," Jake said cynically. "We'd best fuel up good, and then make more shipboard, too."

We discussed this—Making Happy seemed like our best option, which I knew would please Frank and Rain—and then, feeling there was no point in putting off the revelation, I admitted, "It's possible I won't be sailing home with you, Jake."

The captain eyed me keenly. "You stayin'?" he demanded. "Damn me, I didn't look for that."

"I *may* stay," I corrected him. "I've been invited to. I haven't decided yet."

After a moment's thoughtful silence, Jake ventured, "I thought she was kin to you. Ain't she kin?"

"Master Anna?" I asked stiffly. I felt myself flush. "She is—but only by marriage. In fact, not even by marriage, really. It's—complicated." Somewhat defensively, I added, "Her late husband was my best friend."

"Aye, well… You know your own business best," Jake said briskly, shuffling his papers together. "You think it through and let me know what's to be. No reason you can't stay here if you want. The men'll be real sorry, but they're used to partings. All sailors is."

As I went to find Loyal, passing crewmen greeted me with a degree of friendliness that took me off guard. We hadn't seen much of each other lately, and their sudden warmth reminded me of an ancient expression I'd once translated to the effect that to be away from someone makes their company seem more desirable. This seemed to be true in my case.

I wondered whether what the captain had said was also true, that sailors got used to partings. If so, I might ask them for their secret. Whether I went back to the continent or stayed in the Island Forest, I was facing a lot of partings myself soon, and unless I got used to them—quick—they were going to hurt.

Nobody liked to talk more than Tim did, and long before I reached the engine room door, I could already hear him telling Loyal stories about Captain Alcock. However much fun the sailors made of their captain behind his back—and they made a *lot* of fun of him behind his back—"Old Stoney" was a figure of considerable respect on the *Muriel*. He was profane and he was dirty, and the punishments he meted out could be brutal, but the crew was willing to forgive him a lot for keeping them safe.

Given that Loyal's Valleyspeech was limited, I wasn't sure how much he was getting out of Tim's conversation, but I always enjoyed it. Smiling in anticipation, I stopped outside the engine room door to eavesdrop just as Tim was saying earnestly, "He ain't a great talker, except for sometimes. But when he does talk, he's sure to be saying something smart. There ain't much in the world he don't know about. He don't brag on it, but he's real educated."

This was an overstatement, in my opinion. There was much in the world the captain knew absolutely nothing about. (He was also a bit of a braggart.) On the other hand, Jake's knowledge probably did seem prodigious to Timmy, who was illiterate.

Tim said, "He don't think that makes him too good to work, though. He gets his hands dirty as the rest of us."

And let them remain that way. The captain's lack of hygiene no longer bothered me—absolute proof you can get used to anything.

"He's a good shot, too," Tim continued proudly. "Not a dead shot, like Mr. Richard—but he don't claim to be a dead shot. What's important is he makes his shots count."

I recognized this as an almost-verbatim quote from the captain himself, roared out during gunnery practice early in the voyage. Firing speed was more important than accuracy, he'd repeatedly said, because a shell that landed in the water near another ship was as good as a hit if it made the other ship's gunners miss *their* shot. Even sick and sweating in my bunk I'd thought this valuable advice, and I was happy Tim remembered it.

"And I guess I don't even need to say he's the bravest man aboard," Tim added. "You know that time I was telling you about before? When I got my face messed up? He was the one got us out of that, one hundred percent. I mean, we all done pretty good. Nobody shit hisself or nothing." Tim mentioned this fact, with pride, every time the topic of Ant Island came up. "But he's the one got us back to the ship."

With this assessment I largely agreed. In the end, the captain's timely barrage was the only thing in the world that could have saved us.

Thanks to me, it had nearly been in vain. I'd had a few tortured nights since Ant Island dreaming the men had already taken me up on my reckless offer of one shot for themselves from my pistol before the ship's cannon scared the Ants off.

I was recalling this with a mental shiver when Tim added, "But what was *bravest* that he done there was he didn't leave nobody behind. Nobody that wasn't already stone-dead, that is. He made sure *personal* all the wounded was carried along; me in his own hands. Anybody else woulda looked after his own self first."

It was my impression that Tim was still talking, but I couldn't follow what he said after that. I was busy trying to figure out at what point the subject of the conversation had ceased to be Captain Alcock and had become Mr. River. Tim had praised Jake's knowledge, his work ethic, and his wisdom, and given him a little too much credit for our escape from Ant Island (Mr. Jameson deserved at least half). But the only one who had carried Tim on Ant Island was me. No doubt that was a great thing to Timmy—but why had he brought the incident up while he was praising the *Muriel's* captain?

When it occurred to me Tim might have been speaking of me all along, I turned and bolted back up the ladders to the top deck and went into my cabin.

There I sat thinking things over for a long, long time.

After the Ant Army was broken in the Battle in the Valley, the command structure of the United Armies fragmented and never formulated a single, unified strategy against the Ants again. Most of the Men's armies disbanded, in fact, and those that didn't turned on each other like hungry wolverines, eager to take advantage of neighbors whose lands battlefield losses had made vulnerable. Men left finishing off the Ants to those who were on fire with hate and a thirst for revenge, and that included me. I attached myself to some Hunters; quickly became their leader; did things I couldn't live with afterward; and had spent all the years since running away from my shame.

But the Forester soldiers had remained under orders, and the remnants of the Forest Army, though almost as broken as the Ants, doggedly pursued the surviving enemy into the bleakest wastes of the former Antlands. They killed any Ants who turned and fought, of course. That was a simple matter of self-defense. But their post-battle policy was to rely on hunger and want to finish those who retreated before them.

Not because such a policy was better or more merciful for the Ants. It wasn't. They did it because, as a weary Forest subgeneral once informed me, the Ants had to die, *and the Foresters had to live with themselves afterward.*

This remark meant absolutely nothing to me at the time, and everything later.

As far as I was concerned, the fact that I had eagerly embraced the Men's way of finishing the Ants instead of the Foresters' was the strongest possible evidence that I didn't, and never had, belonged in a forest.

But if what Timmy said about me was right, that I showed evidence of having principles, and even virtues, then maybe I'd come to belong in one. Maybe the transformation I'd been assuring my family I'd undergone was that I'd matured into a Forester at last.

Maybe I could stay on Annasland not on its master's sufferance but because I belonged there.

I thought about this until a rap at my door and Timmy's distinctive nasal, "Mr. River, sir?" told me it was time to take Heron's son back to Annasland.

*

On our return trip, Loyal talked faster than he rowed. He had understood a surprising amount of what Tim told him and insisted with great sincerity that steam power was the greatest invention of all time. It even surpassed radio, he said.

"My mother told me many times you were very clever, but you are much more than that," he informed me.

I dryly explained that neither Dan nor I had ever really invented anything. "I'm not as smart as you think. I'm just a re-implementer of old technologies."

"But you read and understand what the Ancestors wrote," Loyal reminded me.

"Well, yes. I'm a bit of a linguist. That's useful."

"I want to be a linguist, too, then," Loyal declared. "Teach me. What is 'booger'?"

When I could finally stop laughing, I explained, "Nobody really knows what 'booger' means, Loyal. We've forgotten for at least a thousand years. It's just a word Men say when they're angry." Unwisely, I added, "You know—like our word 'shit.'"

Only then it turned out Loyal had never heard the word "shit" before, and I had to explain it to him.

"I'm glad you're not a telepath," I sighed as we landed. "Don't tell your mother, all right?"

CHAPTER TWENTY-SEVEN

That night, Master Anna invited the entire island population and the crew of the *Muriel* to dinner, the first time we had all sat down together. The Hall was too small for the occasion, of course, but the weather was beautiful and nobody minded eating outdoors. The sailors groomed themselves for the occasion like lovers going courting, and Jake washed his face and tried hard to curb his language. He sat next to Anna, where I hope he learned something from her example about inspiring respect without resorting to cursing or violence. The island had no large game, so there were no smoking platters of boar and venison to pass, as there would have been in Evergreen, but there were plenty of meaty soups and stews, and every kind of fish. Everything was well-cooked, and the *Muriel's* crew, including me, ate heartily.

After the meal, there was music.

Islanders sang to the accompaniment of island-made flutes and harps, and every tune was one I knew from boyhood, performed just as it had been by the singers and musicians of Evergreen. Ants, as I've probably said before, are not innovators. Afterward came recitations of old forest stories, translated into Valleyspeak for the benefit of the non-Foresters present.

When it was our turn, the same two sailors who had sung at our John's Island feast sang again—unobjectionable songs—and we had more rope tricks and fiddle music. Helen, blushing sweetly, sang too, and Mike finished the program with his spark-leaps. Electricity was a new thing since the islanders had left the continent, and they loved watching Mike.

Then Master Anna said, smilingly, "Your turn, River."

There was a time when I played the flute well, but after the war I hadn't kept up with it. "You play," I demurred, laughing with embarrassment. "I don't remember how."

"We'll play together," Anna answered.

To my surprise, when she handed me a flute, my fingers automatically curled comfortably around it, and when she began a slow air, my fingers remembered the air, too. I fumbled at first, but Anna covered for me, and after a few tunes, I felt confident enough to set a faster tempo.

More musicians joined in, and during a particularly lively set, a few of the *Muriel's* sailors were moved to get up and dance.

The island citizens just watched at first, but when Peregrine and Helen joined in, some of the bolder Annaslanders decided they'd dance too. Before long, there were so many dancers that tables had to be pushed aside to make room for them all. Eventually Helen came and claimed me for a partner, and seeing me being dragged away to the dance floor, laughing, Jake suddenly declared he was damned if he didn't like to dance himself. He held out his hand to the nearest female, who happened to be Masterson's mother, Bird, and hemmed in by the crowd, Jake and Bird and Helen and I danced side-by-side for some time. I am happy to say the near proximity of an Ant didn't spoil my fun in the least.

"You were crazy to leave Evergreen, Uncle River!" Helen cried. "This is wonderful!"

My niece's style of dancing is what we'll call "uninhibited," and probably caused a lot of (mental) comment among our hosts, but I danced with Helen until Peregrine reclaimed her, and then I danced with a lot of other females, all of them undoubtedly Hybrids in one degree or another. I danced with Anna to a slow melody; the one we'd danced to at her wedding. I don't know if she remembered that.

It was late when I slipped away, leaving the young ones still enjoying themselves. I didn't feel like going back to my cabin on the ship. Instead, I lay down in the grass by the radio hut and studied the sky, my arms folded behind my head. We were miles north of the most northerly tip of the continent, and as Helen had pointed out, the stars were different here. Eventually I fell asleep and dreamed my boyhood dream of sailing down a long, long river, stepping out at the end of the voyage onto an unknown continent. In a half-conscious moment, I wondered whether it was Annasland I'd dreamt of.

*

I woke up at dawn, curled on my side, chilly and stiff. Helen was standing over me, poking me with her finger.

Groaning, I sat up. "I am definitely too old to sleep on the ground," I muttered; adding, since Helen was still poking me, "Stop that! Did you ever get to sleep last night?"

"Who needs sleep?" my niece exclaimed. "Come listen to the radio! Come now, or you'll miss it!"

Then she bolted into the radio hut, leaving me to struggle to my feet and follow.

The radio, when I got to it, was emitting its usual static—and, faintly, far off in the background, something else.

I lowered myself onto the chair in front of the radio set. "That's—!" I said, and stopped.

"That's exactly what it is," Helen agreed breathlessly. "It's music." She leaned over me and adjusted the tuner. "It was Deer's idea," she explained.

On Dan's advice, Helen had gotten in touch with Deer about the mysterious "voices" we'd picked up on the radio, and Deer had immediately set out to discover definitively whether they really were voices, and if they were, whether they were "live" voices. We all figured some type of recorded speech from ancient times might have somehow started spontaneously broadcasting again.

After listening for a day, Deer discovered the transmissions followed a pattern. Two hours of voice was followed by two hours of silence, followed by two more hours of voice on another frequency. Reasoning that if they could send, they could also receive, next day during a broadcast Deer made a return broadcast from Evergreen on the same frequency the voices were using. Next broadcast, and the next, he did the same, matching his frequency to the voices' each time.

He did this over and over until, two days into the experiment, the voices stopped changing frequencies and stayed permanently with the frequency Deer had last used. Instead of making regular broadcasts two hours apart, they now seemed to time theirs to "answer" his.

"Yesterday," Helen told me, "just to be absolutely sure he had real, living people responding to him, Deer had the idea of broadcasting music. Or maybe it was Bellflower's idea. Come to think of it, I'm pretty sure Deer said she thought of it."

"Just go on!" I said impatiently. The music had faded, and I turned the tuner-knob slowly, trying to find it again.

"All right, all right. Bellflower had the idea of broadcasting music," continued Helen. "She figured people—real people—might broadcast music back, just to show they'd heard. And now they have! Do you see why I had to wake you up? You'd never have believed it if you hadn't heard it for yourself, would you?"

I probably wouldn't have.

"How long before their next broadcast?" I asked eagerly.

"No, it's Deer's turn," Helen corrected me, retuning the radio. "And here he is!" she announced.

For the next hour, my niece and I listened to Deer's newest brilliant idea, which was teaching whoever was listening to count in Forester. He'd say the word "one," and then ring what I recognized as an Evergreen signal-gong one time. Then he'd say the word "two" and ring it twice, all the way to ten. Then he'd start over.

"This is great," I murmured to Helen. "Unless they're Ants, or as stupid as Ants, they have to catch on."

"They must be far away. We're receiving Deer much better than we receive them."

"Well, wherever they are," I said, "if they teach us to count in their language, with a little research we may be able to identify what language they're speaking. And if we figure that out, we might be able to find an ancient map that shows where that language was spoken. On the continent, the words for things like numbers haven't changed as much as a lot of other words. Let's hope it's the same where they are."

CHAPTER TWENTY-EIGHT

I didn't tell anyone, not even Jake, whom I saw eyeing me speculatively from time to time, but I was pretty sure I was going to stay in Annasland. Life in the Island Forest, I'd decided, would provide me with the direction and purpose my present life lacked.

Of course, my life in Men's Lands hadn't always seemed purposeless. At one time I'd been rooted there by Sarah and the children. Even if, as I hoped, Anna and I someday found our comfort in each other, I knew I'd miss the home that I'd once shared with my family until the day I died.

But that home no longer existed. Now when I was on the continent, I lived in a single room in Coast-town. It wasn't much of a home.

We set a sailing date, weather permitting, and the islanders generously opened their larder to supply us with dried meat and fruit for the voyage. The men of the *Muriel* responded gratefully in kind, giving away knives, tools, and all the clothing they could spare. I contributed my soft bedsheets to the general giveaway—one each to Pearl and another new mother to make baby clothes. My decision to live by Forest Principles meant I'd soon have to sleep on island-cloth like everybody else. However, there was no Forest Principle that said I couldn't use a radio to ask my daughter to ensure there were linen sheets for everybody aboard the *Muriel* when she returned, which is what I did.

Helen, meanwhile, gave the Island Foresters more than anybody: She gave them herself.

Two days before we were supposed to sail, she came to me, asking, "Uncle, can we leave the radio here? May is so sick, and I know she gets a lot of comfort from talking to Aunt Anna. What if we left it for them?"

I was about to remind my niece that the ship's radio wasn't a device for social interaction, but a key piece of the *Muriel's* navigational system, when she added, "I think I can make you something from spare parts that could pick up the time signal, at least. The time signal's what you need most."

It was a good suggestion, but the fact that Helen didn't meet my eye when she made it aroused my suspicions.

"What's this 'you need' thing?" I asked. "*You're* the ship's navigator."

Helen squirmed. "Not... exactly. I mean, I am, but..." Then she burst out, "Uncle River, what if I stayed?"

"What—here?"

"Why not? I like this place," Helen replied—as though that was all it took. You liked a forest, and the forest took you in. Before I could remind her that there was such a thing as Forest Law, she added, "I could be useful here."

It would complicate my plans if Helen stayed on Annasland, too. "Of course you could be useful," I said testily. "You're always useful."

"What I mean is, I think I could be an infirmarian," Helen explained. "I want to stay and learn how. Snow says she'll send books, and she can teach me a lot over the radio. And then later she might come herself when... Well, when she can."

Snow would never leave Evergreen while May lived.

"What about your Papa?" I asked quietly.

Helen was silent for a minute. "Papa has other people to help him," she said finally. "These people don't."

I had to admit to myself Helen did seem almost born to be an infirmarian.

I thought things over. Jake had made good charts on the way out. There was one unknown stretch where he'd have to steer perpendicularly to the current to circle back toward Dead Island, but anybody could do that with just a compass, and any generally southwesterly course after that would put him on a line for home. "I guess they'll be all right," I conceded.

"They?" Helen repeated. "Are you staying too?"

"Yes," I said. "Or—maybe, anyway. I'm not sure yet."

"Auntie?" my niece suggested tentatively.

I didn't know what to say about her auntie, so I changed the subject. "I think you have another reason to stay besides learning to be an infirmarian," I said, smiling.

Helen smiled back. "I might."

To celebrate the *Muriel's* last full day on Annasland, Jake reciprocated Master Anna's hospitality and opened the ship to visitors. Frank and Rain spread the news—which took about one minute—and all day long the islanders came aboard in groups of five or six to see and marvel. Some of them brought fragrant bouquets, which I directed into Jake's cabin, and the Island Forest citizens all behaved much better than I would have under the circumstances— the circumstances being that the *Muriel* was a treasure trove of equipment that, if it had been new to me, I couldn't have kept my hands off. Though I was confident my knowledge and skills would make me a *useful* citizen of the Island Forest, I was pretty sure I wasn't always going to live up to the Hybrid standard of conduct.

In late afternoon I excused myself and went ashore to call Sarah. I owed it to her to make her the first to know I'd decided to stay on the island.

When I got to the radio hut, I found Helen there, wearing a new shirt embroidered all over with flowers and intertwined hearts.

"So that's what he was waiting for," I said, grinning. "I wish you and Peregrine a thousand years of happiness, Helen. And lots of children." Children are very important to Foresters.

My niece threw herself into my arms, laughing and crying at the same time.

"Isn't it beautiful?" she cried, pulling away again immediately to show off the shirt. It looked scratchy to me. "Peregrine did it all himself, too! I feel so stupid that I can't make him one in return. I can make a shirt, but I don't know anything about embroidering."

I explained that it would be perfectly acceptable for her to ask someone else to do the embroidery for her. "You're not expected to know everything. In a forest, if you want something you can't make for yourself, you trade something you have, or can do, to someone who'll make it for you. Here," I added, pulling my old tinderbox from my pocket. "Offer them this and they'll make you ten embroidered shirts. It's from Evergreen."

I was only exaggerating a little about the worth of the Evergreen connection. According to Frank, the Island Forest Hybrids regarded Evergreen as a former "home" to all of them, since they knew the place through Anna's recollections almost as well as if they'd lived there themselves. Consequently, they valued anything—sayings, songs, objects—that had an Evergreen provenance.

Then, because I wanted to have the radio hut to myself, I suggested, "You know who'll embroider really well? The head of the sewing room. That's who can give you the materials to make a shirt, too. Go ask."

Helen brightened immediately. I eased her toward the door.

"By the way," she said, as I opened it for her, "Deer called just a few minutes before you came in. He asked me to have you return the call as soon as you could."

"What's up? Did he sound upset?"

It was always on my mind May might take a turn for the worse.

But Helen said he sounded fine, just eager to talk with me, and then hurried away. As I was closing the door, I saw a Hybrid woman stop my niece to admire her shirt, a knowing smile on her face. Where I might have shrunk away, Helen delightedly embraced her.

Once she was gone, I sat down and turned on the radio—and stared at it.

Now that the time had come to do it, I had no idea how I was going to break the news of my decision to my family. When I told them I was planning to live—probably forever—on an island somewhere off the edge of the map, would they think I'd been lying all the times I'd said I was looking forward to coming home and seeing them again? I thought they might be hurt. Would they be angry?

Luckily, while I was wondering this, I remembered that Deer had asked me to call him. If I called Deer *before* I called Sarah, I suddenly realized, I could get his advice about what to say. In fact, he might even offer to make the call to Sarah for me. I was sure to make a mess of it. Deer liked Sarah. He'd want to spare her that.

Deer was evidently monitoring the radio because I got him right away.

"I have a great deal to tell you, River," he said immediately. "Would you like to speak first?"

As far as my news went, Sarah needed to be the first to know, sure—but she didn't need to know this very minute. I switched over, telegraphed back, "No, you go ahead. What's on your mind?" then sat back with a sigh of relief and got comfortable.

Deer told me what was on his mind, at length—but I couldn't take it in. When he stopped talking, all I could radio back was a stunned, "Say again?"

Deer repeated, slowly and clearly, that the *Muriel* was now the property of the United Forests. "The forests decided in United Council it would be useful to have such a ship. We can't be certain our way of life will be sustainable on the continent as Men's numbers increase."

I knew this. It had worried me for some time, in fact.

Among the million questions that leaped to my mind, the first was to wonder how—how—the United Forests had gotten the *Muriel* away from the shippers. They certainly hadn't let her go cheaply. If things went as planned, the shippers stood to make a lot of money with her.

As if he'd heard the question, Deer continued, "The transaction went very smoothly. The forests are, by Men's measures—which, of course, are not the same as ours—very rich."

I knew this from Fisher.

"The secret of our wealth seems to have escaped the forests, and with acknowledged riches, we find, comes power; and with power, both opportunity and responsibility. We accept the responsibility. With the acquisition of the *Muriel*, we hope to be able to take advantage of certain opportunities, also."

My first horrified thought was that the Foresters were planning to set themselves up as merchants. Nothing wrong with being a merchant, of course.

Some of my best friends were merchants. But they were not also Foresters.

To my relief, Deer went on, "The aim of business is to bring money, and as money motivates Men, we will leave the world of business to them to develop. Exploration, on the other hand, is unprofitable. Thanks to the radio, we know now there are other humans besides us left in the world. We have contacted them. With the *Muriel* and subsequent ships, the forest people will undertake to find these other humans."

He stopped there, and when he didn't say anything more, I guessed it was my turn to speak.

I was almost too stunned to make the switch-over, and when I finally did, all I could think to say was, "That's your 'opportunity'? To explore? Wonderful! More than wonderful!" Then I added, more cautiously, "I hope that forest money you mentioned is a lot, though, because what you're suggesting is going to cost a lot."

I don't like to say that Foresters can be a little naïve sometimes—but...

They can be touchy, too, so I took a minute to try to think up a tactful way to offer some advice.

Straightforward, forthright trade seemed like it would be a safe suggestion to make. The forests had always traded among themselves. "If you're clever, I think you can make exploration offset some of its own cost. You'll need supplies from Men's Lands. Any reason you can't—perfectly legitimately—pick up cargoes while you're exploring, and trade them for what you want? Lumber might be good. Men would happily trade you for any wood you brought in, and imported lumber would have the effect of distracting their attention from *your* trees, too."

Then I added, "Your turn. Go ahead, Evergreen," and switched back over.

To my amazement—to my comprehensive, absolute, unalloyed astonishment—my former teacher and foster-father Deer, who knew me, and knew all my faults, and knew by exactly how much those faults exceeded my virtues, answered, "You are clever, my son. Will you be our agent and guide us in this important enterprise? We—the United Councils—are confident you will do the job well and never urge on us any form of 'cleverness' incompatible with our principles. Please consider this offer."

When he said the word "offer," every hair on the back of my neck stood up.

"Shit, me?" I said—aloud, but not on the radio. "Have they all lost their minds?"

Deer was silent, though I thought I could hear the murmur of other voices in the background.

I knew he was waiting for me to answer, but I didn't switch over right away. I needed a minute to come to terms with the prize I'd just been offered. Accept it—and I intended to—and I'd be like Fisher; an agent of the forests, straddling two worlds, a foot in each. But unlike Fisher, whose heart had always been torn, I'd *like* the life. I'd *love* it. It was direction and purpose enough for anyone's life, not just mine, and the fulfillment of every dream I'd ever had except the secret one where I held Sarah in my arms again.

Just as I reached for the radio, Deer spoke again.

"Leaf has just reminded me that I should mention the other aspect to this endeavor."

Leaf was present? Who else, I wondered?

"As you seek out humans, you will undoubtedly also find Ants. It's our intention to make it a part of the *Muriel's* mission to advance, if we can, the re-integration of Ants with Men. The Island Forest has proven this can be done."

My brief, golden dream turned in an instant to smoke and dust.

I hadn't anticipated this at all. Posthumous, I knew, had believed completely in the concept of Ant "re-integration," but I'd always assumed Deer's attitude was more like John Seaborn's. John had believed re-integration of some kind was possible. The existence of Anna argued for it. But he'd never expressed any desire to help it along or even to witness it happening. Unlike Posthumous, he and Muriel had planned to go home to the continent once Anna's colony was established, not stay and "re-unify" anything. They'd even assumed Anna and Heron would come back with them, though I thought now they'd been wrong about that.

I took my time reconfiguring the radio so I wouldn't speak in haste and regret it.

When I felt I was ready, I answered, tapping out my answer with unintended emphasis, "I'm not the one for you, then. Though the Hybrids here are good people,"—I owed it to them to say that much—"what you call their 're-integration' cost thousands of lives and the brutalization of hundreds of human females to achieve. I can't be a part of anything like that." Then I added, "I'm sorry," though I wasn't.

I had to take a lot of deep breaths before I could bring myself to set up the radio to receive again.

Despite my outburst, Deer was as calm as ever.

"We understand your feelings, River," he said. "Ours are the same. It's the Hybrids who must do this work. If you're willing, from time to time, to transport Hybrids to places where there are Ants living, as when you take Frank and Rain to Making Happy, that will entirely meet our needs."

When Deer said this, the whole project suddenly made sense. Bring enough Hybrids even to a place like Ant Island, and the native population could be reasoned with and controlled. Hybrid minds, as I'd seen for myself, were much stronger than pure Ant-minds.

The process would be slow. I'd personally never live to see many Ants "re-civilized." But each new group of "gentled" Ants and Hybrids would add to a pool that could be dispersed among other Ant-dominated populations until eventually the inhabitants of the whole world would be...

I had to stop to think for a minute. What the inhabitants of the whole world would be, I decided, was—Hybrids.

Hybrids like Anna and like Frank.

However I felt about pure Ants—I hated them—there was no denying that in some ways, Anna and Frank and Hybrids like them were an improvement on pure human stock. Humans were always fighting (even Foresters, who fought their own violent man-natures and—like me—sometimes lost). Hybrids were naturally cooperative. Since their goals and ideals were derived through consensus, they had no reason to fight. Where pure Ants were stolid and dull, I had seen for myself on Annasland that Hybrids produced intelligent, imaginative children.

Telepathy persisted in some of these children. With enough Ants, telepathy might survive the "re-integration" process. If so, consensus might one day be worldwide, and the resulting peace eternal.

Everlasting peace was a pretty ambitious goal, and I wasn't sure I could believe in it. But at the very least Deer's plan would provide the inhabitants of the continent with a chance to seek out and meet other human survivors of the Ant Cataclysm. I wanted with all my heart to be a part of that. It seemed like the mission I'd been inadvertently training for all my life.

As suddenly as I saw that, I saw I'd been foolish to imagine I could stay in Annasland. The Island Forest would take me. Master Anna had made that clear. Maybe I was even worthy of living in a forest now. The thing was I didn't belong there. A forest is a place, firm ground under the foot. I am a river, and rivers flow.

I swung my feet up onto the radio table.

"I accept your proposition," I telegraphed, saying the words aloud as I sent them, just to enjoy their sound. "In fact, I'm with you heart and soul. Who else is there with you, Teacher? You mentioned Leaf… Is Roar there, too? Speak up, everybody. I want to hear your voices again."

Many old forest friends were in the room, it turned out, and we talked for hours.

CHAPTER TWENTY-NINE

awn was breaking when I finally got down to the beach. After getting off the radio to Evergreen I'd called Sarah, and the two of us talked the rest of the night. There'd been no need for me to break any actual news to her. As part-owner of D&R, she'd been a party to the negotiations for the *Muriel*.

Sarah confirmed what I'd guessed—that the United Forests had paid plenty to get the ship. "Danny and I advised waiting, but Deer was determined to have everything settled before you started for home. He wanted every port on the continent open to you. The war may spread, but of course the forests are neutral."

"I accepted Deer's offer."

Sarah wasn't surprised. "I guess you'll be traveling more than ever now," she said, and over the static I thought I heard her sigh. "That's the right thing for you, though. That's what you love."

I started to answer her in my usual way, by saying I loved her and our children more than traveling and so forth, but then I stopped myself. No point in going through it all again.

So instead, I said, "Want to come with me? You used to like to travel, too."

The question took her by surprise. She said she didn't know.

"You'd like it," I coaxed. "I'd like it. Why don't you?"

But Sarah wouldn't say yes—though she didn't say no, either.

"You'll be home for a few months before you leave again, won't you?" she asked. "Let's see how that goes, first."

By "home," she seemed to mean—our home. The one we'd shared.

But I didn't have the courage to ask, and that's how we left things.

*

Not bothering to signal for the dinghy, I swam out to the *Muriel*, where Collin, drowsy and heavy-eyed, tossed down the rope ladder.

To my surprise, Jake was right behind him.

"Thought I might as well stand a watch," he told me, leaning down to give me a hand over the rail. "Nights before we sail, I can't sleep." Then, with a sharp look, he demanded, "What's it to be? You stayin'?"

I turned to wring my shirt over the side—and to hide a smile. "As a matter of fact..." I paused, teasingly. "*No*. I was up all night settling a little ship's business, Captain. The *Muriel* has new owners. We work for the United Forests now."

Both Jake and Collin stared. Collin didn't seem sleepy anymore.

"Say that again," ordered the captain.

"It's true," I insisted. "The Foresters are so happy with the way this island forest is shaping up they want to establish more of them. They want the *Muriel* to look for suitable places to settle and provide transport to them when they're found. I imagine she'll also be making regular runs between here and the continent, but we didn't really discuss that part yet."

"Booger!" Collin exclaimed joyfully. The Foresters' reputation for fair dealing made them appealing employers.

Jake also pronounced his satisfaction with the news, plumbing the depths of human depravity for adjectives adequate to express his pleasure at the unexpected change of ownership. "Rouse the men!" he ordered Collin, while meanwhile thumping me repeatedly on the back. "Tell 'em to come up, but don't tell 'em why. And bring up that barrel! You know the one."

262

"Spirits?" I protested, as Collin darted off. "Jake, are you sure that's a good idea?"

Jake thumped me again. "It's a damn small barrel," he assured me. "And I meant to broach it tomorrow anyhow, when we turned for home."

Looking eastward, he corrected himself. "Today, that is. Damn me, River, you're full of surprises, ain't you? I bet you had this planned all along."

I hadn't, of course, but I didn't have time to disclaim it. The sailors were already swarming the deck.

*

I found Anna sitting at the edge of the Memorial Grove, her eyes tightly shut. Before I could speak, she said quietly, "You're going."

It wasn't a question.

"Yes," I said. "But I won't take Loyal with me, if you've changed your mind."

When she opened her eyes, the tears she'd been holding back ran down her cheeks. "No, take him," the master said. "I'm happy for him, really. He wants to go. He's excited to go. He's like you. Our forest is too small for him."

Sadly, she patted the bench beside her, and I sat down.

"I don't understand Loyal the way I understand my other children. I know my daughters' minds as well as I know my own, of course, and Peregrine is very open, like his father. But Loyal is a stranger to me in some ways."

Privately, I thought a big part of Loyal's problem—if you could call it a problem—was just that he had a sense of humor. There wasn't a lot of humor on Annasland. Humor often depends on an element of surprise, and it's hard to surprise a telepath.

"He's a typical fifteen-year-old male," I said reassuringly. "I know it looks bad from the outside, but it's actually pretty normal for him to be miserable at this age."

"He's lost his father," the master reminded me.

"Losing his father is extra. Loyal would be going through a lot of this even if Heron were..." Involuntarily, I glanced toward Heron's tree, and my throat tightened. "...here. After Loyal's seen a little bit of the world, and had a few adventures, he'll come home, and he won't be sad anymore."

"I hope he won't be sad," Master Anna said. "But what if he doesn't come home?"

No point in lying. It could happen. "I visited my mother. I visited, and I brought my children to visit. Whether he ever lives here again or not, Loyal won't be lost to you."

Anna murmured that this was true, and then she cried—just as my mother had cried for me. I comforted her as well as I could, acutely aware this time that I was also comforting every other telepath on the island. I didn't know anymore how I could have imagined living out my life in the Island Forest among beings who were never private, never alone.

The master and I sat for a long time together, my arm around her and her head on my shoulder. Like two telepaths, we didn't have to speak. Each of us knew what the other was thinking.

CHAPTER THIRTY

There had never been a farewell ceremony on Annasland. No Forester had ever left the island before. But the islanders all knew from Anna's memories how one was supposed to go, and at the proper time, they gathered without being told to for the procession.

Loyal and I were not the only honorees. Before we'd parted at the Memorial Grove, I promised Master Anna I'd make sure the Small People—"her" people, she called them—were living free, and less than a minute after that five Island Foresters had already volunteered to come along and help Frank and Rain bring fairer leadership and "nice things" to Making Happy. Their bundles in their hands, they were leaving Annasland too, coming aboard the *Muriel* with me.

Wearing garlands of flowers and singing, we proceeded slowly toward the shore. I remembered the songs, but didn't join in. I didn't trust my voice to be steady.

As we emerged from the trees onto the beach, most of the island citizens turned back toward the village, still singing, leaving those of us who were departing to say private farewells to our closest family and friends.

Master Anna, looking sad but calm, briefly addressed us all, then moved from one journeyer to another, saying a few words to each. I was senior of the group. She came to me first.

"We'll miss you, River," she said gravely. "I will miss you. I will miss you more than you know."

Was there regret in her eyes? I know there was none in mine as I answered her.

"I'll miss you too, Master. I'll miss you—but we'll meet again."

Anna rested her head briefly against my chest. Then, saying softly, "You will always be welcome here," she moved away.

Helen was next to say goodbye to me—although in fact, she refused to say it.

"It's not goodbye," she insisted, her lower lip quivering. "You'll be back soon."

"What's the latest on the voices?" I asked.

Helen looked grateful for the change of topic. "Did I tell you? Deer and the master have all the Hybrids working together to identify what language they're speaking."

In the chaos of getting ready to sail, I hadn't heard this.

"They taught us to count to ten in their tongue, just the way we hoped," Helen told me. "That's a place to start. And there's a word they say at the beginning of every broadcast we think must be 'hello,' or 'greetings,' or something like that. The Hybrids are taking turns going through all Grandfather's books to see if they can find anything in them that looks like it might be those words. As you said, if we find their words, we'll have found their language! I mean, maybe."

"Maybe." I laughed, but the plan actually struck me as pretty clever. Every book one Hybrid searched would essentially be searched by all. Their telepathy would have a synergistic effect on the project.

"Shall I bring your Aunt Sarah with me when I come back?" I offered. "And maybe your Papa, too?"

My niece's face lit up. "Oh, do you think he'd come?" she cried.

"You're the one who's got the radio," I pointed out. "Start working on him."

Peregrine came to me; then his sisters; then Doe.

As Doe was thanking me for the hundredth time for what I'd done for her leg, a signal cannon fired from the ship. I turned in time to see the

United Forests flag being run up the *Muriel's* stern flagstaff. Master Anna's eyes met mine proudly. The sewing-room had worked half the night to produce it.

Smiling, I turned back to Doe, took her hands, and put my cheek against hers. "Take care of yourself," I said, and she answered me, "Good journey!"

Timmy and Lionel arrived in the longboat then. The tide wouldn't wait, even for a forest master. It was time for us to go. At the boat's side, Anna relinquished her son valiantly and left him to go stand with her other children, who now included Helen. As we pulled from the shore the group began to sing the children's song, "How Fair Is Our Forest." It was the first song Anna had learned in Evergreen and the only forest song Helen knew all the words to now. This time I sang along. Among so many breaking voices, I figured no one would notice mine. Loyal stared silently, face set, at the place on the shore where everyone he had ever loved in his life was getting smaller and smaller, while the *Muriel*, large and strange, loomed up behind us.

The song over, I attempted a little conversation. "What've you done to your hair, Tim? Are those braids?"

Timmy looked back at me and grinned. "I work for Foresters now. That makes me kind of a Forester too, don't it?"

His "braids"—short and greasy—were like nothing ever worn in a forest, but naturally I didn't tell Tim that.

Instead, I turned to Loyal. "What do you think? Should we all wear braids now?"

Loyal tore his eyes from where his mother stood leaning on his brother Peregrine's arm and stared at me vacantly.

I wanted to say something comforting, like Deer would have said to me. All I could come up with was, "Loyal, if there's one thing I've learned in all my travels—and there may only be one thing—it's that no matter where I go, no matter what I do or how I live, I'm still a Forester inside. And you'll always be a Forester, too."

"Yes, and me too," Timmy put in promptly. "Because people is all the same inside, ain't they, Mr. River?"

I had never subscribed to this idea, as a matter of fact, though I couldn't think of a tactful way to make this clear to Tim.

One of the many times my mother and I quarreled about me leaving the forest, she called me, alluding to my name, "a wild river that has burst its banks and is determined to cut its own channel to the sea without regard for the destruction it leaves in its path." I'd been ashamed when she said it, because it was true.

But I thought now that what my mother hadn't considered was that bursting its banks is a natural thing for a river to do sometimes. Rivers burst their banks, run wild, enrich new soils and make deserts of old ones, and mingle their waters freely with the water of the streams and brooks and other rivers they meet along the way. Far outside the forest, my own river had somehow turned to run again in the same channel as the River of Evergreen, which would probably have made my mother very happy. But maybe our confluence was inevitable from the first. Eventually, all rivers meet in the sea.

Timmy might be onto something after all, I thought.

I watched with my usual admiration as Tim and Lionel expertly drew the longboat alongside the *Muriel*, shipping their oars at precisely the right second.

Then I stood up, and offered Loyal my hand.

"Climb aboard, Loyal Anna's-son," I said. "We're home."

NEXT IN THE 'ANTLANDS' SERIES
BOOK 3: FARLANDS

Fourteen-year-old Claire Dunn has a problem.

Her mother is…gone. Claire doesn't know where. Her sailor father is at sea. And now, just by accident, she's killed her only other living relative, her abusive Aunt Jane, in a fight. Murderers are hanged in Fortress City. Until Claire's own injuries have healed enough to allow her to slip away to sea to find her father, she needs to hide. A secret room in the town library seems to provide an ideal refuge—until the day someone slides a key into the lock and walks in.

Claire's visitor is the rich and well-connected Sarah Farmer. Seeing in the girl a kindred spirit to her late husband River's, she offers Claire a chance at a better life. But first there is a disturbing mystery for Claire to solve, lessons to learn, a troubled child to nurture, and smugglers and pirates to defeat before she can accept the gift.

'Farlands' - Book 3 in the 'Antlands' series is available now, in paperback and for Kindle®, from Amazon.

BY THE SAME AUTHOR

The *Antlands* series:
Book 1: Antlands
Book 2: Annasland
Book 3: Farlands

Other writing:
The Complete Raffles (Annotated & Illustrated)

Available now via your local Amazon store

ABOUT THE AUTHOR

Genevieve Morrissey is a passionate student of British and American social history, but through one of those strange little quirks of fate she spends most of her days talking with scientists. In *Antlands*, she explores a future history of societies coping with the loss of civilization—and attempting to rebuild it. She enjoys reading obscure books, travel, good cooking, and solitude.

Stay up to date with Geneveieve and her writing via her website:

antlands.com